TEMPTING JO

Nancee Cain

Serrated Edge Publishing

❧ Praise for *Saving Evangeline* ❧

"*Saving Evangeline* has stayed in my head for the better part of a week. I think the possibilities it opens up and thoughts it inspired is a testament to Nancee Cain's storytelling."

❧ *The Literary Gossip Blog*

Six-Star Review and 2015 Top Pick: "I laughed my butt off and cried my heart out. I swooned with the passion and felt warm & fuzzy with each hug. This book touched me in so many ways. When a book does that I give it 6 Stars without question."

❧ *Smut Book Junkies Blog*

"I forgot how to breathe; this book completely swept me off my feet. I will remember it always. By the time I got to the end of this book it felt like a prayer. Beneath the beautiful imagery, the religious figures, the humor, the sadness, is an epic love story. A 6 star read!"

❧ *After This Page Book Blog*

"If you're looking for a story that is BEAUTIFUL and yet so REAL, *Saving Evangeline* is it. It has the perfect amount of depth and humor. It'll keep your attention and it will captivate you."

❧ *Beauty in the Beastly Books Blog*

Five Stars: "This story had such a unique feel to it and was brilliantly written. It was hilariously funny and incredibly addictive."

❧ *Totally Booked Blog*

In the Top Ten list for 2015.

❧ *Kat Loves Books, A Booklover's Blog*

Serrated Edge Publishing
PO Box 969
Jasper, AL 35502
www.nanceecain.com

First published September 2016

Chapter one of *Saving Evangeline*, copyright © 2015
Used by permission of Omnific Publishing

ISBN: 978-0-9976139-0-2

10 9 8 7 6 5 4 3 2 1

Editor: Jessica Royer Ocken
Book Design by Coreen Montagna

Printed in the United States of America

For my husband and daughter.
I love you even more than the cats.

CHAPTER ONE

"Hey, Rafe. You've got a cleanup on aisle E."

"Not my problemo." I don't bother looking up from the mystery I'm reading. "I'm off duty."

"The Boss wants to see you."

Slamming the book closed, I glare at Remiel. "Why didn't you say that in the first place? Jerk."

He laughs and falls in stride with me as I rush toward the office.

"How's Evangeline?" I ask him, preening my wings and catching a white feather that flies loose. He's either been moping or raising hell with his pranks since returning home last year.

"She's okay." Remiel shrugs, his black feathers rustling. "Taking life by the balls." He hesitates and sighs. "I miss her like crazy."

I nod, sympathizing. My brother risked everything when he fell in love with the girl he was sent to rescue. In my opinion, it was stupid, but he's always been a renegade. Still, he was careless about hiding his true nature. That put all of us at risk. He should have kept his focus on the job. We've all had to do it. Even me.

Personally, I'm a by-the-book kind of angel. Rules bring order. I'm known as the problem-solver. The Boss calls on me when it's something big because of my ability to assimilate into any situation. My favorite was the time I convinced Anne of Cleves that her head would look better on her shoulders. The look of surprise on Henry's face when she agreed to the annulment was priceless. It's been a while since The Boss has requested my services, though. I don't count my recent stint spying on Remiel as a job. That was more for sport, and also unsuccessful because he refused to listen to reason.

"So what's going on? Who's in trouble?" I ask.

"I dunno. I'm just the messenger. Gabe was busy and couldn't deliver the summons. I wouldn't keep the Old Man waiting, though. He's already pretty upset. He hasn't been able to crack level 666 on that candy game He plays on His phone."

"That's bizarre. I mean if anyone could, He could."

"You know how He is. He likes to experience what frustrates the humans." Remiel hurries past me, grabbing Peter's keys. He takes off flying as Peter raises Cain in hot pursuit.

I pause, straightening my wings before knocking on the huge wooden door. The knock isn't needed; it's just a courtesy. He knows I'm here.

"Come in, Raphael."

The door swings open on silent hinges. His bright presence burns like the sun, illuminating the stained glass windows behind Him. Classical musical plays in the background. The Boss's wooly eyebrows are knitted together as He stares at His phone.

He pulls on His lower lip. "Quite annoying. More so than that silly Rubik's Cube from a while back." He looks up, and the blinding light causes me to blink and squint. He motions with His phone. "Have you tried this game?"

"No, Sir. I find it ridiculous and a complete waste of time."

One bushy brow rises a fraction of an inch.

"I mean, it's just not for *me*, Sir."

"You really need to learn to have fun, son. You're much too serious."

Heat flushes my face, and a knot forms in my stomach. There's no way to describe the feeling when you disappoint Him. Despair bleeds into your soul, infusing every molecule of your being. Another long minute passes as He finishes His game — unsuccessfully, judging by His scowl.

"Sorry, Sir. I'll, uh, catch a game of Go Fish with Peter later."

"How can that be fun? We all know that old rascal cheats."

"Yes, Sir." I remain standing at attention.

He sighs and rolls His eyes. "At ease, son. I'm not upset with you, Raphael. I just wish you'd lighten up. It's okay to have fun. I know you and Mary Magdalene had a good time when I sent you after Remiel."

He thinks we had fun? This surprises me. I'm still kicking myself for the way things went down. "We failed in our mission, Sir. Remiel fell in love with Evangeline. He should have left and let me deal with it. I take complete responsibility—"

"Stop." His voice rumbles like thunder. He looks up from the phone, His attention now focused solely on me. I don't like it—not one bit—when He's perturbed.

My feathers stand on end, and my wings flap despite my attempt to hold myself together. Remiel listened to my advice about as well as Marie Antoinette did. I told her she'd regret the cake comment, and I counseled Remi to let Evangeline go. In my opinion, The Boss was a bit too easy on him. And we all know what happened to Marie.

"Do you really want to go there?" He asks softly.

Having an omniscient boss sucks at times. "No, Sir. I'm sorry."

His face softens. "Relax. I've already told you, I'm not angry, nor am I disappointed in you. When was the last time you had a vacation?" He walks around to lean against the desk, facing me.

"Um, let's see…I think it was nineteen fifty-three. Peter and I attended Queen Elizabeth's coronation. Peter enjoyed the pageantry." Personally, I'd been bored to tears and found *I Love Lucy* more entertaining.

"Peter does love the smells and bells. He can be a bit pompous. And that's one of my favorite shows, too. Lucy always gets in trouble, but her heart is in the right place. Good heavens, you're way overdue for some off time, my dear boy."

"I don't need a vacation, Sir. I'm content working."

He studies me, and I lower my eyes for a second under the intensity of His stare.

"*Content?*"

"Yes, Sir. Perfectly content." My wings ruffle, and I shift on my heels.

He raises His brows and folds His arms. "Do you think that's My goal for you? To *just* be content?"

His question throws me. *Is this a trick?* "Uh, yes?" I swallow and add, "Sir."

"You need to live a little, Raphael. Everyone needs time off to relax. Even *I* took the seventh day to — how do they say it now? — chillax? However, there's a problem you need to handle first."

I contain my smirk and stand tall, ready for my assignment. "Yes, Sir." I hope this will be something interesting — like espionage.

The Boss picks up a file folder and scans the contents. "Ah, yes, here it is. That sweet Jolene is getting in a little over her head."

Stunned, I blurt, "Who?" Surely I didn't hear Him right. I do my best to hide my growing trepidation. I'm not prepared to see Jolene again...I was hoping for something a little less *personally* dangerous.

"You heard me. Jolene Sanford. You're her guardian angel. Brown hair, hazel eyes, quiet but feisty young woman. You spent quite a bit of time with her when she was growing up and having a rough go of things with her folks. She seems like a nice girl. How could it possibly be dangerous for you? You always adhere to the rules."

"When I left, she was fine and on the right track. I can't imagine her in a predicament, Sir. She's a little, er, *boring*." I hope He buys my attempt at deflecting as I try to remember how old she is in human years now. Twenty-five?

"Should be a perfect fit." He smiles widely and winks.

Busted.

"Just check on her. After you're sure she isn't headed in the wrong direction, take a week off and enjoy yourself." He cuts me off with a raise of His hand before I can protest. "That's all. Go. And relax; act like a human."

That last remark irritates me. Remiel caused a lot of chaos last year doing precisely that. I'm nothing like him. *I* take my job *seriously*.

"Raphael?"

"Sir?"

"Have fun." He walks back around His desk and picks up the phone, grumbling under His breath about the complexity of the stupid game.

I leave, wondering what the hell Jolene has gotten into. Truth is, she is anything but boring. The one kiss we shared is ingrained in my soul. It's one of the reasons I hastened home when she turned fifteen.

CHAPTER TWO

"Friday."

Over the intercom, the clipped voice sounds tinged with annoyance, sending a shiver down my spine. It's too early to decide if that's in a good or a bad way. But probably bad. I'm two minutes late.

My name is Jo Friday...

No, not really. It's Jolene Loretta Sanford. To my misfortune, my mother's a huge country music fan. My family and friends call me Jo. My boss calls me Friday, because he can't remember my name. I'm not important enough for him to notice, even though I've been his administrative assistant for six weeks now.

But this will change. He *will* notice me, because I'm attentive to details. That's what makes me good at my job.

Administrative assistant. It's actually just a fancy title for flunky or whipping girl. My co-workers refer to my job as the *admin ass*, because they think only a dumbass would take the job. Mr. DeVille goes through admin asses like my daddy used to go through beer before he went to the pen: fast and furiously.

Now that I think about it, *whipping girl* might not be so bad. Being spanked by Mr. DeVille is currently one of my favorite late-night fantasies. Regrettably, this isn't likely to happen any time soon. I'm not exactly his type. I don't look like Barbie, and although I sound like a redneck, my IQ is above that of a drunken gnat. However, I'm taking steps to improve myself, and as I've mentioned, I'm determined to make him notice me. I know this obsession with my boss isn't healthy, but it is what it is. He's the most fascinating man I've ever met. And he has ambition, like me. He owns this business! He's not like the losers back home who are satisfied living and dying in the same boring town, doing the same boring jobs their daddies did.

"Friday, I'm counting. One…"

The dreaded countdown. No one has ever survived past three and kept their job. That's why I'm his fifteenth assistant in three months. This isn't like me. I'm usually competent and avoid the counting altogether, but this morning I overslept. My second job and night school are kicking my admin ass. My brother thinks I've taken on too much, but I can handle it. I know this opportunity presented itself for a reason. How many jobs come with a place to live built in? And working so much helps pay for school, so in that respect it's made my life easier.

Picking up the phone, I hit the intercom button and respond using my best professional voice. "Yes, sir?" Hard as I try, I can't quite curtail the drawl that clings to my words like honey on a Sunday morning biscuit.

"You're late. Has some catastrophic event occurred? A hangnail, perhaps? A run in your stockings?" His dripping sarcasm reminds me of wet quilts on a clothesline, heavy and unflappable.

I grin, picturing steam coming out of his ears like a cartoon character. "No, sir." I glance at my unpolished, bitten nails and comfy black pants. *Note to self: buy stockings and garter belt, get manicure.* "I apologize for my tardiness, sir. It won't happen again."

As my mother would say, sugar wouldn't melt in my mouth. She has all kinds of cliché sayings like this. She dishes them out like fried chicken at a Baptist funeral. Thinking about my mother firms my resolve to improve myself. I refuse to end up like Crimson Bryant Sanford: living in a trailer, miserable and strung out on prescription meds because of some SOB who treats her like dog poop.

I want a man who treats me like a beautiful princess in public and a naughty schoolgirl in the bedroom. And I know just the man for me: *Mr. Lucius DeVille.*

Far from stupid, I know right now I'm so far out of Mr. DeVille's league, I couldn't make it into the dugout, much less out on the field. He's high cotton, and I'm just plain ol' polyester. But this will change, or I'll darn well die trying. I'm saving any extra money that doesn't go for living expenses and school. Someday I'll have enough for some lipo and fake tits. In the meantime I could at least use a new wardrobe. Until then, I'll work on my education and lose the hick accent. A sweet, refined, soft Southern drawl would be okay. Men seem to like that.

Through the phone line, I hear Mr. DeVille's fingers drumming on his desk, and cold fear courses through my veins. *Shoot, the countdown started again. Please don't let him have made it to three!*

"Two…"

The frostiness in his voice makes me break out in a cold sweat. I *need* this job to pay for school. I *want* this job to be close to the object of my obsession.

"Sorry, sir. I'm here." *Phew.*

"Where are the reports I asked for yesterday?"

Although I can't pinpoint his accent, Mr. DeVille's brusque manner is that of a damn Yankee. Yes, that's one word, and it isn't considered cussing when referring to those of the Northern persuasion who have moved south and stayed. No one knows where he's from or why he bought this little company three months ago. All of his employees fear him, except me and my best friend, Rafe Goodman.

Okay, maybe I'm just a *tad* afraid of my employer.

Just after I got this job, I was surprised when Rafe showed up to interview one day — that's another reason I know this is meant to be. We hadn't seen each other in years, yet we reconnected like it had been just a few weeks. Rafe was my best friend growing up, and he gets me like no one else. We share a love of corny sitcoms and movies. It's great to have him back in my life, especially here at work.

"On your desk, sir." I let out the breath I've been holding. I'm on top of things. My middle name should be Efficient. Smiling, I place a single pink rose and a white feather in the vase on my desk. Rafe leaves them for me every Monday. Of course, he leaves the other five women in the office a rose, too. But mine is always pink and always accompanied by a white feather. I pull out today's paper and tuck away the coupons for myself. I don't consider it stealing since I used to dig them out of his trashcan anyway.

"And my coffee?" Although cool, Mr. Deville's voice sends a warm thrill all the way down my body, curling my toes.

Shoot, I have to get my act together. "I will gallivant to serve you, sir." *Gallivant* is today's word on my Word-A-Day calendar. Rafe gave it to me as part of my Christmas present last month. *To roam about in search of pleasure.* I'm not quite sure I've used the word correctly, but I'm too tired to care at the moment. I ignore my boss's growl of frustration. I'm used to it.

I yank open my desk drawer, reapply my deodorant, and run to the break room. Rounding the corner I find Rafe holding court with the twins I've nicknamed Tweedle Ditz and Tweedle Dumb. I doubt they got their jobs based on their typing skills.

Everyone loves Rafe. When I was six, I ran away from home and got lost in the woods. He found me and became my best friend. The man knows more about me than most, including the details of my unhappy childhood. But he's a little older than I am, and we drifted apart after he left for college. By then I was living with my brother, so my home life had improved. I wanted to stay in touch, but it was like he'd disappeared off the face of the planet.

The most popular guy in the office, Rafe has an amazing ability to carry on a conversation about absolutely anything and sound like he knows what he's talking about. Today he's discussing fashion trends on the red carpet. Yesterday he was talking football stats. He's like one of those lizards that can change color to blend into his environment. Back home in our small town, he wore jeans and T-shirts. He taught me how to throw a ball and bait a fishing line, even though I hated doing it. Here in Birmingham he dresses like an upper-crust New York businessman and wheels and deals like a high roller. The man was born to be a salesman, and his numbers reflect that. He's always number one on the board in the break room and could probably sell the Devil ice water in hell.

Tweedle Dumb rubs against him, purring like a feline in heat. Crossing my arms, I stare daggers at her until she leaves. To my credit, I refrain from making a gagging noise when she blows him a kiss. Tweedle Ditz tosses her hair and smirks. She and her sister would love to get their manicured claws in Rafe. Thankfully, he's too smart for that. He's constantly warning me not to get my honey where I get my money, and he seems to live by that rule. To say he doesn't approve of my obsession with Mr. DeVille is an understatement.

"If you need anything, you know where to find me," Tweedle Ditz simpers, straightening Rafe's tie.

"Sure thing. Thanks." Rafe turns his attention to me.

Dismissed, she leaves, her smile faltering. She glares at me on her way out the door.

I stop myself from sticking my tongue out at her. "I think I'll go vomit now."

"Jealous?" He winks at me and pours himself a cup of coffee.

I snort. "No. Except maybe of their fake boobs."

Rafe's intense gaze scans me from head to toe. He shakes his head. "Fake boobs are overrated. Good grief. What's up with your outfit? This isn't nineteen eighty-three, and you're not graceful enough to star in *Flashdance*. Didn't I buy you a new sweater for Christmas?"

I glance down at my worn black leggings adorned with white cat fur and my baggy, oatmeal-colored sweater. I look like a walking advertisement for the local thrift store. In contrast, dressed in black pants, an electric blue shirt, and a striped silk tie, Rafe looks like he just stepped out of the pages of *GQ*.

I roll my eyes. "Your brow's getting an old man furrow from frowning. The sweater is in the wash. Is this your not-so-subtle reminder that I still owe you a Christmas present?"

"Well, now that you mention it…" He grins, and it softens his critique, but he's right—I'm a hot mess.

My two arch nemeses are always dressed impeccably and are probably size zero despite their humongous fake boobs. I don't have money to spend on clothes. Prior to landing this job, I didn't care. *Comfortable and serviceable* was my motto; *cheap* was my standard. I've realized this too must change as I immerse myself in the study of all things Lucius DeVille. I've earmarked this week's paycheck for a trip to TJ Maxx, the poor girl's Saks.

"Thanks for the free fashion critique. Is my current ensemble a step up from when you asked me if I was wearing one of Sophia's sweaters from *The Golden Girls*?" I start a new pot of coffee. I wouldn't dare deliver anything less than fresh to the boss.

"If you say so." His raised eyebrow says otherwise. "Ludicrous the Devil sent you for coffee? What's the matter? Did he break a leg?"

"I don't mind doing this."

"He's a sexist tyrant." Rafe crosses his arms.

"Just stop. Don't *you* have a job to do?"

"I'm doing it."

"Standing around criticizing?"

"Protecting you."

"Oh, for heaven's sake. From what? I'm getting my boss a cup of coffee. He isn't going to throw it at me."

"I wouldn't put anything past him," Rafe counters.

"Mr. DeVille may be demanding, but he isn't evil."

"Trust me, he's evil incarnate. Play with fire, and you're bound to get burned."

I roll my eyes. "Don't you think you're being a little overdramatic?"

"Fine. Don't listen to sound advice." Rafe shoves away from the counter and storms back to his office.

I know he's not really mad. This is just how he gets. Sometimes he acts like I'm still six years old. When the coffee's done, I add three-fourths of a yellow packet of sweetener to Mr. Deville's cup. On the specific china plate he designated for his personal use, I place half a whole-wheat bagel with one tablespoon of light cream cheese. He eats the same thing every day. Once he takes notice of me, I plan to add a little variety to his life—starting with plenty of spice. On my way to his office, I pick up his mail and the paper from my desk. I've folded it so the headline is visible.

Mr. DeVille's on the phone when I enter. He doesn't spare me a glance as he rubs his forehead, barking orders at the hapless soul on the other end of the line. I place two aspirin on his breakfast plate, stealing a peek at the man I've shadowed for six weeks. Well, officially for six weeks. I guess Rafe's right; I'm kind of a stalker, but not the creepy killer kind. Even before I got the job as his assistant, I watched and studied him as I quietly cleaned his office while he worked late. Most people don't notice those who clean up after them, and Mr. DeVille is no exception. That's why I'm so good at this. I paid attention to what he likes.

Without stopping his conversation, he hands me a note with a woman's name and address written on it. One of my jobs is to send Mr. DeVille's thanks-for-the-sex flowers on Mondays. It really griped my butt the time I had to send matching bouquets to the twins. He doesn't care about any of these women, and it's always someone different. He can't seem to find what he's looking for.

I often fantasize about writing a snarky note to accompany the bouquets, such as: "I get lost in your cavernous depths of desire." I'm pretty sure it would fly over the recipients' empty heads. From what I've seen, Mr. DeVille's "dates" only speak in sighs, slurps, and two-syllable words. *Hey, there's an idea.* Maybe for Valentine's Day I'll have Mr. DeVille send his women a Word-A-Day calendar. They'll be half-price by then.

When I become his girlfriend, there won't be any need for these flowers. I'm not a casual sex kind of girl. And I definitely don't like to share. No, when he's mine, it will be for keeps.

Today Mr. DeVille's wearing my favorite gray suit with a lightly starched white shirt and lavender, gray, and black striped tie. Back home, no self-respecting man would wear a purple tie, but it looks spectacular on him. I like the way it sets off his ice blue eyes. Just looking at them makes my heart race. At times, I swear I can see flames flickering in them.

He's in need of a trim, and one strand of his blond hair has fallen out of place. I know for a fact he has an appointment with his barber after lunch. He has his hair trimmed every third Monday at exactly 1:15 p.m. I twist my fingers together to keep from brushing the stray lock from his forehead. I like his hair best on the morning of trim day. I'd love it even more mussed after a night of wild, freaky circus sex.

He hangs up the phone, and his lips press together when he realizes I'm still here. Just once I wish he'd look me in the eye.

"Anything else, sir?" *Me bent over your desk? Or a blow job? I'll even attempt to swallow...*

"No." He picks up a report, ignoring me.

I've just been dismissed without so much as a look or wave of acknowledgment. He never says thank you. I don't think the two words exist in his vocabulary. Hiding my disappointment, I leave quietly, closing the door behind me.

Someday he'll notice me.

The door closes, and I chuckle to myself. Jolene Sanford looks at me like I'm a damn piece of chocolate cake at a weight loss convention. Sometimes she licks that tempting, plump lower lip as she stares, making her appear ravenous. I make a note to research her family and see if there are any Donners lurking there.

I call her Friday because she's so damn efficient. And it keeps her at arm's length. I can't show my hand, yet.

Friday is pretty in an unassuming way, although she isn't at all confident about her looks. Her dark, wavy hair has a hint of auburn in it, and she usually has it pulled up in a ponytail or a bun. She needs very little makeup with her perfect complexion, and I like her natural look. Tall and charmingly awkward, she moves like a coltish tomboy, as if she's not quite comfortable in her own skin. Those golden hazel eyes with flecks of green are her prettiest feature. I like it when they flash with ire after one of my many unreasonable requests. She keeps a lid on it, but I know my assistant is full of piss and vinegar. It's her fiery nature that has started to intrigue me.

Her taste in clothes runs understated and casual, but I have to wonder why she doesn't own a damn lint brush. There's always white fur on her clothes. I'm not fond of animals as pets — the lone exception being my fiendish hound, Black Shuck.

I much prefer people as pets.

Though I haven't revealed it yet, Friday has most certainly captured my attention, and this cat-and-mouse game is proving quite entertaining. More so than I anticipated. The silly girl thinks she's in control. Little does she know, this whole scenario is part of a bigger plan.

I toss the aspirin in the garbage — now that I'm off the phone, my head feels fine — and down my perfect cup of coffee. Grabbing the files I need for the board meeting, I slip out the door, hoping she's at her desk. The office staff scurries to appear busy, like rats on a sinking ship. Do they really think I don't know they've been gossiping and checking their social media? I find Friday with her butt in the air, fiddling with her chair. I clench my fist to keep from smacking her admin ass as it wiggles in front of me. I clear my throat and wait for her to acknowledge my presence.

"Hang on. I've almost got this chair fixed so it'll quit lowering on its own. If that cheapskate would part with some money, maybe I'd get a chair that didn't sink like the *Titanic* every time I sit in it."

The noise in the office stops. It's as if her words hang suspended in the air, and it takes every bit of self-control I possess not to smirk.

Friday stops adjusting the chair and freezes, sucking in air like one of the hapless victims on that ill-fated ship. The clock on the wall ticks off time like a death knell.

"Oh, sho-ot." With her southern accent, the one-syllable word stretches into two.

She slowly stands, and her neck flushes pink, the color working its way to her hairline. Her eyes scan her co-workers in a desperate plea for help. None will be received. They may present themselves as human, but they're actually a bunch of slimy, self-serving invertebrates. It's why I hired them, of course. Only Raphael has any balls about him, and he isn't here. A full minute ticks by in silence, and not one of them offers her a lifeline.

Then Mr. Holier-Than-Thou rounds the corner and pauses, shooting me a death glare as Jolene fidgets in front of me.

"Friday." I keep my face blank, my tone even.

"S-Sir?" Her pupils dilate to the point it's hard to detect their hazel rim. If she doesn't breathe soon, I'm afraid I'll be forced to utilize my rusty CPR skills.

"Have lunch delivered promptly at eleven thirty to the board room, the standard order. Make sure you buzz me precisely at one for my appointment at the barber." I turn and walk away, determined not to smile at the relieved huff of air escaping her lips.

No one dares to look me in the face as I stride past. Out of the corner of my eye, I see one of the workers slip another a twenty. I'm sure it's for the numbers board circulating among the drones. They're betting on how long before I fire her.

That isn't going to happen. As a matter of fact, this is the first morning she's not been on top of her game. Perhaps I should get her a new chair, or at the very least, a lint brush. Not only is she the best damn assistant I've ever had, she's integral to the whole reason I'm here.

I square my shoulders, mentally preparing myself for my tiresome board of directors. A more apt description of our weekly conferences would be *bored* meetings. For the next hour and a half I'll contemplate either killing them in a slow, torturous manner, or a self-inflicted lobotomy.

Everyone thinks I'm a ruthless ballbreaker. They are correct. What they don't know is that I hate everything about this place. I couldn't care less if we're in the black or the red. I'm not a businessman. I'm on a mission, biding my time, toying with one of His favorites. My real job goes way beyond the scope of this petty office.

An hour later, the threat of snow thankfully cuts the board meeting short. Snow in the South is an interesting phenomenon. Just the hint of it has everyone rushing to the grocery store to buy milk and bread, which is asinine. If the power goes off, why would you open the refrigerator to get milk? And don't people usually have milk and bread in stock for normal days? Wouldn't it make more sense to buy condoms and liquor? This is Alabama. They don't get snow that lasts more than two or three days. It should be a party occasion, like Mardi Gras.

Looking up from my computer, I minimize the screen when I hear the timid knock on the door. Mrs. Cabot, the office manager, approaches my desk like a rabbit skirting around a hungry mountain lion. I've contemplated screaming *boo* just to watch her jump, but she's elderly, and I choose not to be responsible for giving her a heart attack. Too much damn paperwork involved. I make a mental note to have Friday schedule a CPR class for the office.

"Yes?" I raise an eyebrow and give her my patented annoyed look. I'd be lying if I said acting like an asshole was an act. The truth is, I *am* an asshole.

"M-Mr. D-DeVille, as you know, we are under a threat of ice and s-snow." She twists a tissue in her hands, blinking rapidly behind her thick glasses. Her corkscrew gray curls bounce with her nervousness.

"And?"

"Some of your employees live quite far away. S-Schools are being released early."

I sigh dramatically. "I suppose everyone wants to go home."

She nods, apparently relieved by my intuitiveness.

Elbows on my desk, I steeple my hands together and glare. "With pay?"

Her throat bobbles, and her face blanches to the color of paste. The shredded tissue scatters like the very snow she's scared of.

I heave another gargantuan sigh. "Very well." I motion her out the door.

"T-Thank you, sir," she snivels, reminding me of Bob Cratchit as she beats a hasty exit.

Just call me Ebenezer.

CHAPTER THREE

The sound of a vacuum cleaner in the outer office pulls me from my computer. I've been engrossed in a genealogy website. I haven't found any Donners in Jolene's family tree, just a few moonshiners. Stretching to ease the kinks, I can feel my neck pop and shoulders crack. A glance at my watch shows I've been working for eight hours without a break. This isn't unusual when I get caught up in a project. I'm meticulous with research.

Outside, the streetlight illuminates big, fat snowflakes falling steadily. I shiver with distaste. I despise cold weather and fucking *hate* snow. For once the meteorologist was right. I've often thought it must be the perfect career for humans. You can be wrong the majority of the time and still keep your damn job.

The vacuum cleaner sounds closer. I smile. Perfect. I'll just stay here and finagle my way into Jolene's apartment. My story will be that I can't get through all the abandoned vehicles on the street, which is probably true. Southerners don't know how to drive in snow. It's rather amusing. I shut down the computer.

Utilizing my best James Bond moves, I quietly inch the door open. My eyes light on my unsuspecting assistant, and I pause to watch her dance with the vacuum cleaner, shaking that moneymaker like her living depends on it. She's wearing a gray sweatshirt and pink yoga pants that say *Kiss It* across her curvy ass. I can't quite contain my grin when she belts out the chorus of Britney Spears' "Baby One More Time," complete with butt smack. Jiggling her cute bottom one more time, she spins around to face me.

Upon seeing me, she shrieks and her cheeks flush the color of her yoga pants. She snaps off the vacuum, and the foreboding sound of the ticking clock is all that's left in the eerie silence. I think she's stopped breathing, so it will be interesting to see how long it takes before she passes out cold.

Her gaze locks on mine, her pupils expanding into liquid pools of darkness. She quickly averts her eyes, clasping her hands together. I can practically smell the fear on her skin, and it flicks the switch to my dick. Hmmm…that's unexpected. An image of her dropping to her knees teases the corner of my twisted, devious mind. I suppress my smile. Victory tinges the air.

"What are you doing?" I demand.

Her throat moves up and down as she sucks in what I'm sure is some much-needed air. Straightening her shoulders, she lifts her chin. "My job, sir."

"Obviously you haven't paid attention to your job description. While I require work spaces to be kept neat and orderly, nowhere have I instructed you to do menial labor."

Her lips thin, but she doesn't respond.

"Forgive me for asking a ridiculous question. Do I, or do I not pay someone to clean the office?"

"Yes, sir. *Me.*"

"You?" Of course I already know this.

"Me, myself, and I, sir. And I like manual labor."

"The word I used is *menial*. You'll find it on October first in your daily word calendar. Now answer my question. Why are you cleaning the office?"

She crosses her arms, almost looking annoyed that I've dared to question her. "Not everyone is born with a silver spoon —" She stops just short of finishing her insult. Her face reddens and her throat bobbles. Posthaste she adds a soft "sir."

"I'll ignore your impudence," I admonish, hoping I don't bust a gut trying to keep from laughing. She really is adorable in a diamond-in-the-rough kind of way.

"Thank you, *sir*."

I raise one eyebrow. *Was that a hint of impertinence in the "sir"?* I give her a curt nod and turn to leave. In the reflection on the elevator, I see her do a mock curtsy behind my back. *Why yes, it was.* Perfect. I love humans with backbone. It makes the conquest more satisfying. Punching the button, I can't contain my grin. The elevator opens, and I step inside, composing my face as I turn around. A small hand darts in between the doors, and my heart damn near stops. I hate when people do that. I don't like, or trust, elevators.

"Wait!" she says, eyes wide. "The roads are closed; you can't go home, sir."

I give her my best haughty, stick-up-my-ass look. "I can, and I will."

She removes her hand, and I once again push the button. As the doors close I hear her mutter, "Idiot."

An hour later, I return: wet, cold, and faking a limp. I stood outside freezing my ass off and threw snow on myself to give the illusion of having tried to get home. She damn well better be worth the discomfort, or He and I will have words. Did I mention I fucking hate cold weather?

I glare at my now-smug-looking assistant. "How in heaven did you get here if the roads are impassable?" I roar, struggling out of my wet jacket and running a hand through my damp hair that didn't get cut today. This is another question I already know the answer to.

"I never left."

"You've been here since eight this morning?" I glance at the clock. It's now close to nine. "Did anyone authorize this overtime?"

"No, sir. It isn't overtime. This is my sex, er, second job." She bites her lip at her faux pas.

I grin, stepping into her personal space. She grips her dust rag, looking everywhere but at me.

"How do you plan to get home?" I purr softly.

She steps back, carefully folding the cloth and placing it on her cart. "I'm going to walk, sir."

I do like her attitude. "Walk? As slippery as it is, it's dangerous. I'll escort you." I gesture magnanimously toward the elevator.

A smile crosses her face and a flicker of something darkens her eyes. "Sure, you can walk me home. I just need to empty the trash cans first."

With an exaggerated sigh, I cross my arms and wait, glaring at her for good measure. Not that my annoyance seems to matter. She takes her time finishing before she presses the elevator button. The doors open, and she pushes the cleaning cart in, waiting for me to follow. I hate enclosed areas. Perhaps I should move the office to a one-level building — ideally one situated below ground and utilizing solar panels on the roof. My heart rate accelerates, and I take a few deep breaths before stepping into the tomb of death.

With the cart taking up so much room, we're forced to stand close together. I can smell the scent I've come to associate with her: summer roses. It's rather intoxicating, and so is the fleeting notion of nailing her right here, right now. This isn't an irrational, random thought. Not only is she much more intriguing than I expected her to be, if I were fucking her, I wouldn't be thinking about all the movies where people plunge to their deaths in an elevator.

I take another, deeper breath in anticipation of the ride and realize her delicious scent is tinged with lingering notes of lemon Pledge and bleach. It's a bizarre turn-on. I imagine dusting her off with my tongue...

"Um, sir?"

Her hesitant voice interrupts my fantasy. Obviously my brain is malfunctioning from food deprivation, claustrophobia, and toxic cleaning fumes. *Damn that lemon Pledge.*

"Yes?"

"Could you press the button for the basement, please?"

"Isn't that your job?" I ask in bitchy-boss mode, straightening the knot of my tie, hoping the sweat trickling down my back doesn't stain my shirt and give away my impending anxiety attack.

She sighs and her breasts press into my back as her arm snakes past me to push the button. The temperature in the elevator rises as we descend. Her fingers whisper across my back, making me jump.

"Sorry, sir. Just removing a twig."

The door opens, and I saunter out as if her touch hasn't just ignited my cock like the engine booster on a rocket. She rolls the cart out behind me, storing it in a closet. We're in the basement, and I'm finally able to breathe easier. I follow her to another door, and she motions me inside with a smile.

"Welcome to my home."

Oh. My. God. Mr. DeVille is in *my* apartment. Miracles do happen! I'm a little worried because he's limping, but he looks so sexy all rumpled and out of sorts. His glacial gaze sweeps my one-room studio apartment with a mixture of disdain and shock. I'm sure he grew up in a mansion that's been in his family a gazillion years. The trailer I grew up in was blown away a few years ago by straight-line winds, not even a real dadgum tornado.

Oh, shoot. His eyes lock on the one thing that isn't put away, and his eyebrows lift. There it sits like a damn Oscar on my rickety end table. *The Academy Award for best orgasm goes to...Jolene Sanford!*

My place is tiny, and every piece of furniture serves a dual purpose. Thus, the end table next to the world's most uncomfortable futon is also my nightstand. Heat infuses my cheeks as I pretend to ignore his interest in my battery-operated boyfriend. Whether he's being a gentleman or is too horrified to speak, I'm thankful he doesn't comment.

"Well, I'm home." I ease toward the table. Taking his wet jacket, I use it as a shield to grab the vibrator and shove it behind a book. There's no place for his coat except on top of my bookcase.

"Interesting decor," he teases with a wicked grin as he loosens his tie.

I want to die. These things only happen to me. "Please, sir, make yourself comfortable. Would you like some supper? Or a hot shower? I can throw your clothes in the wash while you bathe. I'm not much of a cook, but I make a mean ham sandwich."

"Are you suggesting I stay *here* tonight?" He wrinkles his nose as if he's smelled a fart.

Or is it the litter box? I'm positive I shoveled it this morning, but knowing my cat, he's pooped on purpose just for spite.

Reality check: I'm ten pounds overweight with mousy brown hair and real tits that are a B cup, not triple Z like Tweedle Ditz and Tweedle Dumb. I'm *so* not his type.

Yet. I'm nothing if not goal-oriented. Someday I'll be his girl-friend—after I lose weight, have a boob job, and learn the art of seduction. However, if I don't quit eating dessert with every meal, this isn't going to happen. *Note to self: Show more restraint with chocolate.*

I shrug, hoping my hurt feelings aren't broadcast across my face. "I was being polite, sir. If you'd rather camp out in your office, I can loan you a pillow and blanket. I don't think the beanie weenies in the vending machine have expired."

The look of disgust crossing his face is pretty dadgum funny. It would serve him right if he's stuck eating nasty canned food, the ar-rogant, handsome-as-homemade-sin jerk. Except I wouldn't really wish that on my worst enemy. "I'll even throw in that ham sandwich. It's whole-wheat bread, too."

The lights flicker, and I hope he decides to stay with me. Being alone with him in the dark would be a dream come true. The lights blink once more, and we're plunged into total darkness. *Yes!* I fist-pump the air before accidentally-on-purpose walking into him under the pretense of looking for a candle. He grasps my arms. I kind of wish he'd grabbed my boobs. I've been in a major sex drought since I moved…and before I moved, which was part of *why* I moved.

"Careful," he murmurs, his warm breath fanning across my fore-head. He smells like promises of sin—spicy, hot, and all male.

"Sorry, sir." *Not sorry.* "I guess you need to stay here, unless you want to walk upstairs in the dark. The elevator won't be working." My voice seems to have dropped an octave, and I hope my glee isn't too evident.

"I suppose. Do you have candles or a flashlight?"

"Yes, sir. In the kitchen. That's where I was going." Shoot, why didn't I think before I spoke? This would have been the perfect op-portunity to seduce him. No lights would mean an inability to see my body. Maybe it feels thinner than it is; I rub a hand across my bottom. *Who am I kidding?* Regardless, I take the opportunity to slide against him, and he hisses in a breath. I'm relieved the lights are out so I can't see what could well be a look of revulsion on his face.

Finding the candle and matches, I get us some light, but I'm not ready for the vision it reveals. My mouth is as dry as Alabama dirt in the summer. Trying to speak, the only sound I manage to make is "mmmm."

"What?" He unbuttons his cuffs, rolling up his sleeves to reveal strong forearms. Tossing the tie on top of his jacket, he looks down at his damp, dirty trousers and frowns.

"You can take your clothes off," I croak, my mouth finally engaging—though unfortunately before my brain. His eyebrows lift, and I'd almost swear there's a twinkle in his eye. "I mean, uh, you could catch your death of cold wearing wet clothes." I pray that didn't sound too lame.

"Don't be ridiculous. That's an old wives' tale." His eyes scan my kitchen area, lighting on a fresh loaf of bread.

"Fine, but don't whine to me if you die of pneumonia, sir. Peanut butter okay since I shouldn't open the fridge?"

He nods. "Friday, think about how illogical that sounds. How could I whine if I'm dead?"

I make him a sandwich. I'm not hungry for anything but him. "Haven't you heard of haints and spirits?"

"In bad movies, yes." He takes the sandwich without so much as a thank you and heads to the futon, where he collapses. "Aren't you eating?"

I want to eat you, like a big ole piece of lemon pie. I'd bet you'd be tart at first bite, but then sweet. "I ate earlier."

"What the hell?" he barks, jumping up and dancing around like a voodoo priest working some mojo. I hear Atticus hissing and rush over, grabbing my poor old cat before he gets trampled.

"What are you doing? You scared him." I hug Atticus to my chest, petting his head and cooing to soothe him.

Mr. DeVille's gaze narrows as he points at my traumatized cat. "I scared *him*? That beast attacked me." Agitated, he paces back and forth. "Are animals allowed in this building?"

I hug Atticus a little tighter, making him squirm. "P-Please, he's ten years old, sir. I should have warned you he likes that end of the futon. It's my fault."

Mr. DeVille's shadow looms large and scary on the wall. Frantic, Atticus howls and twists, trying to get away, and he scratches my neck in the process.

"Ow! Would you please stop pacing and sit down! You're upsetting my cat." Oh, crap. I just screamed at my boss. "Sir," I add as a suck-up afterthought. Atticus manages to wriggle loose and runs under the bookcase.

Mr. DeVille's brows knit together, and he grabs the candle, raising it in front of me. "You're hurt."

"Of course I'm hurt. This cat has been with me through some pretty bad times. I don't want to have to get rid him, and I can't afford to move." I sniffle, looking away and trying to contain the threatening tears. The thought of not having Atticus to curl up with at night when I'm lonely kills me. Now that I've yelled at my demanding, no-nonsense boss, I might as well start packing. If I'm lucky, he'll show mercy and not throw me out in the snow.

"Jolene, I meant you're physically hurt. Your neck is bleeding. Has that animal had his shots?" He turns my head, inspecting my neck. I smell his spicy aftershave and inhale like a stoner. It takes everything in me to refrain from licking his scruffy five o'clock shadow.

It suddenly registers that he called me by my name. My mouth falls open. "You know my name?"

He frowns. "I sign your paycheck, don't I?"

"Technically, no." Sometimes I forget to keep my mouth shut. *Make that a lot of the time.*

"That's neither here nor there. You need to do something; you're bleeding. What if you get cat scratch fever?"

"Don, don, don," I wail Ted Nugent's guitar riff with the three-tone blues progression.

For the first time ever, he laughs. *Mr. DeVille is laughing!* I hope it's *with* me and not *at* me.

"Not bad. What will your encore performance be?"

Hopefully "The House is Rockin'." I blink, praying I didn't say that out loud. *Phew.* I didn't. "I guess you'll have to stick around and find out."

He follows me to the bathroom and holds the candle so I can see. Blood oozes down my neck. I glance at him in the mirror, and he pulls the candle under his chin, making spooky faces.

"I vant to drink your blood." He grins and waggles his eyebrows.

My knees weaken, but I don't have the heart to tell him he sounds more like the Count from *Sesame Street* than Count Dracula. However, the thought of him nibbling on my neck makes me feel like Alice, lost in Sexy Wonderland. The room seems to have shrunk around us. Thankfully the subdued lighting hides my shaking hand as I cleanse the scratch.

He checks out my tiny bathroom, his face unreadable. My entire studio apartment could probably fit inside his bathroom. He reaches for the book on the back of the commode. *First, the vibrator, now this?* This semester I took easy courses as I learned to balance my schedule. Last night, needing to multitask to get everything done, I read my assignment for my human sexuality class while taking a bath.

"*Sex at Dawn?*" His eyes crinkle with amusement. "Fascinating bathroom reading, Friday."

"It's for school, sir."

"Interesting. What kind of homework is involved?"

"Why? Are you offering to help me study?" My brother always tells me to think before speaking to save a world of worry. Someday I might take his advice. Or at the very least tape my mouth shut—which leads to an image of me blindfolded and gagged...

He laughs. "I guarantee you'd get an A."

Beyond embarrassed, I tear out of the bathroom like a NASCAR driver at the Talladega Superspeedway. I need a moment alone to gather my wits before I end up back in the trailer park. It's way too easy to picture myself back home, trudging to the convenience store where I used to work. Hearing him return, I lift my head, and square my shoulders. I can do this.

Mr. DeVille places the candle on the end table and collapses on the futon, eating his sandwich. He casts the stink eye at my cat. Not partial to peanut butter, Atticus ignores us and licks his butt, unaffected by the events unfolding. The stupid cat might think differently if he knew his catnip supply would dry up if I become unemployed.

From my tiny closet, I pull out bedding for Mr. DeVille and myself. He's finished his sandwich and watches me. The weird sensation of being in a National Geographic documentary comes over me. I'm not sure if I'm the predator or the prey. I think I'd like to be the prey. Atticus's purring on his end of the futon sounds like a motorboat in the unnatural silence.

"I'll make the bed for you, sir."

"For me? Where will you sleep?" He stands, glancing around the dimly lit, cramped room.

"I guess the floor. I'd say the bathtub, but it has a constant drip, and it's going to be cold enough without heat."

"Don't be ridiculous. I'm not putting you out of your bed."

Rats, he's going to walk back upstairs to his office. I shrug. "It's no biggie; I slept on the floor as a kid. I realize this isn't what you're used to and all, but I promise the bedding's clean, and I'll lock Atticus in the bathroom for the night. He'll meow for a while but will eventually quit. Actually, it might be best if I sit in there with him. It might help—"

"Friday, you're rambling. Stop."

I immediately shut up, and a tremor of desire courses through me. With the shadows, I can't see his eyes, but the candlelight plays on those sexy lips. I wonder what they taste like, how they feel. Does he kiss like he owns it, like a conqueror? Or tentatively, like an explorer? I'll probably never know. I sigh without thinking, and those perfect lips shift into a frown.

"We're adults and capable of making rational choices. We can share the bed. There's no need for either of us to be any more miserable than the situation warrants."

My inner seductress-wannabe pants in anticipation of lying next to this ideal representation of the male species. *Miserable?* Sharing a bed with Mr. DeVille, are you freaking kidding me? This is my dream come true. Pulling myself together with a mental, *down girl,* I nod docilely and purr, "Whatever you say, sir."

He watches as I wrestle with pulling the futon out into a bed. It's at least fifteen years old, and if it ever saw some serious action, it would probably collapse. I bend over and make the bed, careful to smooth the wrinkles. I can't do a thing about the lumpy mattress and god-awful iron rod that hits your back just wrong. I shoot a nervous glance over my shoulder.

I'd almost swear Mr. DeVille's been staring at my ass. He stretches, and the yawn is audible behind his hand-covered mouth. *Great.* I've practically put him to sleep before we even get in bed. How depressing. I need remedial homework for my human sexuality class. Maybe I'll get some extra-credit study tonight. Atticus gives me a smug, in-your-dreams cat smile.

CHAPTER FOUR

Jolene bends over to make the futon into something we supposedly can sleep on, and my dick stands at attention. I'd love to be drilling her from behind, rubbing that beautiful ass. I have to say, I'm not entirely certain where this is coming from. At least a few parts of me seem to be taking His project very seriously. Raising the candle, I fake a yawn when she peeks over her shoulder at me with those sleepy, bedroom eyes. If I'm lucky, my crotch is hidden in the shadows. Just to be sure, I turn my back to her and kick off my wet shoes and socks. I don't want to move too fast and scare her. This is way too much fun. The only thing that would make it better is if that sanctimonious prick Raphael were here to watch.

The candle flickers on the bedside table where her dildo once sat like the damn Statue of Sexual Liberty—*give me your poor, tired pussy*...I unbutton my shirt. When I glance up, I catch her staring at me again. The look on her face is that of a hormonal teen at an all-you-can-eat chocolate buffet. Remembering my role, I raise one supercilious eyebrow. "Yes?" *Lick me like an ice cream cone, woman.*

Her eyes widen, and she blinks. "Uh, sorry, sir," she squeaks.

Holding her gaze, I slowly shrug out of my shirt, like a stripper at a bachelorette party. Friday scampers to the bathroom, and a resounding crack makes me wince.

"Hells bells."

Only Jolene can give a two-syllable phrase four with her quaint Southern drawl. I keep my thoughts about belles in hell to myself.

"Are you okay?" I ask, feigning politeness.

"Yes, sir. I, uh, ran into the door."

Shit, I love it when she calls me *sir*. She returns smelling minty fresh and hands me a new toothbrush. Her brown hair now hangs loose halfway down her back. My fingers itch to tangle in those waves as I kiss her senseless. Instead, I grab the toothbrush and head for the bathroom, tripping on her beast of a cat. I'd love to feed that damn animal to Black Shuck.

She follows and hands me the candle. "Here, I don't need it. It's my apartment. I get up to pee in the dark all the time." The soft light enhances her beauty. "Shoot, I didn't mean to say that out loud. How embarrassing." Without another word she darts out of the bathroom.

I grin. She's embarrassed about saying *pee* after I've seen her dildo? She's adorable. While washing my face and brushing my teeth, I contemplate the best approach for Jolene's seduction. I don't want to scare her, but time is running out. That annoying do-gooder Raphael is bound to butt in soon. He's always been a cock-block.

I grab the candle, on guard for that sneaky attack cat, and make my way back to the living area. Jolene's already in bed, arms wrapped around her knees.

"Are you ready for bed, sir?"

I close my eyes for a second to get a grip on my raging desire for this woman. *Slow and steady wins the race.* Unzipping my wet trousers, I toss them to the chair and hear a hiss. Good. I'm having an effect on her. My pants move like an alien being, and that damn cat works his way out, flicking his tail with measured annoyance. Apparently it wasn't Jolene hissing with desire. I blow out the candle and dive under the covers with an undignified grunt. Pain radiates through my body. *Holy crap, I think I just broke my hip.*

"Sorry, sir. I know this isn't very comfortable," she whispers.

No shit, Sherlock. "There's no need to say *sir*. We're not in the office." No, we're in bed. Together. So close I can smell her minty breath.

"What should I call you?" she asks, softly.

"I think, considering the fact that we're sharing a bed, you can use my nickname, Luc—though not in the office, of course."

"Luc," she tries. "I like that, the hard *k* sound at the end, rather than the soft *s* sound of Lucius. Did you ever get teased about your name growing up?"

"Teased? Me?" The thought is ridiculous. Scorned maybe. Shunned, definitely. "No. No one dared." *Except that asshole, Raphael.*

"I can imagine."

I hear the smile in her words and grin in return.

We lie there for what seems like an hour, staring at the ceiling. The only sound is the motorboat purring of her damn cat, which stares at me, probably plotting his revenge.

"Do you like snow?" she asks.

There's something about lying in the dark that makes even benign talk about the weather sound seductive. Perfect. "Nope. I detest cold weather. I'm more of a tropics kind of guy. Give me heat over cold any day."

"Where is your favorite place in the world?" She snuggles onto her side, facing me.

I could make a move now, but she isn't ready. Seduction begins with the mind, which women think means discussing feelings. Ridiculous and highly overrated—but if it works? Worth it. I plan to reel her in so smoothly she'll never know she's been caught. "The Grand Cayman." I prop my head on top of my folded hands. "Have you ever been there?"

She snorts. "Sure, I fly there every year to soak in the sun, do a little shopping."

"You could—"

Her phone interrupts me. *Dammit.* I know who it is. She reaches over me to answer. Under her sweatshirt, her nipples are hard. My dick follows suit. My hand might accidentally-on-purpose now rest on her delightful ass. Just to steady her, of course.

"H-Hello?" Her voice sounds strained.

I grin, happy she can't see my Cheshire cat-like smirk of impending triumph.

"I'm fine." She scoots back onto her side of the uncomfortable so-called bed.

My glee dissipates like bubbles from flat champagne. Sure enough, it's that irritating do-gooder Raphael checking up on his precious little Jolene. I resist the urge to grab the phone and assure him she's in *good hands.*

"The power's off." She pauses, listening. "No, no, there's no reason to risk your life coming over. I'm fine." She sighs. "No, I'm not alone." Now she huffs. "Not that it is any of your business, but Lu — er, Mr. DeVille got snowed in, so he's here. Oh, uh, no. It hasn't really been brought up yet." Again, she's silent as she listens. "*Stop*, you're not my brother. I promise I won't be stupid. *Good night.*" She hangs up with a defeated sigh.

The jerk asked her about protection. Damn that cock-blocking fucker. From her disappointed look, she doesn't have any. Not a problem. It isn't like I'm not prepared. But the mood has been killed.

She rolls over, her back to me. "Good night, sir."

"Luc."

I'm not sure she's heard me until she whispers, "Good night, Luc."

I hang up with Jolene and hurl my phone across the room. I should have seen this coming and stayed late at work. Luc has made his move, and I can't interrupt without blowing my cover. I berate myself for failing her; it's my job to protect her. I can't dabble with her free will, but I'm supposed to influence her away from temptation. She'd never been any problem until Luc set his sights on her. I blame myself. Because of my neglect, she's become curious.

Not that sex is bad. Contrary to what some believe, The Boss is all for it. He invented it so life can continue. If I were in charge, I might have put in a few more safeguards...

The lights flicker. *Sorry, Sir.*

The problem is who Jolene's considering having sex with. I know Luc. He'll use her and cast her aside. With her family genetics and low self-esteem, this could throw her down a dark path. I should've paid more attention to her over the years, but the fact is, she never complains. Ever. Despite a tough childhood, she's everything good about the human race. She was lonely and isolated as a little girl, so I took her under my wing, so to speak. However, to keep up the human pretense, I had to move on.

Who am I kidding? When she was a teenager, I started to develop feelings for her beyond the realm of my duties. I left more for my sake than hers. Because she wasn't a rebellious teen, I'd convinced myself everything was fine—until The Boss sent me back to check on her. Turns out I suck at being a guardian angel.

But now I'm here to rectify the situation. It shouldn't be too hard to get her back on track. Jolene's a bright young woman, just stubborn.

Standing with my hands on my hips, I debate what to do with this latest development. Trusting Luc is out of the question. I could break the rules and fly to her place, but I don't want to upset The Boss.

I retrieve my phone to call her back. Maybe if I keep her talking, Luc won't have an opportunity to try anything. Jolene is smart, but no match for my fallen brother. I'm puzzled as to why he's even interested in her. Good girls aren't his type. There's enough strife in this world to keep him occupied. And I'm sure there are plenty of folks willing to walk on the dark side without him having to work so hard. Why Jolene? Despite being twenty-five, she's too naïve and trusting for her own good. For Pete's sake, she doesn't even have any *condoms*. My gut wrenches with worry as my thumb hovers over redial. *Help me*, I pray silently. I can't fail her. I'll never be able to forgive myself.

My lights flicker again. He's heard me, and a sense of calm comes over me. At least for now, she'll be okay.

Something jars me, and I tighten my eyelids. My feet feel like chunks of ice, but I'm having the most amazing dream. I try with all my might to resist waking.

Mr. DeVille barks over the intercom for me to bring him his coffee. I enter his office, shaking—not because he's mad, but because I'm stark naked and freezing. He sits at his desk fully dressed, and I notice he's wearing my favorite gray suit and purple-striped tie. I approach slowly, praying I don't spill the hot coffee on myself. A tingle of anticipation shivers down my spine as I wait for him to look up...

"Friday."

"Sir." *I'm surprised I don't feel self-conscious about my nakedness. I don't even like looking at myself in the mirror after a shower.*

"Friday." The exasperation sounds more pronounced this time, and my eyes fly open. I'm lodged between my boss and cat. Judging by the loud sigh to my left, and the tail lashing to my right, both are annoyed. My head rests on Mr. DeVille's shoulder, and my arm is wrapped around his warm waist. Maybe I'm still dreaming. I close my eyes and snuggle in closer.

"Aaghhh! Shit!"

The voice is real; it wasn't part of my dream. I sit up, startled, pushing my hair out of my face.

"What?" Clicking the lamp, I realize the power remains off, so I relight the candle.

Atticus jumps down with an aggravated kitty *harrumph*. The temperature in the room is almost as icy as the demeanor of the man next to me.

Shivering, Mr. DeVille pulls up the covers, rolling in them like a cocoon. "Your f-feet are like damn icicles. Put some s-socks on, woman."

"Sorry, sir." I scramble from the bed. When my feet hit the cold floor, my molars chatter like wind-up fake teeth. Positive he's horrified by the entire situation, I grab some socks, not daring to look at him. I know what I look like in the morning, and it isn't a pretty sight. My hair always looks like I stuck my finger in a socket, and I usually have a raccoon mask from not fully removing my eye makeup. Plus, my dream is still fresh in my memory. Despite the frigid condition in my apartment, heat scorches my cheeks like a beach bonfire.

Perching on the chair, I slip on my socks and another sweatshirt. Finding an old, roomy blue sweatshirt, I toss it to Mr. DeVille. "Do you want a pair of socks?" I ask, holding up my favorite pair of Hello Kitty knee-highs.

He frowns as he struggles out of the covers to pull on the sweatshirt. The blanket falls to his waist, and my eyes take in the glorious sight of a half-naked Mr. DeVille. Despite being covered in goose bumps, his sculpted chest could easily grace the cover of a sports fitness magazine. Now hot and bothered, I regret putting on the extra sweatshirt.

"No th-thanks. I'm not a c-cat lover."

Slipping into the sweatshirt, his teeth clack together so hard I'm afraid I may have to pay his dental bill. Atticus glares at him, apparently not amused by the cat lover statement.

"When will they get the power back on? This is ridiculous," he mutters, sounding more like his grouchy self.

I shrug, unable to formulate a coherent sentence while looking at his bed-rumpled hair and the sexy morning-stubble on his face. He's too beautiful for words. To keep from staring, I leave to visit the bathroom. It takes me a minute, but I find another candle in the vanity drawer and light it. As I brush my teeth, I worry about my lack of groceries and what I can make him for breakfast without power. *He could have me.* Should I take a cold shower, just in case? One glance in the mirror tells me it probably won't be needed.

Oh well, a girl can dream. I send up a quick prayer, begging for the power to stay off forever—or at least for one more day. As I leave the bathroom, I run into a wall of a delicious male chest, and immediately regret giving him the sweatshirt. But it's probably for the best. I'm sure he'd be horrified if I licked his bare pecs. I bite my lip and hug my ribcage to keep from wrapping my arms around him.

"Easy now." His hands grip my shoulders to steady me, and yet my world still reels. The sound of my harsh breathing saws between us, and despite the frigid air, I'm pretty sure steam comes off my skin.

"Sorry, s—"

"Luc." He taps my nose with his finger.

"Luc."

"Good girl." I hear the smile in his voice. My feminist side chafes under the sexist term. My inner sex-kitten-wannabe wants to rub against him, purr, and offer to be his bad girl. Instead, I step aside as he shoves past me into the bathroom, slamming the door. With haste, I make my way to the kitchen area and panic when I realize he won't have his morning coffee.

This is a fiasco waiting to happen. A caffeine addict, Mr. DeVille jonesing for java could get ugly. I wonder briefly if Atticus will mourn my demise and stand guard over my dead carcass. I read about a dog doing this when his owner died. My cat looks at me with a typical *as if* look of feline indifference before stomping away with an angry slash of his tail.

Already jittery, I jump at the piercing sound of Atticus howling outside the bathroom door. He's clearly upset that his routine has been interrupted. First a stranger took his side of the bed, and now he's barred from his bathroom. It must be six in the morning. I can set my watch by my cat's morning litter box visit.

The bathroom door opens with a whoosh. "What the hell is that god-awful caterwauling?"

"Um, a cat?" I offer, unable to stifle my giggle. Mr. DeVille jumps when Atticus streaks past him.

"Did I mention I hate cats?" He runs a hand through his hair and wrinkles his nose. The scratching sound from the bathroom is obviously Atticus's response.

"I believe it was implied, sir. Would another peanut butter sandwich be okay for breakfast? I'll try to make you some coffee on my Hibachi grill."

"A sandwich is fine. Don't worry about the coffee; the weather is frigorific, you don't need to risk frostbite."

"Frigorific? That sounds like something from a cartoon."

"Frigorific is a fine word, and I don't watch cartoons. I believe you'll find it on your calendar under November third."

I check my calendar, and sure enough, he's right. It's an adjective that means *producing extreme cold*. It's also archaic. How did he know that? It isn't November...I glance back at him, but turn away so he can't see me grinning at the sight of him in my sweatshirt and his boxers. Apparently the frigorific condition in my apartment hasn't affected his morning wood. Snickering at my own crude thoughts, I wish for the umpteenth time he was naked. But this isn't a fairy tale, and wishes don't come true. He climbs back in bed, pulling the covers up to his chin.

"It isn't that cold. I don't mind trying to make you a cup of coffee," I offer as I slather peanut butter on bread for our less-than-stellar breakfast.

"Weren't you ever told lying is a sin? Goddammit, cat, quit hogging the covers."

Grumpyboss really needs his coffee. I hand him his sandwich and head back to the kitchen to get the grill. I'll brave the cold if it gets his majesty some caffeine and a better mood.

"Where are you going?" He glares at me, and his voice sounds colder than the air around us.

"To try to make coffee. Or I could walk around the corner and see if the coffee shop is open. Sometimes businesses have generators."

"Friday, get your ass back in bed, *now*."

Heck yeah!

"I don't want you getting sick. I need you at the office. No one else can make a decent cup of coffee," he grumbles.

"Yes, sir," I reply with a defeated sigh. He says I make decent coffee, yet he doesn't want me making him coffee. Bipolar much? The fact he doesn't want me in his bed *like that* stings a bit. I guess I still have a way to go before I'm girlfriend material. I climb back in, careful not to get too close. I can't risk my job.

Atticus begins to head-butt Mr. DeVille. I try shoving my pushy pet off the bed, but he ignores me. Clinging to the covers with his claws, he lavishes attention on my cat-hating boss.

"Sorry, sir. You know what they say: cats always take up with the people who hate them most."

To my surprise, Mr. DeVille scratches Atticus behind the ears instead of pushing him away. "Since we're stuck here, what should we do?" Finished with his sandwich, he wipes his mouth with his thumb. I'd have been more than willing to lick it clean for him.

A pounding on the door interrupts us. Dadgumit, just when things are about to get interesting with Mr., er, Luc. I scurry to the door, intent on getting rid of whoever it is. I find Rafe holding a bag of food and two cups of coffee.

"Hey, I figured your power was still out, so I brought you some coffee and breakfast." His eyes scan my small apartment, narrowing when he spies Luc.

Mr. DeVille smirks. "What impeccable timing. Goodman, is it?" He casually swings his legs over the side of the bed and steps into his pants.

"Yes, sir." Although polite, Rafe's voice has an edge to it. The tension in the air snaps like an impending storm. "The roads are clear, although Mrs. Cabot called and said not to come to work today since schools are still closed and the power remains off for much of the area. Here included, I see."

"How astute of you to notice. No wonder I pay you the big bucks. Of course Mrs. Cabot said to stay home. It isn't her losing money, is it?"

Mr. DeVille pulls off my sweatshirt, revealing those cut abs. I stare unabashedly, and Rafe snaps his fingers in front of my face. Luc buttons his shirt, glaring at Rafe the entire time.

"Well, Friday. Thank you for the hospitality. I'm sure since Goodman *flew* here on the icy roads to check on you, I'll have no problems getting home. I suggest you take today to study for your classes, and remember I'll be more than happy to help with your homework assignments." His eyes flash with desire, and my cheeks heat.

Rafe snarls, looking positively feral.

"A-Are you sure the roads are okay? Would you like a cup of this coffee before you go?"

"I only brought two cups," Rafe protests.

Shocked by his rudeness — and to our boss, no less — I quickly offer, "*Mr. DeVille* can have my cup." *What has gotten into him?*

Ignoring Rafe, Mr. DeVille turns to me as he shrugs into his coat. "That's quite all right. Thank you, Friday." He gives me a conspiratorial wink and a smile.

Rafe, in comparison, receives a cool nod. The hair on my arms stands on end when Mr. DeVille stops and turns to face my friend. I must be having some sort of low blood sugar event because I swear it looks like the rims of his blue eyes have turned the color of a hot stove eye. I blink and find him glaring at Rafe, and the look is returned in kind. Good thing we aren't living in a century past. If we were, I'm quite certain there would be a duel at fifty paces. He leaves without saying another word.

Rafe slams the door with a muttered, "Good riddance."

I cross my arms in front of my chest. "Thanks a lot."

"You're welcome." He ignores my sarcasm.

I sigh and gratefully accept the warm to-go cup. I can't stay mad at him for long; he's my best friend.

And he has coffee.

CHAPTER FIVE

"I was being sarcastic," I clarify. "What's up with the clam jam? Why are you really here?"

I walk to the kitchen area, and Rafe follows. I add powdered creamer to my coffee. The heat from the cup feels good, warming my cold hands.

"Clam jam? What are you talking about? A friend can't drop in on another friend?"

"You know full well what you interrupted."

His eyes flash with annoyance before he composes his face. My stomach rumbles, and he smiles. "At least I'm able to satisfy *one* of your baser needs."

He hands me the bag, and I grin at the smell of freshly baked donuts. We automatically move toward my rumpled futon. I feel a little self-conscious about Rafe having almost caught me in bed with our boss. However, practicality wins over embarrassment. It's the warmest place in my apartment, and I dive under the covers. Rafe throws his coat on the bookcase, kicks off his shoes, and using the candle, inspects the sheets.

"What are you doing?"

"Making sure I'm not getting into something that will make me puke."

"God, you're sick. I just told you *nothing* happened, thanks to your impeccable timing."

He snickers and puts the candle down before climbing in bed.

Digging into the sack, I grab my favorite: a Bavarian cream. "My hips need this like an alcoholic needs a beer."

Rafe nudges my shoulder. "Stop it. You're not fat." He dunks his plain cake donut in his coffee. "So what are we gonna do today?"

"I need to study."

"Pfft. You don't have classes tomorrow, just work. We can play today. Wanna make snow angels?"

"I thought you said it was melting. Besides, I don't have heat, and I'm already freezing."

"Come here; I'll warm you up." He holds out his arm as he sips his coffee, and I cuddle in close. He's always provided such a sense of security. It's more than just his height and the fact that he has guns that won't quit. It's a feeling of comfort, like the warm breeze across the lapping water of the pond where we used to hang together as kids.

"You know, it occurs to me that while I know your favorite Golden Girl and what brand of tampon you use—"

I punch his arm. Only once did I ask him to buy them for me, and it was an emergency.

"You haven't told me much about your life after I left Hicksville."

I snicker at our nickname for our hometown, but hesitate before answering. I don't talk about my home life. *Ever.* I shrug and place my coffee on the nightstand. "There isn't much to tell."

"Come on. You always said you were going to leave as soon as you turned eighteen; what took you so long? Share your deep, dark secrets."

"I have no secrets." I refuse to admit my irrational anger when he left for college. I'd never felt so alone.

He puts his coffee down and pushes me back on the bed. Propping his head on his hand, he grins. "Somehow I doubt that. Everyone has secrets. We haven't got anything else to do with no power."

It's not lost on me that this is the second guy in my bed in less than an hour, and that there are plenty of things we could do besides talk.

Funny, I haven't thought of Rafe like that since I was a teenager. His dark, wavy hair is longer than Luc's, and there's a touch of premature gray at the temple. I love his designer-stubble beard. His lips are full and generous, just like his heart. Staring at those perfect lips, my brain turns to mush, and my nerves seem to tingle with a sudden awareness of this man as potentially so much more than a friend.

Startled at this turn in my thinking, I begin my pathetic story. "Well, after you left, I pretty much just minded my own business. You know I was living with Johnny Waylon and his wife, Lynn, by then."

"Yeah, your brother's a great guy. How is he?"

"Fine. I talked to him a few weeks ago. He's now the sheriff back home. Lynn got sick with ALS two years after they married. I worked part time, took a few classes online, and helped take care of her until her death six months ago." I try to remember when Rafe might've met Johnny Way, but I can't think of a time their paths ever crossed. My brother's ten years older than me, so he and Rafe weren't in school together.

"I'm sorry about Lynn. I didn't know," he murmurs.

My teeth chatter, and to my surprise, Rafe draws me in closer, wrapping the quilt up to my neck. I use his shoulder as a pillow and wrap my arm around his waist. With my thigh resting on top of his, I'm no longer cold—far from it. Heat courses through my veins.

What's wrong with me? Have I really contemplated intimacy with two different men this morning? These convoluted feelings for my friend *and* my boss must be the result of hypothermia. It's the only explanation.

"Heard from your parents lately?" Rafe asks.

I pick nervously at the button on his shirt. "Do you really want to talk about my ignominious family?" *Ignominious* is today's word of the day. I saw it on my calendar, and it describes my past perfectly: *causing disgrace or shame.*

He raises his eyebrows, and one corner of his perfect mouth rises. "Continue, Scheherazade."

"Bless you." I hand him a tissue.

"What?"

"Didn't you sneeze?"

He laughs, making me smile in return. I love his deep, hearty laugh.

"Didn't you ever read *The One Thousand and One Nights?*"

"No. Is it a good book?" I didn't realize Rafe had a penchant for erotica…

"It's like a collection of fairy tales. Scheherazade was brought before the king of Persia. The guy was a horny horror who would marry a virgin every day, bed her, and then have her beheaded. But Scheherazade was smart. She knew the real way to capture a man's attention was with her mind. So she told the king a story, ending it with a cliffhanger just as dawn broke. The king was intrigued and allowed her live, with the stipulation that she must finish the story that night. Every morning, Scheherazade left the story hanging. This continued for many nights until she confessed she had no more stories. However, by this time, the king had fallen in love with her, so her life was spared. They lived happily ever after."

My mind wanders back to Mr. DeVille. I'd tell him a story every night, but I have a feeling it would take something more than a good yarn to hold his interest. I add researching tantric sex to my mental to-do-list.

Rafe nudges my shoulder, and I pull my thoughts away from sex with my boss. "Go on," he says. "Do you have any contact with your parents?"

I snort my derision. My parents were parents in name only, and he knows it. "Last time I saw her, my mother was playing the role of genteel Southern lady. She's taken to wearing fake pearls and serving tater tot casserole at church dinners, saying things like 'mercy me' and 'bless her heart.'"

"I hear a *but* in there." His hand rubs my back in lazy circles, encouraging me to continue.

He's rubbed my back before, and I thought nothing of it. But today I'm hyperaware that he's a single, attractive man—and in my bed. He smells good, too. Unlike Mr. DeVille, who smells of hot spice and promises of sex, Rafe smells like cool water on a still night. It's soothing and makes me want to unbutton the button I've been playing with and snuggle closer.

I snap out of it and sit up, glad when Atticus hops on the bed, demanding attention. "The only reason my mother joined the church was to garner sympathy after Robert Earl—you remember my dead-beat father—got sent off to the pen. She relishes her role of victim.

The truth is Crimson's still addicted to pills and won't be winning Mother of the Year any time soon."

"You know you're nothing like her." Rafe kisses the top of my head. It's as if he knows being just like her is my biggest fear.

I realize I don't know much about his family, except that he was a latchkey kid. It's weird now that I think about it. In all our years growing up together, our families never met. Unlike me, he said he came from a stable home, despite his mom not being in the picture and his father's lengthy absences for work. My upbringing and his were so far apart they're not even on the same road map. Not that I'm complaining. Like Johnny Way says, you just gotta play the hand life deals you.

"After I moved in with Johnny Way, he kept my butt in class with threats until I graduated," I say, resuming my tale. "He and Lynn did the best they could to make up for our lousy parents. Even after Lynn got sick, he taught me to be grateful for what we did have. He's a good man." I sigh, missing him.

"That explains a lot," Rafe murmurs.

"What?"

"Nothing. What's new with your dad?"

I snort. Robert Earl's name may be on my birth certificate, but he ain't — I mean *isn't* no father. At age six I quit calling him Daddy after he kicked me off the front porch like a stray mongrel just because I didn't bring him a beer fast enough. Angry and hurt, I ran away from home and got lost in the woods. That's when Rafe rescued me.

My leg bounces, and I force it to stop. I don't like talking about my past. The past is best left behind. I'm more interested in the future — a future I plan to make for myself.

"I don't have much contact with him," I finally say, looking away. The last time I made the effort to do the Christian thing and visit him in prison, he refused to see me. Even after all these years, his rejection still hurts. "Robert Earl resides at the William E. Donaldson Correctional Facility on account of his agricultural interest in growing non-medicinal marijuana."

Rafe's eyes remain focused on me, and although I sense anger simmering just below the surface, his face doesn't reveal a thing.

I grin and try to lighten the mood. "Johnny Way says hauling his butt to jail was the highlight of his career as county sheriff. I heard he threw in a few extra wallops takin' the SOB down. I figure it was to make up for us being Robert Earl's punchin' bags growin' up."

Rafe laughs. "Good for him."

"I need to call and check on him, maybe even go home for a weekend soon. I know he must be lonely. And he's always been there for me. Remember when Johnny Way and Lynn took me to live with them, and Crimson didn't even notice I was gone for two weeks? All because it was the first of the month, and she had a ready supply of her prescription meds. And Robert Earl was too drunk or stoned to care." I laugh to hide my true feelings. My parents' indifference has always hurt a lot more than the beatings from my no-count father.

"Anyone special in your life—aside from your ridiculous fascination with that jerk Lusty DeVillain?"

I punch his arm but giggle at his ridiculous name for our boss. "No, Johnny Way's the best, but Lord, he's so overprotective. Make him mad and he's got the temperament of a chained pit bull bred to fight. I didn't date much back home. The guys all said he was too good a shot—not that I had much free time anyway."

I heave a sigh, thoroughly finished with this topic. "Enough about me. Tell me something I don't know about you. How's your dad? Is he retired yet?"

Battling a flash of panic, I take a moment to collect my thoughts. I can't tell Jolene about my life without blowing my cover. It's strange. On other missions I've told plenty of stories to cover my true identity. But with Jolene, it's different. I hate lying to her, so I give her an abridged, vague version of the truth.

"Let's see. Uh, Dad still works all the time, but I talk to Him every day. He still loves gadgets. The last time I saw Him, He was stuck on some game on His new phone. I've had a few different jobs before landing here..." Distracted, my voice trails off.

She's playing with the button on my shirt, as if she wants to unbutton it. I'm not sure if she's even conscious she's doing it. My obvious physical reaction is disconcerting. Sometimes pretending to be human can be embarrassing. I roll onto my stomach, dislodging her before she becomes aware.

"Jo…"

"Yes?"

"I'm sorry." Guilt eats at me. I should've done more to protect her from the aftermath of her crappy childhood. Knowing I've failed as her guardian angel unsettles me deeply. "I'll make it up to you," I blurt.

"Sorry for what? Make what up to me?" A puzzled frown furrows her brow.

"Um, all the hard things you've been through."

She laughs. "Silly. It wasn't your fault." She shivers. "There is one thing you can do."

"Anything."

"Get closer; I'm freezing."

Burrowing back under the covers, I pull her soft, willing body into my arms. Her mewl of satisfaction triggers an intense desire to feel skin on skin. I grit my teeth and clench my fists to keep from ripping her clothes off and burying myself deep within her. I need to get control of myself, focus on the job I'm here to do. This longing for a girl I'm supposed to protect goes against everything I believe. I shouldn't be having these feelings. But then again, maybe I've had them for a long time.

"They say if you get naked, you stay warmer by sharing body heat." Jo shivers.

Did she just read my mind? She rises on her elbows and stares at me. Her eyes crinkle at the corners, and a smile plays across her full lips. I think she's teasing me, but my thinking is so muddled, I'm not sure. I've never experienced anything like this before.

"I've heard the same thing," I whisper. The temperature seems to increase as we play our sexual waiting game.

In the wake of this complicated awareness swirling between us, I only distantly recall that I'm here to protect her from precisely this: an act of lust, not love. Right now I want to kiss that plump lower lip and connect with her on more than a cerebral level. This feeling is primal, and I've never felt so alive. It takes every bit of self-control I can muster to keep my human cover. I'd love to flaunt my feathers like a preening peacock.

By nature, I have keen eyesight, which doesn't help my situation at the moment. I force my eyes from Jo's glorious breasts, rising and falling with each audible breath. I have difficulty swallowing when I realize she's staring at me like I'm a triple-decker ice cream cone in August. Her cat-like eyes darken, and her tongue teases across her lower lip. Curiosity lingers on her face, and I pray she never develops a gambling addiction. She'd lose her shirt. Which would be fine right now. Cupping her cheek, I trace my thumb around her mouth.

"Y-You're beautiful," she whispers, brushing a strand of hair off my forehead. "Why have I never noticed that before?"

"I've noticed."

Her lips curve into a wider smile. "You've noticed you're beautiful?" she teases.

"N-No. I've noticed *you're* beautiful." I feel myself falling into a dangerous abyss of emotion, and if I'm not careful, I'm going to drown. Lines are blurring. Jolene is no longer just a job. *Was she ever?*

The last time this happened, I left.

I should leave again.

I don't move.

"Me? I'm fat." She looks away but grips me tighter.

I continue to explore her face with my fingertips. I'm not the only one sinking like lead in these uncharted waters. "Yes. You. Stop it; you're far from fat. I don't like those stick-thin girls; most men don't. We like softness, curves. You're wonderful just the way you are, and don't let anyone convince you otherwise." I inhale her warm, intoxicating scent. "You always smell like the wild summer roses that grew by the pond. Whenever I see pink roses, I think of you…"

Jolene sucks in a ragged breath. It's my undoing. The pulse in her neck pounds as I cup her cheeks in my hands, pulling her closer. I tease her lips with mine. They're softer than I imagined, and they smile before opening, allowing me to deepen the kiss. She doesn't close her eyes, and like a magnet, my eyes are riveted to hers. I see her soul hungering for mine. The soft sigh from the back of her throat pushes me over the edge. I'm gone. I feel one-hundred-percent human, and it's heavenly.

The harsh overhead light flicks back on, and the groan of her ancient refrigerator coming back to life breaks the spell. Awkwardness takes over.

Jolene hops off me, her face flushed. Without saying a word, she hurries to her kitchen area. She refuses to look at me, and her hand shakes as she measures coffee, spilling it on the counter. Under her breath, she hisses, *fork*. I know the word she *could* have used, and it seems apropos, considering the situation. I run a hand through my hair and try to rein in these human feelings and physical reactions.

"Coffee will be ready in a few." She wipes the counter, still not making eye contact.

I sit on the side of the futon, feeling embarrassed and full of remorse. With the lights back on, we've switched from almost-lovers back to friends and co-workers. The old roles now seem boring and incongruent with these new feelings, but I know they're necessary. I'm not really here to be her friend, or co-worker, and certainly not her lover. I'm here to guide her away from the pain and suffering sure to follow if she continues her obsession with Luc.

"I guess I'll head home and let you study." I look over my shoulder at her, hoping she'll ask me to stay as I put on my socks and shoes.

She doesn't say a word. Her hair is a tousled mess, and she's still shivering as she stoops to pet Atticus.

I shrug into my coat and walk over to her. "Jo?"

She stands before me, holding her cat like a shield over her chest. "Yes?"

"I, uh —"

"Shh…" She shakes her head and finally looks up at me. "It's okay. We got carried away in the moment. It was just a kiss." She shrugs nonchalantly.

Just a kiss? An unfamiliar pang grips my heart. "Exactly." I reach out and give Atticus a scratch behind his ears. "Well, I guess I'll see you at work tomorrow."

"'Kay. Be careful." She opens the door for me.

I leave, resigned to being a crappy friend and the world's worst guardian angel.

CHAPTER SIX

I collapse on my futon, wondering if I'm in shock, or at the very least living in some sort of parallel universe. Maybe I'm dreaming. Atticus head-butts me, purring like a jacked-up motorboat. Nope, not dreaming. My bossy cat is once again happy as the sole male competing for my attention.

Just thinking about Luc and Rafe makes my insides heat and flip. One man I want desperately to kiss, and I've just sampled the lips of the other. *And what a kiss.* It was like being zapped by a jolt of electricity. Remembering makes me feel tingly and hot. It also reminds me of when I was fifteen and overrun by hormones — I tried my untested female wiles on Rafe. I kissed him, but it was uncomfortable and left me feeling silly and embarrassed. He left for college soon after, so I quit thinking of him as boyfriend material. We've always had a more sibling-like vibe in our relationship, and it's worked for us.

Today's kiss had to have been a fluke, a by-product of the ambiance created by the power outage and the testosterone-laden one-upmanship between him and Mr. DeVille. The more I think about it, the more I convince myself what happened wasn't about me. Shoving the strangely disappointing thought away, I focus my attention back to my original plan: moving from boss's assistant to boss's girlfriend.

I just hope I haven't blown my chance. In the light of day, Mr. DeVille—Luc, I remind myself. He told me to call him Luc. Oh wait, that was just when we were in bed, not in the office. But what about in my fantasies? *Agh*, I'm so confused. Regardless, he may very well be horrified by what almost transpired between us. Was I too aggressive? And my butt is about the size of Vermont. Oh my God, what if he fires me for sexual harassment? Jesus take the wheel—even though I'm halfway through my twenties, Johnny Way will tan my hide.

"Oh, Atticus, how did my life go from mundane to exhilarating? What do I do?" Typical of my cat, he ignores me. It's the response I'm used to from men.

Now that there's been an unexpected turn in my journey to becoming everything Mr. DeVille wants in a woman, I'm lost. It's like I skipped a step and don't know where to pick back up.

Sighing, I give up trying to figure out my now-complicated life. I don't have time to waste. I've been given the gift of a few extra hours to get caught up on schoolwork. With a last scratch behind Atticus's ears, I head to the shower. Today's goals are to finish my homework, get a good night's sleep, and see what tomorrow brings. This is doable.

Doing my best not to trip in these ridiculous heels, I enter Mr. DeVille's office the following morning. I pause to admire the object of my affection. He's had his hair trimmed, and his tailored black suit showcases his broad shoulders. His crimson tie contrasts with his ice blue eyes, which are fixed on me as I approach. I run a hand over my pencil skirt and glance down, making sure my blouse is buttoned. I attempt a sultry approach, channeling a runway model. Judging by the sloshing of the coffee, I don't think it's working. At least I don't stumble and fall.

I place his coffee and newspaper on his desk, inhaling the hot, spicy aftershave that makes me think of sex.

To my surprise, he says, "Thank you."

Thank you? For what? Thinking about sex? *No, dummy, the coffee.* I pull in my wayward thoughts and await further directions.

He pauses with the cup halfway to his lips, staring at me as if he just read my horny thoughts. His brows knit together, and a bubble of panic forms in my Spanx-flattened stomach. Have I forgotten something? I heated his coffee and added the right amount of sweetener. The newspaper is folded precisely, headline up…

"Stop fidgeting."

"Sir?"

"You heard me. It's your tell when you're nervous. Learn to control it."

I take a deep breath and release it. "Yes, sir. Is there anything else you need?"

"Yes. I want you to fly with me to New York."

Crimson once caught Johnny Way looking at porn and smacked him, screaming that he'd go blind. I thought this was an old wives' tale, but now I'm wondering if it's true—and other senses are involved, too. Surely my lust has affected my hearing. There's no way my dream lover and boss just asked me to fly off with him for a rendezvous.

"W-What?"

"You know I don't like to repeat myself."

That sounds more like the Mr. DeVille I know, but my mind is still reeling, and I blurt, "I-I can't."

"Why not?"

Why not, indeed? *Because I'm not ready.* "I don't know if I can get the time off." What. The. Fork? Have I lost my ever-loving mind?

"I'll clear it with your asshole boss," he replies with a smirk.

That almost makes me giggle. "I don't have anything to wear." What the heck is wrong with me? My dream is to see him naked. *Exactly.* I want *him* naked; he doesn't want to see *me* naked with my dimply butt.

Shut up, I chastise myself.

"I beg your pardon?"

Oh shoot, I said that out loud!

"Uh, I meant, shut the front door! You want *me* to go to New York?"

"At times you have a charming way of phrasing the English language, Jolene."

I mentally slap my doubts aside. Mr. DeVille just invited me to go with him on a trip! This is my dream come true. I bite my tongue to keep from saying anything else. I'll ask Rafe to help me. He used to be a jeans and T-shirts kind of guy, but now he dresses like a *GQ* model. Surely there's hope for me too.

Mr. DeVille smiles, and his gaze travels down my body. I feel visually undressed. "We'll go shopping; I'll buy you a dress. A wardrobe if you want." He shrugs as if it's nothing.

"Why me?" My brain feels muddled, like when your GPS hasn't updated and has to recalculate. I have no idea which direction I'm headed right now.

"You're my assistant, aren't you?" He raises one eyebrow. "I need you on this business trip."

"Yes, sir. Of course." *Duh.* A business trip. For work. I'm not girlfriend material, yet. I make a conscious effort to school my features. "But I can't afford to fly up there." Has he lost his mind? *No, obviously I have.* This is still a step in the right direction. We'll be together regardless of the reason. I'll be able to prove myself as an invaluable employee and, perhaps if I work hard at it, a witty and charming companion.

"Jolene, I'll take care of all the expenses. Now come here."

I approach his desk, thinking he's going to hand me the file he's been reading.

His hand cups my bottom, and he pulls me closer, giving me a quick kiss. I taste the coffee on his lips and see desire flicker like flames in his mesmerizing blue eyes. A vague uneasiness settles over me. This smacks of something sleazy. Months of fantasizing about this kiss dissipate like junk mail run through a shredder.

"No, thank you," I tell him.

"Hmm?" He nuzzles my neck, hitting the spot that makes my knees weak and turns my brain to mush.

"I said, no thank you, sir." I step back. I need distance to remain strong. Wrapped in his arms, I want to fall to my knees and worship him. I'd do anything for him, with him, and to him, if he asked.

"Why not?"

"I don't want to be *that girl.* The cliché office girl used by her boss and tossed aside. I don't want to send myself the thank-you-for-the-sex flowers." In the light of day, the night of the power outage is an embarrassment. Shame heats my cheeks. I'm better than this, and I deserve better. Johnny Way has always cautioned me that men don't buy the milk when the cow is free.

"Mixed signals, much?" He sips his coffee.

He's right. But I'm not in so deep that I can't stop and rethink my plan. I want Lucius DeVille like I've never wanted anything in my life. But I want him to want me because I interest him, not because I'm readily available. I refuse to be a one-time fling. I want the fairy-tale ending. I want to be Julia Roberts in *Pretty Woman*. Except for the prostitution part. *Eww.*

I lift my chin, meeting his gaze. "I apologize if I've given you the wrong idea."

"Don't make this a big deal. I have to attend a party and make nice with some business associates. You'll serve two purposes: my assistant and my date."

But this *is* a big deal to me. I refuse to be just a booty call. "Why me? Why not take Tweedle Ditz or Tweedle Dumb—uh, I mean, someone else?"

His eyes crinkle, and a grin splits his face. "Because I need someone who can carry on an intelligent conversation."

I blink, pondering his statement. *He thinks I'm intelligent?* Maybe he does see me as girlfriend material. Now I don't have a clue what to do. I want to go and be with him. But I'm also intimidated by the thought of socializing with the upper class.

"Friday, you're my assistant. I am in need of your services on this trip. It's as simple as that."

I tell myself he's talking about my organizational skills, but part of me hopes he means something entirely different. *No wonder I'm sending mixed signals…*

"Say yes." His blue eyes hypnotize me, and my resolve slinks into the gutter.

I'm enticed but fearful. A shiver runs up my spine, but I'm not sure if it's a premonition or anticipation.

"No sex, and I don't want your money or new clothes. I'm not a prostitute," I blurt out, instantly regretting not engaging my brain before speaking. My inner feminist pats me on the back. My broke sex-kitten-wannabe rolls her eyes.

"I would never think that about you. Don't insult me or yourself."

"Sorry, sir. But, I mean it. No sex." *Unless he begs for it.*

One condescending eyebrow rises, and his lips curl at the corners. "Agreed."

I smile with triumph and manage to walk back to the door without taking a spill in these horrible shoes.

"Unless you beg for it."

Sweet baby Jesus.

"You're going where with whom?" Stunned, I put my fork down and stare at Jolene.

"You heard me." She takes a bite of her sandwich, licking a crumb off her bottom lip. I'm glad we're sitting at the table in the break room so she can't see the effect that innocent gesture has on me. This being human gig is harder than ever. Pun intended. She's all I've thought about for the past two days.

"Why you?" I'm losing control of this situation. If I'm not careful, Jolene's going to slip into Luc's snare and be another casualty of his game playing. Somehow I have to get her to realize this is a horrible idea.

"Why not me? I'm his assistant." She huffs with annoyance. "In case you haven't noticed, I'm quite good at my job."

"That isn't the point." I clasp my hands together and level my best don't-do-this look at her.

Unfazed by my disapproval, she smirks. "Quit being so overprotective. And stop frowning, you look like a guardgoyle."

"A what?"

"You know, those ugly troll-looking things that guard the cathedrals of Europe."

"Gargoyle."

"Isn't that what I said?" She looks with longing at my apple pie.

I shove it toward her, and she starts to take a bite, but pushes it back toward me.

"You can have some," I assure her. "I don't mind sharing."

"That's what he said," she quips, mimicking Michael Scott.

"I was talking about the pie, not *you*. Mr. Devil has a reputation. I don't want you to get in over your head…"

"You sound like my brother. I wish you and Johnny Way would acknowledge that I'm no longer a little girl. I can handle Mr. *DeVille*."

"That is precisely what I'm afraid will happen," I mutter.

"Stop it. I can take care of myself, and I know what I want." She stands.

I hold my breath, watching her wobble like a three-year-old wearing her mother's shoes. Her middle name certainly isn't Grace. If she makes it through the day without twisting her ankle, it'll be a miracle.

I pinch the bridge of my nose, knowing I'll never talk her out of this. Maybe I should just throw in the towel and notify The Boss I've failed. There has to be someone He could send who would have more influence over this headstrong, beautiful girl.

"Look, this is just work. It will be fine."

Skeptical, I shake my head.

She shifts back and forth like a tower of blocks about to tumble. Throwing her arms out, she sinks back into the chair opposite me. "Okay, so maybe I dream of it being more than work. But I'm not dumb. I won't let him use me, and I know I have a lot more to accomplish before I'm suitable for him long term."

I slam my hand on the table, rocking my bottled water. Her eyes bug as she steadies it. I've never been so irritable and short tempered with her, but since that kiss, I can't help it.

"Don't," I hiss. My jaw clenches so hard my back teeth hurt, and I narrow my gaze, doing my best impersonation of Peter when Remiel hides the keys to the Pearly Gates. That look makes every angel around sit up and take notice, except Remiel. Unfortunately, it doesn't faze Jolene, either.

"Don't what?" She cocks her head to the side and faces me across the table, as if spoiling for a fight. Truthfully, I love her spirit and tenacity.

"Why would you think you're not good enough for *him?*" I roar. "He's not good enough for *you!*"

Using her fingers, she ticks off a list. "I'm not college-educated. I need to lose ten pounds. My hair tends to frizz. I have small boobs—"

"Stop it," I growl through gritted teeth, grabbing her hand. "Jo, why would you worry about those things? That's ridiculous. You're perfect just being you." I stand, ready to do battle. She has no idea what's at stake here. "I'm gonna go kick his ass for even making you feel that way."

She rolls her eyes and pulls her hand away. "Now you're the one being ridiculous. You can't just go in there and beat up our boss. And no, he hasn't made me feel inferior. As a matter of fact, he makes me feel...*special*."

"Well, you are, but he's manipulating you—"

Her brows draw together, and her pretty mouth tightens. "You must be the one who doesn't think very highly of me if you believe I can be swayed by a little attention. I'm going to New York. It's part of my job." She clasps her hands and looks away for a brief second. "I-I was going to ask you to help me shop for a few nice outfits."

"Me? What do I know about women's clothes?"

"Don't be silly. You have a knack for dressing. Even in sloppy clothes, you always look nice. I don't want to ask any of the girls here for help. They might get, you know, the wrong idea..."

"What? The idea you're trying to nail the boss?"

She huffs with annoyance, and her cheeks flush the color of the rose I left on her desk. I always associate roses with Jo—beautiful and able to bloom even in terrible conditions.

"Whatever. For your information, I stipulated this as a no-sex weekend."

"If it's just work, why did that even come up?" I splutter.

Jo merely pauses a moment, offering no response. "Now, back to my clothes. I have a friend at school, but she's all tied up with her boyfriend and is kind of young. I just need to find a business suit and a cheap cocktail dress." She bites her lower lip. "Please?"

I close my eyes for a second and sigh. She isn't going to be swayed. When her mind is made up, it's a done deal. With reluctance, I nod.

Maybe I can also convince her to buy a chastity belt and give me the key.

CHAPTER SEVEN

The next day I sit at the bus stop, shivering as I check my watch. I'm meeting Jo during our lunch break to shop for clothes. She's late because Luc sent her on another ridiculous errand. A bus pulls up, spraying cold, muddy water everywhere, but I blink, and it avoids me. It's a subtle move; no one even notices. Except Him. The wind picks up, and I silently mutter, *Sorry, Sir.*

The bus doors open with a loud swish to reveal legs that seem to go on forever, encased in black boots with six-inch stilettos. My eyes roam up them appreciatively, admiring the good eight inches of skin below the black leather miniskirt.

The woman descends the steps and joins me in the bus shelter. "Hello, handsome. I hear you're in a little over your head." Her low, seductive voice makes the guy sitting next to me shift and cross his legs.

I meet her eyes, both relieved and a tad annoyed. *Why her?* "What are you doing here?"

Bright blue eyes, heavily lined in black, crinkle as her husky laughter rings out. Looking at the star-struck guy next to me, Madge flashes a smile. "Excuse me, sugar. Do you mind if I sit with my friend?"

He hops up, practically tripping on his tongue. "N-Not at all. Aw shit, that was my bus!" The guy runs, leaving me alone with Mary Magdalene.

"So, darling, The Boss sent me to help." She peers at my crotch and grins. "What happened to your balls?"

"What?" I gasp, outraged, but not surprised, by her directness. I shift away from her.

"Are you really going to let Jolene fly off alone with Luc? You know that's a disaster waiting to happen. She's smart, but she's no match for him. You have to save her."

"Tell me something I don't know." Placing my elbows on my knees, I rub my face. "Jolene has this asinine fascination with that jerk. And he's playing her like a fine instrument. It's going to be a mess to clean up."

"So prevent it from happening."

"Uh, hello. He's the Prince of Darkness. How am I supposed to stop him? He pretty much does whatever he wants, and always has. Jolene's my first job as a guardian. I'm used to dealing with bigger issues that require actual force. Not..." I shrug and wave my arms around. "Not babysitting sweet girls with feelings. That's more Remiel's line of work. Although considering how he screwed up his situation, I'm relieved he isn't Jo's guardian."

"Don't be such a negative Nancy. And using the term *girl* is sexist. Remi's a much better angel for his experience. Being human does that; it changes you, screwing included."

"I didn't mean it like *that*."

She peruses me with a knowing eye, and I shift uncomfortably.

"You need to get in touch with these feelings you're experiencing," she says. "Only then can you relate to Jolene and help her."

"And how do I do that?"

"For one, relax and enjoy your time here. You're so uptight. I hear things got a little heated the other morning." She nudges my shoulder, waggling her penciled brows. "Tell me about it."

"What? No! It's none of your business." I'm a little irritated He told Madge. *So much for confidentiality.* A cold blast of wind hits the bus stop. *Sorry, Sir.*

She chuckles. "You wussed out when the lights came back on, didn't you? Remiel owes me."

"You bet on me?" I'm horrified that my personal life has become a topic of conversation, much less the subject of a betting pool. "That was Remiel's idea, wasn't it? When I get back home, I'm going to kick his ass."

"No, I bet against you. Actually Peter set it up."

"Peter?" I sputter.

"Yep. Said he was tired of betting on Go Fish."

"That's just great." I mentally flick through the guardian angel playbook. What she's suggesting is that I toss it out and play Luc's dirty game. Madge is female and has had the human experience. Maybe I should set my angelic male pride aside and ask for her advice. "So what do you think I should do?"

"Get your act together and quit being so holier-than-thou. Think like a human; react like a human. Only then can you understand what Jolene's going through. You know Luc is going to pull out all the stops. You can't play fair. Real life isn't fair, and you have to be real to her. By the way, I can get us into that party Luc's attending with Jolene."

"You're just full of tricks."

Madge laughs and winks. "That's the rumor."

She's always been a good friend, and a lot of fun. Plus, she's right. I've got to get in the game if I'm going to win. Losing Jolene isn't an option. She's too important.

Madge nudges my shoulder and smiles, murmuring, "Well, speak of the Devil's girlfriend…"

And with that, she's gone. I hope no one noticed her disappearing act. She and Remiel always take risks on Earth.

Jolene honks and waves. I hold my breath and watch as it takes her four tries to do a passable job of parallel parking. I stand and smile as the object of my frustration approaches, nearly getting hit in the process.

"Sorry I'm late; I had to drop off Mr. DeVille's dry cleaning." Concern crosses her face. "You okay?" Pulling off her glove, Jo does the mom thing, placing her hand on my forehead and cheek. I stare at her, enjoying the soft scent of roses and the warmth of her hand. But I pull away before doing something stupid, like kissing her.

"Yeah, why?"

She shoves her hand back in her glove. "Were you talking to yourself?"

"Huh? Oh, uh, yeah. I was just going over everything you'll need to buy for your trip." I grab her hand, thankful for the knit barrier between us. "We need to get going."

"I knew I could count on you. You're always so put together. I'm clueless when it comes to mixing and matching clothes."

"I agree." I pull her sloppy ponytail and grin.

A smile spreads across her face. "You could've at least protested a little. I'm not that bad."

I snort. "Come on. Your sense of style gives new meaning to the term *fashion disaster*." She smacks my arm.

"Just keepin' it real, hon."

"You're so mean. I like to think of my style as shabby chic."

"Shabby for sure."

She sighs. "Seriously, thank you for helping me. I know you don't approve of this trip."

"You're right, I don't. But this is your decision, and you're my friend. I'll always be here for you, no matter what. Now, let's go."

She swings my hand as she talks excitedly about the trip from hell. I nod every now and then, but in fact I'm focused on the way the curls have fallen from her ponytail and the pretty shade of pink on her cheeks. I'm thankful for the long winter coat that once again hides my very physical reaction to this very human girl.

Jo looks as lost as Moses in the desert as she stares at the racks of clothes. "I don't even know where to begin."

"A lint brush?" I pull out a white sweater and winter white pants and hand them to her. "Here, Atticus's fur won't show up on this."

"White? What if I spill?"

"Tuck a napkin around your neck like a two-year-old." I put the white sweater back and hand her a lavender one.

"Wouldn't black be more slimming?"

"Are you going to a funeral or a business meeting?"

She sighs.

"Better yet, don't go at all," I suggest.

"I'm going. Wouldn't a dress be better?"

"No, too much access—er, I mean, don't you want to be comfortable?"

Her eyes narrow but she nods. "I need some new underwear."

My head spins like I'm being exorcised. "Why?" I hiss through clenched teeth. "You said this was a no-sex weekend."

A woman on the opposite side of the rack smiles and purrs, "If you don't want to have sex with him, I volunteer."

I grin as Jo gasps and turns to face my admirer.

"Back off, sister. He's not interested."

The woman winks at me and slinks away.

"How do you know I'm not interested?" I goad.

"She's not your type," Jo responds, sliding clothes down the rack.

I glance back at the surgically enhanced, bleached blonde. Jo's right, but I'm interested to hear more. "What kind of woman is my type?"

Jo pauses and looks at me. "A nice girl."

"That sounds awfully judgmental. How do you know she wasn't nice? And how come women can call other women *girls*, but if a guy does, it's considered sexist?"

She shrugs. "You're not the worst sexist. That woman was staring at you like you're a piece of prime rib."

"Hmm, sort of like the way you stare at Lucifer the Devil?"

Her cheeks flare, and she shoves the clothes with more force than needed. "I thought we were talking about you, not me."

"Honey, this is all about you, and I'm worried. This guy is out of your league."

"I knew it. You don't think I'm good enough for him!" She grabs several outfits and marches to the dressing room.

I run in after her, causing a pandemonium of outraged screeching. This must be how dogs feel with those high-pitched whistles. One woman smacks me with a hanger as I run past her.

"You're wrong, Jo. Like I told you, I think you're much *too* good for him."

Jo turns and her mouth drops open. "Get out! You can't be in here."

I push her into one of the dressing rooms and bolt the door behind us. She holds the clothes to her chest.

"He doesn't deserve you."

She swallows. "Th-Thank you. But again, I can handle this."

Someone pounds on the door. "Sir, you need to leave," an authoritative female voice commands.

Madge said I needed to break the rules. I'm off to a good start. Might as well finish with a bang. I grab Jo and stare into her eyes. I want to kiss some sense into her. Not that I have much sense to impart at the moment. My thoughts scramble as I gaze at her tempting mouth.

"Rafe—"

The pounding on the door intensifies. "Sir, security is on the way!"

Finally, I dig deep and find enough will power to take a step back. Or maybe I just wimp out. At this point I have no idea of the right thing to do.

"You're incongruous," Jo whispers breathlessly.

"Incongruous?"

She nods. "You know, bad beyond correction."

I chuckle. "I think you mean *incorrigible*." Though I feel a little incongruous as well…

"This is security. You need to leave *now*."

I take another step back and straighten my shirt. "But in this case, perhaps both words work."

Three minutes later, I'm outside the store freezing my ass off. The security guard glares at me through the window. A roll of thunder lets me know he's not the only one watching.

Jo and I return to the office, and Luc sends her on another stupid errand. Why can't she see how he uses her? And I'm afraid it's only going to get worse. I march into his office, slamming the door behind me.

"I quit."

Smiling smugly, he steeples his hands together, and his irises burn red. "Good, and totally not necessary, since we both know *I* never hired you."

I lean across the desk, wanting to throttle the life out of him. Except there is no life in him; he's evil incarnate. In this moment it's hard to remember we once played on the same team.

"Why? Why Jolene?"

He shrugs. "Why not?" He cocks his head to the side. "She reminds me of that brown-noser, Job. Ah, that was a fun case for a while."

I slam my fist on his desk. His coffee sloshes. "She's been through enough. Just leave her alone. And you lost with Job, remember?"

"But the torment I put him through was totally worth it." He grins and kicks back in his chair, putting his feet on the desk. "What's the matter, Raphael? Has our sweet little Jo cast her spell on you? Didn't you learn anything from Remiel's experience with Evangeline?"

"This is about me doing my job," I say coldly. "And if you're not careful, this will turn into one ugly holy war. One I promise you won't win."

"Do you really think your *Boss* cares that much about one individual? He has to consider the greater good. If you get in my way, I'll wreak havoc on this pathetic planet. What's one unimportant human compared to, say, millions? Besides, did you ever consider that this might be predestination? Or that Jolene's free will may allow her—perhaps even encourage her—to choose me? It just depends on your viewpoint. Don't threaten me, asshole. I have the means to destroy a good portion of the population if I so choose. And trust me, I've hung out here on *terra firma* more than you have; it wouldn't be much of a loss."

"I'm not going to argue theology with you. I'm warning you to back off. I promise I will utilize every means possible and stop at nothing to protect her." Turning, I stride toward the door. I refuse to let him provoke me into doing something I'll regret later.

"See you in hell, my brother," he says with a laugh.

"If that's what it takes, I'll be there."

I slam the door behind me.

CHAPTER EIGHT

"Here are the reports you need."

Rafe doesn't look up. Things have been strange between us since our shopping trip two days ago.

"Thanks."

A lock of his dark hair falls over his forehead, and I push it back. His iron grip catches my hand.

"Don't," he growls.

"Don't? Don't what? Don't touch you? Don't talk to you? Don't look at you? I think we need to discuss whatever is bothering you. You didn't invite me over for the *Golden Girls* marathon last night."

He studies his desk. "I figured you were too busy. You know, getting ready for your big trip."

"What does that have to do with you and me? Are you still mad you got thrown out of the dressing room? It was your own dadgum fault."

He stands and throws his pen down. "I can't stand by and watch you make the biggest mistake of your life. Tell Looney DeVille you're not going on this trip."

I slam my fist on the desk between us. "For the last time, this is *not* your decision. Back off."

"If you play with fire, you're going to get burned. Can't you see I want what's best for you?" His eyes soften, and he looks away.

"Rafe—"

"You need a keeper."

He's crossed the line on this one. "A keeper? Don't you have any regard for my intelligence? I'm twenty-five and fully capable of making my own decisions. I *choose* to go on this *business* trip."

"Is that your final decision?"

"Yes. You can either support me, or…" I don't want to think about what the *or* could lead to. A full minute passes before he answers.

"Fine." He sighs.

"Fine?"

"I think you're making a poor decision, but I'll always be here for you. Remember that." He grabs his coffee cup and storms out of his office.

I hate this rift between us. I run after him to try to fix things, but Mr. DeVille's door opens and he leans against the doorframe, folding his arms.

"Did you lose your way to the copier, Friday?"

"No, sir." I glance toward the break room, where Rafe has disappeared.

Mr. DeVille clears his throat. I sigh and head toward the copier.

I need this job. But I'm starting to wonder if the price I'm paying is worth it.

"This is risible, sir."

"Call me Luc; it's just us here," I remind her, smiling at her misuse of today's word of the day. Although I have to agree, this *is* an amusing amount of silverware.

She chews her bottom lip as she studies the table. I shift, easing the strain on my pants. I've got to get a grip. Better yet, I wish she'd get a grip on me.

"I need to hurry," she says. "I've got homework to finish before I go out of town."

"Anything you need help with?" I tease with a leer.

Color blooms in her cheeks. "Not unless you want to help me diagram sentences."

Damn. Grammar. Not sex. "*Risible* is an adjective. There, done."

"Gee, thanks," she mutters, staring at the place setting. "Why are there so many? All you need is one fork, one spoon, and one knife."

I happen to agree with her. "Damned if I know, but that's how it's done. Just follow my lead. You have to nail this by tomorrow." *I'd rather be nailing you. On the table, under the table, beside the table...* I pull my wayward thoughts back. Why does this woman make me act like a horny teenaged human? She's not even wearing anything revealing — just an oversized gray sweater and black pants covered in white cat fur.

I'm pretty sure she just called me *Borgia* instead of *bourgeoisie* under her breath. It takes everything in me not to laugh at her accurate description.

She folds her hands, clearly waiting on me to get my mind out of the gutter. Ever since she said no sex, it's all I can think about. Jolene Sanford is proving to be a better adversary than I'd anticipated. The cheeky little minx even thinks she's in control.

I pick up the cocktail fork and spear a shrimp. Mimicking me, her eyes close as she savors the bite. All the anxiety on her face dissipates into a look of pure bliss. Her tongue darts out, leaving her lips glistening, inviting.

"Yu-ummmm." Of course she stretches the word into two syllables. "This is delicious. I've never eaten shrimp that weren't fried."

For two days now, I've been giving Jolene crash courses on etiquette after work. It's been difficult with her crazy schedule, but she's a trooper. She's continued to refuse my offer to buy her clothes, so I just hope she allowed Raphael to help pull her wardrobe together. That fucker has an innate sense of style even the fashion Nazis can't fault.

After seven courses, the catering staff clears the dishes, leaving us alone. Being a quick study, Jolene did well following my lead on which forks and spoons to use throughout the meal. Her only faux pas was gagging after her first bite of the seared sea scallops with *crème fraîche* and caviar. She scraped off at least two hundred dollars' worth of sturgeon eggs, declaring it "nasty" before she returned to her meal—I mean, her lesson. I hid my grin behind my napkin.

She rubs her eyes like a sleepy little girl, and I sigh, knowing the evening is over. Tempting her with sex will have to wait. I want her awake when I seduce her. There's nothing worse than a non-responsive woman. Smeared mascara now streaks the purple rings of exhaustion resting on her cheekbones.

I stand and hold out my hand. "Come."

"Now what? Do I have to walk with a book on my head?" She's too tired to check the whine in her voice.

I chuckle. "No. Do women still do that?"

"I don't know, and I'm too worn out to care."

With my hand on her back, I guide her to the elevator and press the button for the basement. The doors close, and my heart pounds as I breathe deeply, attempting to ignore the panic welling within me.

Her phone beeps with an incoming text. I glance over her shoulder.

Three's Company marathon tonight.
I promise not to burn the popcorn.
Come on over.

How appropriate. This jackass is definitely a third wheel.

Friday texts back:

I wish. Too much to do,
but thanks for the invite.

I smile. *Take that, Raphael.*

Jolene turns off her phone. "Where are we going? Please not dancing. I always land on my butt when I twerk, and freaking is just tacky. I don't know how to waltz or foxtrap."

"Foxtrap? You mean foxtrot? Quit babbling." The elevator doors open, and I escort her to her tiny apartment.

She looks at me, uncertainty written on her beautiful face.

"Good night, Jolene. We'll leave tomorrow morning at seven sharp."

"Good night." Unlocking the door, she enters and turns to face me. "It makes me nervous when you call me by my actual name."

I sidle up close, enjoying her nervousness. Her throat bobbles, but she stands her ground.

"What if…" I let the sentence linger, watching her eyes widen just a bit as I run one finger along her jaw.

"S-Sir?"

"What if I asked you to pretend to be my girlfriend for the weekend?"

Her cheeks turn the shade of a hothouse rose, and her breathing accelerates. "You said this was business, that I'm your assistant—"

"This is, and you are. I just thought maybe…" I leave the suggestion hanging, reeling her in slowly but surely.

She stares at me, and in the space of ten seconds uncertainty, curiosity, and desire cross her face.

"Please? As a favor? These men I'm doing business with are family-oriented, married. It might help seal the deal if they think I have a serious relationship. Not to mention, it could be fun. Just for the weekend, of course."

I can think of lots of fun things to do with Friday, and my patience is wearing thin. I want her like no one in recent history. She fascinates me and makes me smile. One of her wispy curls escapes her ponytail, and I tuck it behind her ear.

She looks away, fidgeting with the pathetic chain lock on her door, taking time to weigh her options. "Okay."

"Okay?" My pleasure is laced with a thin veil of disappointment at her acquiescence. Because I do so love a challenge. Still, it will be a blast lording this over that sanctimonious fucker, Raphael.

Nodding, she looks up. "But no sex. This is still just business."

Atta girl. "Thank you."

Atta girl? What the fuck? I give myself a mental shake. Her courage and strength of character simply makes the chase more interesting. It isn't like I'm developing feelings for a human. No way. I don't do feelings. *Game on, love. I will have you this weekend, no matter what.*

"You're welcome." She crosses her arms over her chest.

"And no sex," I reassure her.

Satisfied, she smiles at me, closing the door. "Good night."

Before it shuts, I add, "Until you beg for it."

I turn and grin as the door slams behind me.

CHAPTER NINE

"No."

I roll over, covering my ear to stop the incessant beeping. I slap at the hand shaking me.

"Honey, you have to get up." The irritating beeping finally stops, and a hard smack to my butt has me awake and fighting mad.

"Ouch! That hurt." I glare at Rafe and rub my behind. "What are you doing here?"

"You loved it, and you know it. You're just mad it was *me* who spanked you and not that douchebag, Lucius Loser. Now get your *tuchis* out of bed and into gear. While you're in the shower, I'll make sure you packed everything."

Shocked by his almost-risqué comment, and relieved that things seem more normal between us again, I scramble out of bed.

"I haven't started packing yet," I mumble. I look down and realize I still have on one shoe and both socks. I toe them off. I must've fallen asleep before I could change. I didn't even pull the futon out, and every bone in my body aches.

"What?" Rafe shouts, throwing his hands up. "See? I think subconsciously you don't want to go. It isn't too late to change your mind."

"No, I just overslept. I'm going. If you're just here to harass me, you can leave. I'll manage on my own."

"Go shower; I'll pack. He's going to be here in less than an hour. Don't get your hair wet; it'll take too long to dry. It's clean, right?"

"Yeah, I washed it yesterday. How am I going to know what shoes go with what outfit? You know I suck at all this." I peel off my sweater, and Rafe quickly turns his back to me, rummaging through my closet. He folds my new clothes with military precision.

"I've made a list, and I'm going to correspond it to color-coded dots that I'll place on the tags."

Thank God. Rafe's even more organized than I am. *Why is he here?*

"Make sure you pack my new underwear," I holler as I jump in the shower.

Rafe swears.

I grin. "Don't worry. It's a no-sex weekend, remember?"

"From your lips to God's ears," he yells back.

In record time I'm squeaky clean and silky smooth. Wrapped in my terrycloth robe, I dash back to the living area. The look on Rafe's face is thunderous as he picks up one of my new bra and panty sets. It's white and silky, with a touch of lace. He jumps when he realizes I've caught him.

Rafe throws me the new underwear and again turns his back as I shimmy into them. I've never owned matching underwear in my life, unless you count white cotton panties and cheap white bras. The new bra makes my boobs look great, but nothing will help this butt. The two scraps of silk held together by strings sit lower than my usual panties and feel weird. I plop on the futon to lotion up, but stop mid-stroke when I see Rafe staring at me, looking as if he just witnessed some horrific crime.

"What?" *Maybe I should have gotten a spray tan? My diet has been going pretty well, I only have one dimple in my thigh…*

Sweat dots his forehead. I've never seen him look this flustered before. He blinks and swallows. "N-Nothing." Turning away, he finishes packing my suitcase.

"What's wrong? Oh my God, do I have a zit?" I feel my face for unwanted bumps.

"No," he replies hoarsely.

I go to him and stroke his back. His long-sleeved navy T-shirt fits him beautifully, outlining his broad shoulders. "Tell me what's wrong—aside from the fact that I know you don't want me to go on this trip. I've told you I can take care of myself."

"Whatever." He shrugs away as if I've got some sort of contagious disease. "Stop. And get *dressed*. Hurry, for Pete's sake."

"What's crawled up your butt? You've seen me in less." I slip into my new dress pants. "Remember that time I went skinny-dipping and a snake scared the be-geezus outta me?"

He ignores me and throws down the blouse he's been folding. I keep poking, wanting acknowledgment that there's something going on between us, even though I'm not sure what it is. I thought things were better, but now I'm not sure. I miss my friend.

"Rafe, what's wrong with you?"

He winces as if struck. "What's wrong with me? *What do you think is wrong with me?* Look at you—you're fucking beautiful."

What's with Rafe cussing? He never cusses. Ever…My mouth drops open. "What? Me?" The pain on his face flusters me. What's he so mad about?

"Yes, you."

I close my mouth and quickly dress. I've never seen him this angry.

"I'm sorry," I squeak.

He hesitates. "Listen, I'm trying to support you, be a good friend, but are you sure you don't want to cancel this trip?"

The hopeful look on his face is like a knife to my gut. He's more upset than I realized, but I don't understand why. "I can't. It's too late. I promised Mr. DeVille." My head feels like a vinyl record being scratched at a dance club. "And you *are* a good friend. I can't believe you're here this morning to help me—"

"Fuck me."

"What? I'm not going to—" I gasp.

"I didn't mean it like that. It was just an expression. Fuck, fuck, fuck." His profanity sounds kind of funny, but the tortured look on his face checks my nervous laughter.

"But—"

He sighs, but doesn't make eye contact. "Please don't go," he says softly.

I'm more tempted than he knows. All my feelings are muddled between my friend and the object of my obsession now. But I need this job.

At my continued hesitation, he sighs and angrily refolds one of my blouses for at least the seventh time. "Just once I wish you'd heed my advice. If you'd listened to me when you were eight, you'd have kept your clothes on and not been scared by that water moccasin. I've known you forever, loved you — never mind. I can't do this; I'm done…" His voice trails off as he places the precisely folded blouse in the suitcase.

Loved me? He means like a friend, doesn't he? Would he throw it all away over this trip?

"I can't back out this late. But I don't want this to come between us. Please don't leave me…" I whisper, my voice choking. I need him. Aside from Johnny Way and my mean old cat, he's all I've got. I open my mouth to speak, but he interrupts me.

"Never. And just so you know, you deserve nothing but the best. If Mr. Devil has coerced you in any way to go on this trip or tries anything you don't want, I'll kick his ass to hell and back. I mean it. Understand?"

Speechless for the moment, I simply nod and look at my friend. Really look at him. He's a great guy. Funny, handsome, caring, willing to fight for what's right — he'd be perfect boyfriend material. *He's also a great kisser*, something deep inside reminds me. Whoa, back up — that was a fluke. Wasn't it?

I press my fingers to my temple. I can't think about this right now, not with my trip. "It'll all be fine. As soon as I get home…"

He nods, his face falling.

"I do love you, you know," I blurt, trying to make things right.

He presses a hand over my mouth. "I know. But stop talking now or I'll tell Luc DeVille you wear white granny panties."

I giggle, and we hug, the tension between us lessening.

"Now do something with that mop of hair and apply some makeup," Rafe barks, back to managing my morning. "You can't go to New York City looking like trailer trash."

I laugh. "But I am!" As he finishes packing for me, I tame my waves into a loose bun at the nape of my neck. I put on more makeup than usual and hope it isn't garish or cheap looking. I look to him for approval, and he nods, tight lipped.

I sigh. "I wish you were going, too. Mr. DeVille may be expecting too much from me. I'm nervous about using the wrong fork or saying something stupid."

"You'll be fine. Just guard your heart, and be yourself—"

A sharp rap sounds, and my stomach flip-flops.

Rafe opens the door and sneers, "Speak of the *Devil.*"

I elbow him out of the way and press one heel into his foot.

"I resemble that remark." Mr. DeVille's eyes dart between us, but his face remains unreadable. "Ready?" His rich, smooth voice warms my body like a cup of hot chocolate.

"Yes, sir."

He nods an acknowledgment to Rafe and picks up my suitcase.

I give Atticus a scratch behind his ears and hug Rafe. "Thanks for everything."

"Anything for you. And I'll see you soon. Promise." Rafe pulls me into his chest and presses a kiss to my forehead. Aware Mr. DeVille is watching, heat floods my face. I'm quite sure I didn't need to apply any blush.

I pull away, and Rafe's dark eyes twinkle with mischief. *Is he trying to make Mr. DeVille jealous?*

Or is it a not-so-subtle reminder that this is a no-sex weekend? He probably figures it will protect my nonexistent virtue if my boss thinks I have a boyfriend. Jeepers, why did I agree to this stupid trip? Shrugging into my coat, I push my worries aside. It's too late to change my mind. I even said I'd pretend to be his girlfriend. My word is my bond, as my brother would say.

Mr. DeVille places a hand on my back. "She's in good hands. See you Monday..." He hesitates a fraction of a second, looking puzzled. "Riff-raff, er, Rafe, is it?"

Mr. DeVille knows Rafe Goodman's name. This situation has once again deteriorated into a testosterone-driven standoff.

I roll my eyes and decide to ignore them, marching to the basement parking lot. My mouth drops a little when a chauffeur steps out of a limo and opens the door. Mr. DeVille gently pushes me toward the car.

I can't contain my grin as I settle onto the luxurious black leather seat. It seems roomier than my apartment and is certainly nicer with its TV and wet bar. "Where's the stripper pole?" I ask. I really need to get a filter for my mouth.

Mr. DeVille smirks. "My, my. You never cease to surprise me. I guess I requested the wrong limo. Would you like a drink?"

"Before breakfast?" Appalled, I pull back a bit. Because of Robert Earl, I detest alcohol. Even when I go out clubbing, I drink diet soda. I'm always the designated driver. Does Luc have a secret drinking problem?

"You haven't eaten?"

"No, I overslept. I haven't even had coffee."

"What would you like?"

I look at him and laugh. "What are you gonna do? Have the chauffeur hit a drive-thru for breakfast?"

"We can. Your wish is my command." His gaze flickers down my body and back up to my face, his expression offering more than breakfast. I feel stripped and naked, as if he knows my fantasies.

I shore up my weakening defenses. Beautiful baby blues will not sway me from my decision. I will not be an easy one-time lay. "No, thanks. I'm fine."

Mr. Bossy Pants makes a quick phone call asking that breakfast be served on the plane. He doesn't bother to ask me what I want to eat, and I'm too keyed up to protest. We arrive at the airport, and I'm surprised when we don't have to go through normal security. As he discusses the weather and estimated time of arrival with one of the crewmembers in our private check-in area, my mind invariably wanders to one of my late-night fantasies…

"Hands against the wall, feet apart." I do as I'm told, and Mr. DeVille pats me down, his hands fondling my breasts, lips tickling my neck…

"Ready for some fun?"

I jump and snap out of my daydream, realizing he actually just spoke. Mr. DeVille's hand lingers on my hip as he leads me to the plane. My tingling body tells me I'm already on board.

CHAPTER TEN

"Mr. DeVille, Ms. Sanford." The perky flight attendant smiles at my boss and avoids eye contact with me.

Mr. DeVille nods, loosening his tie as he guides me to the luxurious chairs that look more like recliners than the airplane seats I've seen in movies.

"As soon as we reach cruising altitude, I'll serve breakfast." She points to a small table.

"Holy smokes, there's a dining table, too? This thing is huge. It doesn't even seem like an airplane. All of this just for you?" I turn a full circle as I take in my surroundings.

"Actually, there are better ways to fly, but it will have to do," he mutters. The smile he gives me looks more like a grimace. The flight attendant hands Mr. DeVille a bottle of water, and he digs a prescription bottle out of his pocket.

First he mentions alcohol before breakfast, and now he's breaking out one of my mother's favorite recreational drugs. My stomach twists. His face appears pinched, his eyes shadowed. It's the same look he gets when riding in the elevator.

Turning to me, the perky blonde says, "The bathroom is behind you, as is the bedroom. Please buckle up and prepare for takeoff." She exits and closes the door, leaving us alone. I scan the back of the plane as I contemplate the stories I've heard about the mile-high club. Why did she tell me where the bedroom is? Does Mr. DeVille routinely bring women on board and retire to the bedroom?

I push my unease aside and concentrate on my surroundings, amazed at how this looks more like an apartment than a plane. Buckling up, I bounce in my seat, unable to contain my excitement. "This is my first time to fly. Do you fly often?"

"If I never flew in a plane again, I'd be happy." Mr. DeVille closes his eyes as the engines rev.

"You're scared to fly?" This is a tidbit of information I didn't know. Maybe the prescription meds are legit.

"Of course not," he snarls as the plane gains speed down the runway.

I'm pretty sure he's lying, and I feel a little smug to have found a weakness.

"We're off!" I do a victory air pump and clap. "Oh my God, this is amazing. We're flying. *In the air.*"

"Where else would we be flying? In the ocean?"

I turn from the window and face the scowling man next to me. With his eyes closed, he white-knuckles the armrest. I gently pry his iron grip loose and give his hand a comforting squeeze.

His eyes snap open. Surrounding their icy depths, a ring of fire burns red. Before I can ponder what I've seen, it disappears. "What are you doing?" he snarls.

"Sorry, sir." *Geez, I'm just trying to be supportive. So much for acting like his girlfriend...*

"For fuck's sake, stop it." He pulls his hand from mine.

I lower my eyes and stare at my clasped hands, literally biting my tongue. I may have overstepped, but I'm confused by his mixed signals. I have no guidelines for this weekend. What does he want from me?

"Jolene."

His voice sounds softer, and I pull my gaze to his, trying to keep my face neutral. I'm not known for having a poker face.

"I'm sorry I snapped at you. It isn't the flying that has me on edge. And it isn't you. Just relax and have a good time. I don't want you continuously bowing and scraping to me."

Without thinking, I roll my eyes. "Since when, sir?" *Great, Jo, kiss your job good-bye.*

"Don't be a smartass. You agreed to pretend to be my girlfriend. That means no *sirs*. Call me by my name. Unless we're in the bedroom, then by all means, call me sir." He waggles his brows and manages a lopsided, goofy leer, but his lids appear heavy, and his speech is just short of slurred.

"This is all very confusing, sir, I mean, Mr., er, Luc."

"Just do as I say."

"Is that an order from my boss or my supposed boyfriend?"

"Both."

The flight attendant rolls a cart with covered dishes into the eating area behind us. I follow Mr. DeVille, I mean *Luc*, to the table, where he pulls my chair out for me. The attendant pours Mr. DeVille coffee and places it in front of him.

Maybe she's new and doesn't know how picky he is. "Please heat this for fifteen seconds and add three-fourths of a packet of the yellow sweetener," I tell her.

"What the hell?" He stares at me and stops her from taking his coffee. "It's fine. Leave the coffee, and leave us alone."

She nods in a subservient manner and shoots me a questioning look before disappearing behind a closed door.

I face his angry glare with confidence. I've prepared his coffee too many times to count. "She didn't do it right. I know how you like your coffee."

"Don't be ridiculous. I'm not that picky," he murmurs, shaking his head.

My mouth falls open. This from the man who barks orders every day and has slung more than one cup of coffee into the garbage?

He scowls and one haughty eyebrow rises. *Haughty* is today's word. It means full of contempt and arrogance. I'm surprised his picture wasn't next to the definition.

"Eat."

I look at the silver bowl over my food. "What's this dome thingy called, sir? I mean, Luc."

"A cloche. It keeps the food warm."

I lift it up to reveal fluffy scrambled eggs, grits, and toast with a slice of crisp bacon. I gag at the smell and replace the cloche.

"What's the matter?" He wipes a spot of cream cheese off his perfect lips. Lips I'd normally love to lick, but not now. Not with the smell of those awful eggs lingering in the air.

"Nothing. I'm not hungry." I don't know how to tell him I hate eggs and grits. I don't want to seem like an ingrate. I guess I could eat the toast and bacon.

His mouth sets in a grim line and annoyance lurks behind his glassy eyes. "You said you were hungry."

I wrinkle my nose. I can still smell those nasty eggs. "Yes, sir."

"So eat."

"I, uh…Have you been to New York before?" I ask conversationally in an attempt to stall before having to lift that cloche and be assaulted by the stinky egg smell.

"Eat your goddamned breakfast."

I sit back with a huff, refusing to cry. What is his problem? He invited me, not the other way around. I stand and throw my napkin beside my untouched plate. "Don't cuss at me, you haughty jerk. No wonder you can't get a real girlfriend. I don't like eggs *or* grits. A gentleman would have asked before ordering." I storm back to my seat and pull out my book. I halfway expect him to follow and offer an apology.

Good thing I'm not a gambler. Behind me I hear the bedroom door open and slam shut.

God, I hate enclosed places. My chest feels like I'm caught in a vise. I've got to calm the fuck down. Why is she acting so crazy? She said she was hungry; I ordered her food.

Women.

Now I remember why I never bother with *relationships.* Jolene, while a pleasant diversion, is still a human with that damn free will. It's annoying to have to pretend to care, especially when horny. It's easy enough in this day and age to get laid—and without the drama. As Jolene herself noted, I should have just asked Tweedle Ditz or Tweedle Dumb to come with me. Maybe both.

I pull my mind back from memories of banging both those girls and remember this isn't a pleasure trip. It's a business trip set up by

The Man Himself. I'm here, toying with this girl, to help Him make a point. The knowledge that He and I work together from time to time would blow the minds of most people. But you can't have good without evil. It's like white and black, peanut butter and jelly; they go hand in hand.

Jolene is proving different from most humans I've encountered. Much as I hate to admit it, she intrigues me. I've got free will too, you know. Raphael thinks I'm here to ruin her and cast her aside. The Boss's plan is more involved than that. And thanks to my growing attraction to Jo, it's getting more complicated by the day.

I throw myself on the bed, willing the drugs to take hold. Heaviness sits like an elephant on my chest. It isn't the flying. It's the claustrophobia. I'd hate this skinny tin can at any height or depth.

Just when I think my pounding heart will explode, I'm finally able to take a deep breath and exhale, relieving the pressure. I relax and close my eyes.

It seems like just minutes later when the bedside lamp switches on. I blink, disoriented for a moment.

Jolene stands over me, frowning. "Mr. DeVille, you need to get up and put your seatbelt on."

"What?"

"The flight attendant said we're landing. You need to put your seatbelt on."

She tugs at my hand. I yank back, and she collapses on top of me. The sound of her harsh breathing and the feel of her body pressed into my chest triggers my dick to stand up and take notice.

Delicate fingers push my hair out of my eyes, and her full lips curve into a smile. "We're not a mile high anymore." Her voice sounds husky.

"I can have them turn the plane around," I murmur in response. My cock seconds the motion.

"Get up! They said we have to buckle up, sir."

I hate landing almost as much as I hate taking off. If I move, I'll get sick. No way that's going to happen. "Trust me, we'll be fine." I wrap my arms around her, more for my sake than hers.

The plane bounces as the wheels hit the tarmac, causing my stomach to roll in protest. Friday wrinkles her nose and sighs. I'm disappointed, too. Or is that a look of relief on her face?

"Now what?" she murmurs, staring at my mouth.

My dick suggests sex. He's always been a persistent bastard.

I cradle the back of her neck, capturing those petal-soft lips. Instead of pulling back with horror, she smiles against my mouth, and I swear, she purrs in the back of her throat. I'm done. Fuck the no-sex promise. It's not like I'm known for honoring promises, anyway. She's a smart girl. I'm pretty sure she knew it wasn't going to fly, so to speak.

I explore her mouth, hinting at the multitude of things I want to do to her body. Our tongues dance in a teasing game of give and take. When I nip her lower lip, her sigh is gasoline to the fire burning inside me. My hand works its way down her neck to a soft breast covered by sweater. Giving her hardened nipple a pinch, I smile when her breathing hitches. She wants this as much as I do.

A timid knock sounds on the cabin door. My hand stops its exploration as my foggy, prescription-and-lust-filled brain tries to catch up to the interruption.

"There." Jolene smiles and sits up, fixing her hair as if we've done nothing more than share a cup of coffee.

"There?" I manage to croak. My blood has pooled below my belt, leaving me unable to think, much less articulate more than a single-syllable word.

"Do I look thoroughly kissed? Maybe even, you know…" She pauses and whispers huskily, "Fucked?" Her use of the word *fucked* throws me for a moment. Friday never cusses, preferring ridiculous Southern colloquialisms. Her beguiling hazel eyes stare at me, and a smirk stands poised on those luscious lips. Inwardly I applaud her bravado. She's a worthy opponent.

"I'll be blessed. I never took you for a tease," I mutter, sitting up and straightening my tie. *Women.* It all started with Lilith, then Eve. I need to regain control. Perhaps I should present her with a contract that outlines what is expected of her—with distinct boundaries and penalties for not adhering to the plan. It works in those romance books women seem to love…An image of me spanking her ass for some infraction teases the corner of my mind.

Fingers snap in front of my face. "Hello? Jeepers! Whatever pill you took has made you drunker than Cooter Brown."

"Who is Cooter Brown?"

"Never mind. Don't we need to disengage?"

I'm fairly sure she means *disembark*. However, at this precise moment, *disengage* actually is the more appropriate term. I need to pull back and rethink this entire weekend before it ends up a fiasco. Could it be I'm starting to have *feelings* for Jolene? This is bad. I can't be conceived as sensitive. I'm Lucifer, for crying out loud. First step to desensitizing myself will be no more mind-altering drugs.

"Quite right." I stand and pull myself together. "And trust me, Jolene. After I fuck you, it will be obvious even to a blind man."

She blinks and her face goes blank.

I smile. It feels good to be back in control. "We need to set some ground rules."

That stubborn chin rises, and her eyes narrow. "We did. You said I'm to pretend to be your girlfriend. I said no sex. That doesn't mean we can't give the impression of having had sex. That is what you do with your *girlfriends*, isn't it?"

She has a valid point—if I had a girlfriend. I stare at her, taking a step into her personal space. To her credit, she doesn't back away, but her sharp intake of breath belies her show of bravery.

"No sex," she squeaks.

"Until you beg for it."

She huffs and folds her arms. "Does that rule apply to you, too?"

I smile. "I never have to beg for sex."

"You haven't dealt with me before, *sir.*"

Holy shit.

Like a typical small-town hick, I turn a full circle when we get to the hotel, surveying the opulent lobby. I can't help it. The chandelier alone probably cost more money than I'll make in my lifetime. This place reeks of pretension with its white marble floor, crystal lighting, and expensive brocade-upholstered furniture. I feel woefully out of place and a little sick.

"Earth to Julia." Fingers snap in front of my face.

"M-My name is Jo—" I squeal my surprise, causing more than a few people to glare in my direction. I throw my arms around Rafe and hug him tight. "What are *you* doing here?" He's the last person—aside from my no-count parents—I ever expected to see. I don't know how he's managed to be here, or what he plans to do, but his strong, steady arms are reassuring. He's dressed in an impeccable black suit and gray striped tie, and more than one female turns to give him a second, appreciative glance. "And who is Julia?"

"You look lost, like Julia Roberts in *Pretty Woman*," Rafe replies with a smirk. His grin widens as Luc approaches. Usually I think Luc's eyes are gorgeous, but at this moment they look almost reptilian under his furrowed brow. A shiver runs down my spine, and Rafe places a comforting hand on my lower back.

"What are you doing here?" Luc parrots my question. However, where I'm excited to see Rafe, he looks downright angry.

"Didn't you receive my resignation? I'm working for Madge Loveman now. I'm here as her assistant. Just like Jo is in New York as yours." Rafe looks pointedly from Mr. DeVille back to me.

Our boss—well, now he's just *my* boss—smiles, but it doesn't quite reach those arctic eyes. He pulls me away from Rafe and rests a hand on my hip. I swear to God, I can almost hear the snorts and pawing of hooves.

"Interesting. Jo is so much more to me than an employee. Madge is here, too? My, my, the big guns are out for this *meeting*. What a lovely conundrum. Will Number One Son be joining us as well?"

I feel like I'm watching a foreign movie, and the translation doesn't quite capture the meaning of the dialogue. I look at Rafe, who, judging by the smirk on his face, is perfectly in touch with the underlying plot.

I bombard him with questions. "What? You quit your job? You didn't tell me you quit your job. When did this happen? I just saw you this morning! What's a conundrum? And how did you get here before us? We flew on a private plane."

Luc pats my hip and winks at me. "You'll find out what a conundrum is on December seventeenth. It's the word for that day." He smiles, and my insides turn to goo. He turns to Rafe. "I guess I overlooked your letter of resignation. No loss."

No loss? Rafe was his number-one salesman. The electricity in the room makes my hair stand on end. These two are sparring like the banty roosters in my brother's backyard. I can practically hear feathers ruffling.

Rafe shrugs. "I quit because I had a better offer. As a matter of fact, Madge would love to talk to you, too, Jo. I'm sure she can propose a wonderful position."

"What? No. I like my job." I glance nervously at Luc, who has stiffened.

"I'm sure Madge has many interesting *positions*," Luc mutters.

A statuesque blonde approaches, diverting our attention. Her hair is styled in an elegant French twist, a far cry from my haphazard bun. She's gorgeous, and every male in the room watches her. Red lips part into a wide smile, and her false lashes flutter over bright blue eyes. I stand a little taller.

"Well, if it isn't that handsome *devil*, Luc DeVille. What a pleasure to see you again." Her sultry voice teases and tempts as she looks quite openly up and down his body. She licks her ruby red lips.

"Madge, what a delight, as always. It's been *years* since I've seen you. You look beautiful." Luc takes her hand in his, brushing it with his lips. "Have you had work done, my dear?"

My mouth drops.

"Aw, Lucius, you evil creature. You know a woman never reveals her true weight, age, or hair color and never, *ever* admits to any plastic surgery." She pulls her hand away and sweeps an amused look between the men. "I can't believe I was fortunate enough to hire Raphael away from you. I treat my employees like family. You should try it." She glances at me. "Starting with this smart young woman. Rafe tells me she's dedicated and hard working. If she came to work for me, I'm sure she'd move quickly into management."

Luc's looking at her like a wolf sizing up a tasty rabbit. She loops her arm through Rafe's and bats her false eyelashes. I dig my nails into my palms to keep from prying her gel nails off of him. *Wait, why do I care? I'm here with Luc.* The beginning of a headache creeps behind my eyes.

Luc smiles. "Jolene is indeed very bright and has a promising future with me. Come along, darling. We need to get settled, perhaps do a little sightseeing before the party tonight. Or we could just stay in and…" He pauses dramatically. "Rest." His hand pats my butt.

"Jo, if you need me, call." Rafe shoots Luc a withering look, which is ignored.

"I will. As long as the color-coded dots coordinating my clothes and shoes are still there, I'll be fine." I grimace. My big mouth has just announced that I'm a fashion disaster to three people who could model on a Paris runway. I hold out my hand. "Nice to meet you, Ms. Loveman."

Rafe's shoulders shake with suppressed laughter, but Ms. Loveman shows class and ignores my blunder. She squeezes my hand in a friendly manner.

"We'll talk later."

Her kindness warms me toward her. She really does seem nice, and Rafe says he likes her and his new job. He looks relaxed and at ease, if you don't count the death glares he keeps shooting Mr. DeVille, er, Luc. With a final wave to me, they walk away, leaving Luc and me alone. I twist my purse strap in my hands, wondering what happens next.

"Let's unpack, grab a quick bite to eat, and then you can decide what to do with the rest of afternoon." He smiles and my knees weaken. "I'm looking forward to getting to know you better."

Does he mean know me, or *know me?* Why is this devastatingly handsome man so focused on me? Is this just a seduction or is he sincere?

Swallowing my nerves, I draw in a sharp breath. *Stay strong, Jo.*

"Or, if you'd like a trip to the spa to get ready for tonight, I can arrange that." He steers me toward the elevator. "Whatever you desire, I can fulfill."

A spa? Does he think I need to go? I thought I looked okay; I mean, maybe I'm not the same caliber as Ms. Loveman, but I'm just an assistant. But I'm supposed to be Luc's girlfriend; I don't want to embarrass him...

He presses the button for the elevator. "Stop overthinking this."

He knows me better than I realized. We step into the elevator. "What do you think I should do?"

"Kiss me."

"What?" My heart hammers, and I wonder what happened to the oxygen supply.

"It's all you've thought about since the plane. Admit it, and just get it over with."

"No, it isn't." I cross my fingers behind my back. "This is discomfiting, sir."

A grin spreads across his face. "I think *disconcerting* fits better, but that almost works. That was last Monday's word, wasn't it?" He steps closer and places his hands on the wall of the elevator, caging my body. His head dips, and I feel his warm breath tickling my neck. "I'd rather fit inside you," he whispers, thawing my resolve.

The elevator doors open on our floor, saving me from dissolving into a puddle of need at his feet. It's *disconcerting* to realize he's going to pull out all the stops to get me to beg for sex this weekend. I take a deep breath, straighten my shoulders, and shore up my determination.

"Here we are," he says.

I cheerily duck under his arm and walk into the hallway. There's only one door. I swallow. "Where will you be staying?"

He smiles. "Right here." He opens the door to reveal a magnificent room with two couches, a huge coffee table, and a grand piano.

The view of the city is breathtaking. I pause at the doorway. Luc brushes my arm, making me jump.

"Easy now."

"Where's my room, sir? I mean, Luc."

"Here." He smiles, and his eyes flash with latent lust.

I turn to leave, intent on finding Rafe, but Luc closes the door and blocks it.

"This is a suite, Jolene. Separate bedrooms with a common living area. You're perfectly safe."

"Somehow I doubt that."

He laughs and tweaks my nose. I follow him as he opens the door to a magnificent bedroom with the largest bed I've ever seen. "This is your room, and the bathroom is over there. And no, we won't be sharing it, either." He pauses. "Until you ask me to join you, that is."

My mouth waters, and I can't seem to find the ability to do more than whimper. I clench my jaw and squeeze my thighs together at the thought of him naked in the shower. I'm sure he's picking up on every nuisance of sexual frustration crossing my face. Or is that *nuance?* I make a mental note to check the definitions later, when I can actually think.

He stands in the doorway, leaning against the jamb. "So what will it be? Spa or sightseeing?"

I know being alone with Luc, even in a public place, will lower my defenses against his full onslaught of seduction tonight. Better to have some time alone to regroup.

"Spa, please." *This way I'll be* ready *for tonight.* Great. My mind is obviously not on board with the no-sex plan.

As if he's able to read my thoughts, a smile forms on Luc's perfect mouth. "I'll make sure you're pampered like a princess." He kisses my forehead and leaves me alone to dream about his impressive scepter.

CHAPTER ELEVEN

Two hours later, I look up from a ridiculous business report I don't give a damn about and frown. "What the hell are you doing here? What if Jolene catches you?"

Raphael's wings ruffle. If I were human, I'd be unsettled. I'm not, so I'm just a fraction past irritated.

"I know she's at the spa, and you and I are going to talk. This needs to stop."

I look down and pretend to study the document. "Stop? What precisely needs to stop? Haven't we had this conversation? Damn, you're like a nagging wife."

"She's naïve, out of your league."

I put the file down and lean forward, clasping my hands. He stands tall, but his power-play move is a waste of time. Very little intimidates me.

"*Au contraire, mon ami.* Jolene is proving to be a worthy adversary. That cheeky minx has made this a no-sex weekend." I smile. "I, in turn, have promised to make her beg for it."

Raphael moves so fast I don't see him coming until I find myself pinned to the wall by his death grip.

"Do not harm her. I'm not playing games," he says through clenched teeth.

His anger burns deep. I haven't seen an angel riled like this since Remiel fell for Evangeline...*Perfect.*

"Ah, now I understand," I whisper with a smile.

His brow furrows, and his grip loosens a bit. "Understand what?"

"Funny, you recognized it in Remiel."

"This is nothing like Remiel's situation." He glances away for a nanosecond. "Don't hurt her."

Time to reel him in. "Interesting. I love a challenge, and seducing the fair, sweet, not-quite-but-almost-virginal Jolene is proving to be very entertaining. She's quite a prize."

"This isn't a game, you insufferable bastard. It's a human life."

I shrug. "Yeah, yeah, sanctity of human life, blah, blah, blah. I know you and your kind set great store by that. Me? Not so much. But we were once brothers, so here's what I'll do: Let's even the playing field."

Rafe lets me go and begins to pace; his expansive white wings flap with barely controlled anger. "I told you, this isn't a game."

"Life is a game and a gamble. You know that. Now either listen to what I have to say, or leave, and I'll go about my *business.*"

"Get on with it." His hand flexes and fists.

No doubt he's ready to deck me, so let's see just how far I can push him. I've tapped into his darkness for perhaps the first time ever. I want to see what he's made of.

"Seduce her away from me."

His nostrils flare and eyes widen before his face settles into a composed mask. I've surprised him. I contain my grin of victory. "You're on Earth. You can do what you want—free will and all that mumbo jumbo your Boss holds dear."

"I can't; she's my charge. I'm her guardian angel."

His crestfallen face tells a different story. He's in love with Jolene, even if he doesn't realize it yet. I can practically see his mind working, strategizing. The poor sap probably hasn't been laid in ages.

"My offer is on the table. Take it or leave it."

"And if I refuse?" he challenges.

I shrug. "Then as the cliché says, all's fair in love and war. Jo's free will might have to go by the wayside…"

His eyes blaze as he paces the room, his feathers beating with controlled measure. "Fine," he growls, holding out his hand.

I clench it, and the energy generated by two polar opposites connecting causes a power outage. In the dark, we're lit by an incandescent glow seen only by those of our ilk and the rare human gifted with *the sight*. Raphael's wings spread in challenge, and mine do the same.

I smile. "Game on."

His eyes pierce the darkness with an almost fiendish light. Maybe there's hope for the old boy yet. "When I win, you have to promise to leave her alone," he snarls.

"Of course."

"And you cannot physically hurt her or cause her psychological damage."

I roll my eyes. "Fine, fine, I won't hurt her, unless she's kinkier than I think and wants to go in that direction—"

He slams me against the wall. The impact cracks the sheetrock, and my neck feels ready to snap. This is the Raphael I used to know.

"Let go. I won't hurt your precious human."

"Brother to brother."

"Brother to brother. And may the best angel win."

We separate, and the lights snap back on.

Raphael smiles. "I will."

He's gone in a flash. I pick up the phone to make the call. When the Voice from my past answers, I grin and say, "He took the bait."

A sharp rap on the door makes me jump, and eyeliner streaks down my cheek. Just great. Now I look like some sort of high-society Goth girl. "Sorry, sir. The lights went out on my way back from the spa, and the elevators weren't working. I'll be just a few more minutes."

"You know I don't tolerate tardiness, nor excuses."

"I know, sir." I'm exhausted from taking the stairs forty-one floors, and my knees feel like rubber. My shower may have eliminated the stink after my Mt. Everest-like climb, but it did nothing to boost my energy, and it also made me late. I scrub the eyeliner off and start over. My second attempt is better. Grabbing my lipstick, I throw it in my purse, slip on my shoes, and open the door. Sweet god of hotness, Mr. DeVille's wearing a tux.

His eyes start at the top of my head, pursuing my body with leisure, or is that *perusing?* I think the word is *perusing.* I want him to *pursue* me. But I also want him to keep me. He motions for me to turn, and I spin like a redneck kid in a beauty pageant. If asked by a judge, my platform would be staying strong in the face of overwhelming temptation.

"You've always been beautiful, Jolene. Tonight you are stunning. Thank you for accompanying me. I predict every man in the room will be insanely jealous of the gorgeous, intelligent woman on my arm."

I snort, but heat creeps up my neck into my cheeks. "Thank you, sir. I'm afraid my dress isn't fancy enough."

"*Luc.* Simplicity is always a sign of true refinement and beauty. Hold your head high, Friday."

His compliment sends a tingle straight through my body. I'm not used to compliments, and it's like a sugar rush, making me lightheaded. "Thank you—" He raises one eyebrow, and I catch myself just in time. "Luc."

"Ready?" He holds his arm out.

Feeling like a little girl playing dress up, I'm determined to be a competent assistant and engaging companion tonight. And if I do well enough, perhaps he'll see me as actual girlfriend material.

As we leave, I notice a crack in the wall behind the desk. I know it wasn't there earlier. "That's odd. Did you see that?" I point. "What happened?"

"I tripped when the power went out. Let's go."

"Do we need to report it? Or will you get in trouble? Will you have to pay for it?"

"Don't worry about it." He smiles and pulls me out the door.

When we step into the elevator, he backs me into the corner. This man has a thing about elevators. They either make him nervous as a long-tailed cat near a rocker or horny as a rabbit in heat. "Do you have any idea what I want to do to you right now?" His hand cups my butt and squeezes. "Maybe we should skip the party," he whispers, his tongue tickling the shell of my ear.

as I try to wrestle with these new feelings *and* function at a party I couldn't care less about. I'd much rather be at home wrapped in a quilt, eating popcorn and watching an old movie with my mean old cat.

And Rafe.

I wish I could dial back time and start over.

Luc glances at me, and I can practically feel the heat from across the room. One eyebrow lifts and that adorable, snarky smirk plays at the corner of his mouth. Rafe's face darkens. Compared to Luc, I used to think Rafe was too safe and boring. But now I'm beginning to think I've been wrong.

Shaking his head, Luc waves off whatever Rafe just said and strides toward me. I feel like a deer during hunting season, and my mind scrambles into defense mode. The lights flicker, and rain pelts the windows ferociously. A crack of thunder makes me jump as lightning arcs across the sky. Odd, I don't remember hearing about bad weather moving in to the area.

"Come. I want you to meet some associates of mine." Luc nods to Madge and places a proprietary hand on the nape of my neck as he steers me toward a group of men.

"Stop it," I hiss.

"Excuse me?"

"You're acting like some dominant lion or something. Are you going to bite my neck next?" I shrug loose from his grip only to have his arm snake around my waist, pulling me next to him.

"Trust me, Jolene. I plan to bite your neck on my slow, leisurely descent to nibbling on other tasty bits," he whispers. "I'll have you begging by the end of the night. Mark my words."

His tongue flicks my earlobe. His smugness is starting to irritate me.

We join a group of men, and I smile during the introductions, attempting to keep up with the boring conversation. All of these businessmen look the same in their elegant tuxes, and my mind is on anything but business. Luc appears to listen to the conversation around him, but his interest remains focused on me. It's seductive and powerful to be the sole recipient of such blatant attention. Even if he weren't standing next to me, I'd be aware of his presence. Luc keeps a hand on me at all times, whether it's resting on my hip, settled around my waist, or holding my hand. But rather than feeling wanted, I feel strangely constrained.

The gray-haired gentleman talking to Luc ogles my breasts. I ignore his rudeness and look across the room, searching for Rafe. I find him standing with Madge and a model-thin, gorgeous redhead. He laughs at whatever she's said. She's doing all the things women do to get attention: twirling her hair, watching him from under her lashes, and rubbing a hand down the sleeve of his jacket. For some reason, I want to vomit with jealousy. As if he's aware I'm watching, Rafe looks at me with a sad smile. I glance away and see Luc staring at me with an almost feral possessiveness. I'm sure my cheeks have gone from green with envy to the color of Madge's lipstick.

"I'm so lucky to have you," Luc says, running the backs of his fingers along my jaw. He smiles, and it's as if the temperature has risen fifteen degrees. The heat is suffocating, and I can't breathe.

"Lucky girl," says the woman standing next to me, under her breath. She's staring at Luc like he's a movie star.

"Are you ready to go, my dear? You've had a long day."

Four days ago, my toes would have curled in my shoes at the term of endearment; now it's confusing. I nod, and he squeezes my hand.

"I must whisk my beautiful companion away. I'm afraid she'll lose a shoe or something at midnight," Luc says with a wide smile to the group. Everyone bids us good night, and holding my hand, Luc maneuvers us through the crowd.

"Did I do all right?" I ask.

"Of course. I had no doubt. You were absolutely charming, and I do believe old Mr. Guthrie wanted to eat out of the palm of your hand. That sale is virtually a done deal. Thank you."

"I don't know about eating out of the palm of my hand. He was too busy staring at my cleavage."

Before us, Rafe blocks the doorway, and Luc sighs. "Move."

"I want to say good night to Jo."

"Say good night, Jolene," Luc instructs, his hand moves possessively to my hip.

I glare at both men. The argument between these two is tiresome.

"Good night, Rafe." I nod and smile. "Good night, Madge. It was nice meeting you."

"You, too, honey. Breakfast in the morning? We can make it a foursome if the guys want to join us."

"I'm quite certain Jolene will be exhausted…" Luc pauses and grins. "And *sleeping* in."

Rafe's breath hisses between his teeth. Although Luc hasn't said anything dirty, it could certainly be taken that way, and I don't like it. Luc draws me toward the elevator, and Rafe catches my other hand. I feel like a rope pulled between two opposing forces.

"Jo." Rafe's haunted gaze sears straight to my soul.

"Yes?"

He leans in and whispers, "I care about you. Listen to me. Please."

I nod and swallow my fear.

"Don't rush into anything, okay? Go with your instincts." Brushing a gentle kiss on my cheek, he lets go of my hand.

"Tsk, tsk, Raphael. Didn't you learn anything from history? A kiss on the cheek is never a good omen." The smile on Luc's face doesn't reach his eyes.

"Call if you need me," Rafe says, ignoring him.

I nod. The elevator opens, and I follow Luc inside. Turning to face the lobby, my heart sinks at the look of devastation on Rafe's face. Madge pats him on the back, whispering something as the doors close.

"Would you rather be with him?"

Startled, I swing around to face Luc. "I—I don't…" I sigh. "N-No. I'm just…" I don't know who I am or what I want anymore.

"Just relax. Remember, you're here because you want to be." A soft smile warms his mouth, and his eyes twinkle. The elevator lurches a bit. His face pales.

I nod, feeling more confident. "Right. I'm in control."

He cages my body against the wall of the elevator. "I don't normally swing that way, but I could be persuaded. What would you do to me if I were under your control?" he purrs in my ear.

Thump, thump, thump… Surely he can hear the sound of my heart echoing in the enclosed space. I smile. "Easy. I'd make you beg for sex." My words sound a lot braver than I feel. In truth, I kind of feel like I'm on that ride at the fair where you go round and round real fast and the floor drops, leaving you plastered against the wall, dizzy and drunk feeling.

Before I can react, Luc slips to his knees. He raises the hem of my dress, and his warm lips follow his hands, trailing kisses up my thigh. I suck in a ragged breath, wondering what has happened to all the oxygen. Looking up at me, his blue eyes flare with passion.

"I'm on my knees, Jolene…"

I'm saved by the ding of the elevator as the door opens. Thank God we're on a private floor and no one's there to see my boss on his knees between my thighs. He stands and escorts me out. My legs feel like jelly, and I take a moment to kick off my heels. There's no way I can walk in them, and if he were to pick me up, I know where we'd go.

Inside the suite, he immediately loosens his bow tie and tosses his jacket on the back of a chair. The storm continues to rage outside, and lightning flashes across the city like a child playing with a light switch. Luc moves to the bar and pours himself a drink, offering me one. I shake my head and toss my purse with his jacket.

"Do you mind if I have just one?"

His thoughtfulness gives me pause. Sometimes he surprises me, adding to my confusion. "No, go ahead." I tread to the window and stare down. The cars below look like tiny fireflies, magnified by the raindrops on the window. Luc sneaks up behind me and nuzzles my neck. The smell of his spicy aftershave and his lazy strokes on my back intoxicate me. He wraps his arms around my waist, and together we watch the storm raging.

"I love the way you smell," he says after a moment. "Sweet, innocent, and sexy all at the same time."

And so it begins.

"I'm not begging…" My voice trails off as his hand strokes down my hip to my thigh, raising the hem of my dress higher and higher. Every nerve in my body is on high alert, screaming *Danger! Danger!*

"Not yet. But you will." He smiles against my ear, and his teeth nip my earlobe.

Pulling a pin, he loosens my bun. I giggle from ticklishness and nerves. He scoops my hair over my shoulder, and his mouth scorches my skin as he kisses down the column of my neck. Somewhere in my lust-induced fog, I realize he's unzipping my dress. He nips between my shoulder and neck, and I jump and squeal in response. I'm afraid he's right; it won't be long before I'm begging.

CHAPTER TWELVE

Luc's hand kneads my breast as he eases my dress down one shoulder. The room phone rings, disturbing his slow, deliberate seduction.

"Shouldn't you get that, sir?" My voice sounds husky and distant. I roll my head back, allowing him greater access to my neck. I keep telling myself I can stop this any time I want. The mind is easily fooled.

"Mmm, don't say *sir* unless you plan to submit to my every whim," he whispers with a smile.

My body whimpers yes and shoves the flitting remembrance of a no-sex weekend aside.

The incessant ringing continues. Exasperated, Luc stops and grabs the phone.

"What?" he answers.

"Does it have to be done right this moment?" Running a hand through his short, gold-tinged hair, he glances at me. Annoyance lingers around his eyes. The mood ruined, I straighten my dress, wondering if it's something I've done wrong. I used three towels after my shower — is that against the rules? I also peeked in the stocked refrigerator, but I didn't take anything. Did I say something wrong to those boring businessmen? Or is he in trouble for the cracked wall?

"I can't rectify this in the morning?" He listens and his eyes narrow. "You can't send anyone up to handle the situation?" He paces, clearly annoyed. "Oh, I have a good idea what's wrong. Fine. I'll be right down, and be prepared to have this resolved within five minutes. Not one minute longer, do you understand me?" He slams the receiver down so hard I'm surprised it doesn't crack.

"Anything I can do, sir?"

Fury flares in his eyes, and a loud fluttering sound fills the room, like the sound of Johnny Way's chickens ruffling their feathers before being fed. The temperature feels ten degrees warmer than five minutes ago. Still, I find myself shivering. The room also seems extra bright, and I squint. Luc closes his eyes and takes a deep breath. The room returns to normal lighting, and a cool breeze comes from somewhere. I rub my eyes, concerned by my wild imagination. I must be more exhausted than I realized.

"No, no. There's apparently been a mix up with the hotel computers and my registration. They want me downstairs to fix the situation. I won't be gone long. Go ahead and relax..." His smile reassures me, and he kisses my forehead, cupping my cheek with his hand. "Need anything while I'm out and about?"

"No, thanks." I paste on a smile, hiding my relief. This will give me a little time to pull my resolve back together.

"Back in a few." He pauses at the door and blows me a kiss. "I wouldn't be opposed if you slipped into something more comfortable."

The door closes, and I sink onto the overstuffed couch, closing my eyes. *Stay strong, stay strong, stay strong...* A pounding on the door startles me, and I race to open it. Luc has the key card. Is it the hotel staff coming to evict me for using three towels?

Rafe barges past me so fast it feels like a strong breeze ruffling my hair. I'd think it was my imagination, but even the curtains billow. Fury stamps his face, and his hair stands on end, as if he's run his hands through it several times. No longer wearing his jacket or bow tie, he looks rumpled with his shirt half tucked in and half out — so unlike my usually well-put-together friend. I pick a white feather off his shoulder, and he blanches.

"What's wrong?" I ask.

"*You*," he roars. Pointing at the door he just stomped through, he growls, "Why did you answer that door?"

"Because you knocked." I flinch and step back when he pounds his fist into the palm of his other hand.

"And you say you can take care of yourself. Never, *ever* open your door without checking who's there first. You're about as prepared to take care of yourself as you were when I met you."

"How do you know I didn't look through the peephole? And I was only six when we met."

"Exactly my point. Grow up! And I know you didn't check first; you're too impulsive."

I turn so he can't see the tears blurring my vision. The stress of this trip, combined with Rafe's crazy behavior, takes me back in time to being that unloved, lost little girl. I'm drowning in my convoluted emotions and too tired to fight the sinking feeling of worthlessness.

Rafe sighs behind me. "Jo, I'm sorry." His voice is softer this time, more like my friend. It almost makes it worse.

I dash my tears away and turn to face him, holding my chin high. "I think you should go."

"Honey, I'm sorry. I'm just worried…" He runs a hand through his mussed hair and closes his eyes as if he's praying.

I swallow the knot of uncertainty strangling my throat and pick up my pride, dusting it off. "I know you think I'm a stupid, redneck little girl. I may be two of those things, but I'm twenty-five and perfectly capable of making my own decisions."

"You don't understand —"

I cross my arms as if to somehow protect my heart. "You're right."

His scowl lifts into a hopeful smile.

"I don't understand how my friend could think so little of me. I'm going to ask you again to please leave. Good night."

His face falls. "Look, I can't explain. But you need to believe me. You're no match for that bastard, he's —"

"I do believe I heard Jolene ask you to leave. Do I need to call security? Nice work getting me out of here. How much did you pay the stooge at the front desk to fake a problem?" Luc leans against the door, glaring at Rafe. Goose bumps skitter across my skin.

"Jo, please. Trust me on this. You've known me for years and this…jerk for just a few weeks. He isn't what he seems." Rafe stares with an intensity that makes me feel awkward.

"Who is, Raphael? Everyone has secrets. I daresay you included." Luc propels himself away from the door, making his way to my side. Placing an arm around my shoulders, he kisses my temple. "It's been a long day, my dear. Say good night, and I'll escort *your friend* to the door."

Rafe shakes his head, his eyes pleading with me, but I'm done. I'm too tired to sort this out. I glance up at Luc, who smiles and nods toward my room.

"Good night."

Rafe grabs my hand, and I search his troubled face. "Jo, I haven't always been there for you. I've let you down, and I'm truly sorry. I may never be able to forgive myself. But know this: If you ever need me—"

I smile, thinking about his favorite movie. I can't stay mad at him. "I can take care of myself. But yes, if I need you, I'll just whistle. I know how."

He shakes his head as he leaves. "Make sure those lips just whistle, no blowing…"

My mouth drops, and Luc howls with laughter. Mortified, I dart to my room and slam the door, sinking to the floor and hiding my burning cheeks against my knees. It isn't two minutes before a knock sounds.

"Who is it?" After all, Rafe told me to be sure I know who's at the door before answering. I'm nothing if not a fast learner.

"May I come in?" Luc asks softly.

"No."

"Ever?"

"Not now." *What?* I should have said never. Obviously my body has taken possession of my mind. I hold my breath, hoping he goes away. I need to just get in my new silky pink pajamas, crawl into bed, and call it a day. This trip has been a disaster. The last thing I need is to end up in bed with my boss.

Luc moves away from the door, and I breathe deeply as I drag myself to the bathroom. A quick hot shower refreshes my resolve. Now that I'm alone, I feel more in control. Settling in on the luxurious, gazillion-thread-count sheets, I snap off the light. My toes wiggle, rejoicing at the thought of tennis shoes tomorrow for the trip home.

Another knock sounds, and I pull the covers up to my chin.

"Jolene?"

"Y-Yes?"

"Come join me in the sitting area? I have hot chocolate and cookies."

I sigh. I'm doomed. How can a girl resist hot chocolate and cookies? Especially when offered by a sexy guy who asked you to pretend to be his girlfriend for the weekend? A guy you've dreamed about since meeting him.

"I'm in my pajamas." I don't even sound convincing to myself. Rafe insisted I buy pajamas instead of a nightgown as an extra layer of protection.

"So am I."

The thought makes my mouth feel like I've just eaten chalk. My curiosity runs rampant and wins against common sense. Some hot chocolate might remedy the Sahara condition of my mouth, I justify.

I slip into the bathroom and comb my hair. There's no need to pinch my cheeks; they're already flushed. Tying my robe tightly, I open the door into the sitting area. The room is awash with candles, giving it an intimate, romantic feeling. A single red rose lies across an empty china plate next to a silver teapot. I prefer pink, but I appreciate the gesture. My stomach growls when I spy the three tiers of decorated cookies. I'm sure each delicate confection has at least seven hundred and fifty calories, just what these hips *don't* need.

Wearing black pajama pants, Luc stands at the window with his back to me. The flickering light highlights his muscles as he stretches, and I stop to admire the view. He looks like a Nordic god. I pray I have the willpower to restrain myself from falling on my knees to beg for what I know he has to offer. Chocolate has nothing on him; he is one-hundred-percent pure temptation.

He turns, and a slow simmer of uninhibited passion burns bright in his eyes. The seductive, sinful look contrasts his easy, boyish grin. I allow my gaze to drift from his face to those exquisite pecs, slowly making my way to that delightful feast of six-pack abs. Butter my biscuit; he looks good enough to eat.

"Hey," I manage to croak.

"Hay is for horses. Good evening, Jolene."

He doesn't move, but the compelling intensity of his gaze makes me feel naked, even though I'm wearing silk pajamas and a robe. I collapse on the couch before my rubbery legs give out.

"Would you like some hot chocolate?" I ask, wanting him closer.

His smile seems to light up the room, and his eyes flicker with amusement. "Would I have ordered it if I didn't?"

True. When has Mr. DeVille, er, Luc, done anything he didn't want to do? He's pretty much in charge of everything around him. The cup rattles in the saucer as I pour the hot cocoa. I concentrate on steadying my hand.

"You look beautiful, Jolene. Much more tempting than anything on that plate."

Sweet mother of confections. Hot, steamy chocolate sloshes over the rim, and I wince at the stinging pain.

Luc rushes to my side, taking the spilled cup from me. "You've burned yourself. That's my job," he teases, licking the chocolate from my hand. It's a good thing I'm already seated, because I'm quite sure I would melt otherwise. As it is, I can't seem to catch my breath as his lips follow his tongue, teasing circles on my wrist. When he takes my fingers into his mouth and sucks them, I whimper. Stick a fork in me, I'm done. I'm his.

He cups my cheek, and flames flicker in his eyes. I blink. This isn't the first time I've seen this, and it's a bit unnerving. I shift to put some distance between us. For all my bravado and well-laid plans to catch my boss and keep him, I realize I'm woefully unprepared.

"Shh," he whispers, leaning close and kissing my forehead. "You're in control, remember? We only do what you want."

His reassurance eases some of my anxiety, and I force myself to relax. He pulls me into his lap and holds me. It's a weird sensation. I've sat in Rafe's lap and felt safe. In Luc's arms it's different—almost like being trapped.

"Thank you for coming with me this weekend. You were a flawless assistant and companion. Mr. Guthrie read the proposal and said he'll have the signed papers delivered to the room."

A part of me wonders if this is true, or if this entire weekend was a ruse to get me to go away with him. *Ruse* is next Saturday's word.

"That's great," I tell him.

"That means we can *sleep in* tomorrow; no need to rush to get to a boring meeting."

I may be ignorant, but I'm not stupid. I know he has no intention of *sleeping.* My heart races as his hand caresses my back in slow circles. There's no way to ignore his prominent arousal beneath me. Luc tips my head back and trails kisses up my neck to my jaw.

"Why me?" I blurt out.

He pauses. "Why not you?"

"I'm not your typical, uh, date. My IQ is more than that of a Barbie doll, and I'm ten pounds overweight."

"You are so much more, my dear."

I gasp my outrage. "Are you saying I'm fat?" I'm all for honesty, but in this case I wouldn't have minded a little white lie.

"No, I'm saying you're the complete package. Brains, beauty, and a hell of a lot of fun." Picking me up, he takes me to his room where a lone candle lights the opulent space. As he stands me on my feet, I slide down his body. At this rate, I'm pretty sure one of us will be begging soon.

My robe slides to floor, and he cups my face in his hands, his forehead touching mine. His lips curve into a lazy, seductive smile.

"Luc?" I whisper, grabbing his wrists.

"Yes?"

"I want this to be special. I mean…this *is* special, right?" I can't seem to control my trembling.

"Very special. And, we won't do more than what you want. Okay?"

This is it. This is the moment I've dreamed about and planned since meeting this man and falling under his spell. As they say, go big, or go home. And I have no way to get home.

I nod and grin. "I want the full she-bang."

He throws his head back and laughs.

This girl is a delight. I adore her sense of humor, her unaffected, easy manner, her determined spirit—and she's cute as hell. Jo looks up at me with those huge, trusting eyes, and some strange sensation gives me pause for a fraction of a second. I shove it aside, not having felt an inkling of remorse in too many years to count.

This is just a job, and I don't want to lose my position by fucking it up. Besides, fucking Jo is much more tempting.

"The full she-bang, huh? That fits right into my plan." I kiss the tip of her nose, and she runs a tentative hand across my chest. Her shyness intrigues me. Sure, she's always been subservient as an employee, but there's also a *je ne sais quoi* about her I find appealing.

"You're so freakin' hot," she murmurs.

"I know."

She laughs and swats my chest. I press soft, gentle kisses along her jaw. My fingers linger on the top button of her ridiculously modest but surprisingly sexy pajamas.

"May I?" I whisper, nibbling on her earlobe.

Her nails dig into my biceps, but she nods. With painstaking care, I unbutton the four buttons. She stares at me, wide-eyed, and her breathing quickens. If I wanted to, I could take her pulse by the pounding in her neck.

"Jolene?"

She blinks.

"You're mine." Her breathing stutters, and she releases that enticing lip she's been chewing. I capture it with my teeth, giving it a quick nip. Her whimper is like an aphrodisiac. She *will* be mine, no doubt about it. I deepen the kiss, my mouth taking hers, as our tongues dance in the age-old mating ritual. Her kisses fit her personality: timid, mixed with a bold curiosity. I'm starting to wonder if I'll ever get enough of her. Jolene Loretta Sanford is unlike any woman I've ever seduced.

Pulling away a bit, she closes her eyes, inhaling deeply. I take the opportunity to slip her top down her arms. Color works its way from her flushed cheeks to her spectacular breasts. I cup them, running my thumbs over the hard peaks. She sways a bit, and I pick her up and place her on the bed. The feel of those nipples against my chest makes me want to rip her pajama pants off and bury myself deep inside her. But patience is a virtue—and perhaps the only damn one I have.

"You are a beautiful creature," I whisper. She giggles and looks away, her nervousness making her a skittish kitten. I soothe her with a reassuring stroke here, a butterfly kiss there. "Look at me."

"S-Sorry, sir." Her breath hisses as I take a nipple in my mouth.

I suck hard enough to make her moan. Her mouth is beautiful, and I envision it wrapped around my cock within the hour. I nibble, lick, and kiss across her chest. She squirms underneath me and giggles as I trace a finger down the blue vein of her biceps until my hand intertwines with hers. Giving her a gentle tug, I roll to my back, bringing her on top. Surprise registers in those amazing hazel eyes, followed by what can only be called a shit-eating grin. I'm more than a little curious to see what she has in store for me.

She giggles. "I never thought you'd let me be on top."

"Why is that?"

"Because you're so bossy."

She knows me well. "I could deny that, but I won't. It's true. However, tonight you're in control. Use and abuse me any way you like." I tuck my hands behind my head and wait. I know she's been thinking about this since the day we met. I've felt her energy and fostered her interest.

But as always, she surprises me. She shakes her head, frowning.

"What? No. I'd never abuse you, or my power. I mean you wouldn't... hurt me either, would you?"

I roll my eyes and place a finger over her lips, scoffing at her seriousness. Not my smartest move. Too late, I realize she isn't talking about sex. She's talking about fucking *feelings*. Shoving her bed-tousled hair behind her ear, she sits up, covering those delicious pink nipples with her hands. "I think we need to talk."

"Fuck." Being a fiery, passionate being, I don't like the murky sea of emotions. I'm drowning, and Jolene isn't sending over the life raft. She rocks back, and I swear by the fires of hell my balls scream at me to *hurry and do something*. I start dog paddling to save the evening from an inevitable hand job later, if I don't get some relief. "Come here, Friday. You're being much too analytical. Let's just have fun."

"Fun?"

"Yeah, fun. You know, I do you. You do me. Then we'll give it a go together."

"That's it?"

"I won't even make you beg," I tease, gripping her hips and bumping her a bit with my cock, right where I know it will make an impact. I see the indecision in her eyes and whisper the most seductive line known to mankind: "You're in control, Jolene."

Hopefully this will bring her back to the moment and out of her head. This girl thinks entirely too much. *Wait, what's wrong with thinking?* Fuck, she has me thinking too much, too. I sit up, wrapping one hand in her hair as I kiss that pouty mouth.

"Wait." She pushes away from me, and we tumble back on the bed, facing each other.

Ah. She's one of *those* girls—the type that likes to play hard to get. Fine. I'm game. "You're adorable. You know that, right?" I kiss her forehead, mentally calculating how long it may take to wear down her resolve. Five minutes? Ten, just to make her feel like she didn't give it up without a fight? And then the unthinkable happens. I look into her eyes and see complete and utter trust. *And I feel guilty.*

"Am I special?" she whispers, searching my face for answers. "Or just another notch in your belt?"

It's on the tip of my tongue to say *of course*, but for some perverse reason, I glance away and hesitate. For the first time, I find myself unable to offer a glib lie. *Or is it a lie?* Jolene sighs and springs out of bed. When she bends over to pick up her top, her ass beckons to be spanked, but before I can act upon it, she stands, re-buttoning her pajamas.

"Of course you're special," I offer, too late.

She shoots me a sharp glance, and the disappointment written on her face feels like a dagger thrust into the cavernous place where my heart should be.

"There's no need to lie. I, um, well…" She grabs her robe and ties it securely around her waist. "Thank you. For everything. The trip, the spa…and the lesson on douchebags."

"I doubt that's in your Word-A-Day calendar." I leap out of bed and grab her hand. "Jolene, please don't go." Holy mother of Him. Am I about to beg this human girl to stay? *What the fuck is wrong with me?* Remembering who I am, I use my boss voice. "Stay."

She shakes her head. "This is for the best. I mean that kiss was nice and all…"

"Nice?" I gasp, more than a little outraged.

"But I realize you don't really care for me as a person; it's just lust. And actually, I think what I'm feeling is the same thing…"

"What's wrong with lust? I can live with lust."

"But I want more. I want the whole package, not just the illusion of love."

This is too much. How dare she deny *me?* Who does this girl think she is? Unmitigated fury burns deep within, and like lava from an active volcano it spews forth, unconcerned about the destruction it will cause. The door to the room slams shut, and in an instant it feels like a sauna. Jo jumps and stares at me.

"I did not give you permission to leave," I grind out between clenched teeth, willing my anger to drop to a low simmer before it singes her skin. As it is, her color has deepened from rose pink to tomato red. Sweat dots her brow and upper lip.

"I didn't ask for your permission. I don't need it. Haven't you ever heard that *no means no?* I don't know what your deal is, but I'm done for the evening." Her eyes blaze with righteous anger, and her show of spirit makes her even more fascinating.

"Thank you for the feminist bullshit speech." I clap three times and hold out my hand to her. "Now get back in bed."

Her eyes narrow, and she clenches her fists. For a moment I picture her in black leather and thigh-high boots, snapping a whip.

"Thanks for the hand." She smiles, but her eyes sparkle with indignation. "Now why don't you use it on yourself? I'll be sure to have flowers sent to you tomorrow, sir." Tossing her hair over her shoulder, she flounces from the room.

The slamming door blows out the candle, leaving me alone in the dark with a grudging new respect for Jolene Sanford.

CHAPTER THIRTEEN

Confused and hurt, I somehow manage to leave with my dignity intact. I figure I have about fifteen seconds to hold it together while I walk to my room. Once inside, I fling myself on the bed and cover my burning cheeks with my hands. I feel stupid and ashamed. Stupid for thinking I'd managed to become more than a good time in bed, and ashamed that I led him on. I hate to admit it, but this is as much my fault as his. Maybe more so — I'm the one who stalked him.

I hear the front door open and bang shut, and I can tell by the eerie silence he's gone. I wonder if he's going to leave me stranded in New York City. After shopping for new clothes for this trip, I have about twenty bucks in my wallet. I suppose I'll have to call Johnny Way and ask him to book me a flight home. It's not a conversation I look forward to.

A tear slides down my face, and I brush it away. The apple hasn't fallen far from the tree. Here I was pretending to be something I'm not, just like my mother — acting stupid for a man. Instead of picking up the phone, I bury my face in my pillow. I can't bring myself to call my brother. Humiliated, the thought of disappointing him makes me feel sick. And I really don't want to hear the lecture, no matter how much I deserve it. I wish there was someone I could talk to.

The bed dips, and the familiar, clean scent of fresh water surrounds me as a comforting hand strokes my hair. It's my undoing, and the single tear turns into a torrent of uncontrollable sobbing. How Rafe knew I needed him, and how he got into the room, I have no idea, but I'm grateful. He's the anchor in my emotional whirlpool, and always has been.

He doesn't say a word, letting me get it all out. I don't think I've cried this much since Robert Earl kicked me to the curb and out of his life.

I choke out my bitter admission: "It seems the adage that you fall for men like your father holds true. Luc DeVille might not be a raging alcoholic, but he's a self-serving, good-for-nothing jerk, just like Robert Earl. What's worse, I'm just like my pathetic mother, falling for the crummy guy."

Rafe chuckles softly. "Hush, you're nothing like your parents. You're good and kind, albeit a little too trusting."

"You're the only person I know who uses the word *albeit*," I say, sniffling. I can always count on him to be honest. When I can finally breathe and talk without sounding like a sputtering engine, I accept the tissue he waves in front of me. Wiping my eyes and blowing my nose, I manage to choke out, "I'm so sorry."

"Sorry? For what?"

I sit up and lean my head against his shoulder. "For not listening to you. I've been such a fool."

"You're not a fool." He stretches an arm around me and kisses the top of my head. "Maybe a little headstrong, but not a fool. I won't lie, though, I wish you'd listened to me."

"I fell under his spell." I sigh and my shoulders sag. "He can be really charming, and you have to admit he's devilishly handsome."

Rafe coughs and growls at the same time. "He's not my type." Brushing the back of his fingers under my chin, he turns my face toward his. His face is a mask of fury. "Did he—" He stops and takes a deep breath, and I sense his anger simmering.

I push the lock of hair that's fallen on his forehead back in place, smoothing my favorite bit of gray at his temple. "I'm okay."

"Did he hurt you?" His voice is softer, more controlled.

"No. I'm just embarrassed." I look around at the luxurious room. "Looks and money aren't everything, are they?"

"Nope."

"I'm going to have to call Johnny Way to see if he can get me a ticket back. There's no way I'm riding on that plane with Mr. DeVille."

Rafe stands and runs a hand through his hair. "Get up and pack your things. I'm taking you home."

"No, I can't do that." It's nice of him to offer, but my brother would kick my behind if I borrowed money.

"Don't argue with me." Rafe grabs my suitcase and begins throwing my clothes in it, so unlike the careful packing he did yesterday.

I'm tired and emotional, and it suddenly hits me that I'm going to have to face Luc at some point. Or quit my job. I feel lost and a little sick at the mess I've created for myself. Rafe pulls me to stand in front of him.

"Get your ass moving. He's not here at the moment, and that's a good thing. I don't want to face him right now. It could get nasty, and no one needs to be around when it happens. I'm taking you to my room, and tomorrow we'll fly home. One more person on Madge's plane won't make a difference, and she won't mind."

Too tired to argue, I nod and scurry to gather the rest of my belongings. In five minutes, we're ready to leave, and I realize two things: At least fifty candles are still burning, and I'm in my pajamas. I run over and start blowing out the flames, but Rafe grabs me by the hand. He makes a sweeping motion with his other arm, and something sounds like a bird rustling its feathers as we're plunged into darkness.

"What just happened?" I'm beginning to wonder if this hotel is haunted.

"Nothing. Come on," he urges, tugging me toward the door.

"But I'm in my pajamas." I attempt to pull away.

He throws my robe at me. *How did he find it in the dark?*

"It's late; no one will see you. Now hurry."

I shrug into it and get it tied just as the elevator dings and opens to reveal an older couple in formal evening attire. *Just my luck.* We enter and they shift away, as if I have cooties or a scarlet letter on my robe. The woman sniffs and turns her nose up, but her husband rakes his eyes over me. He looks like he wants to congratulate Rafe with a frat-boy thump. Our silent descent is uncomfortable, and I'm positive my cheeks are pinker than my nightclothes. The woman stares daggers at me, but I hold my head high, trying to rise above my embarrassment.

Rafe gives my hand a squeeze and places a chaste kiss on my temple. The woman beside me huffs as her husband snickers and stares. Rafe's eyes narrow, and he moves to block the old perv's view. When the doors open, he places a hand on the small of my back and steers me off the elevator.

Holding the door open with my suitcase, he turns to the couple. "Things aren't always as they appear," he says. "People can hide money in foreign accounts. Or they can keep two sets of books—one with supposed charitable donations for the sake of appearances and another that shows the money is spent on useless material things like cars and jewelry. But sometimes the IRS gets wind of this." The woman's face pales, and her husband gasps. Rafe moves the suitcase, and the doors close.

"How did you know that?" I ask.

"I didn't. Just a lucky guess."

We walk in silence to his room, and my feet feel like I'm wearing lead work boots instead of satin slippers. The room isn't nearly as big or luxurious as Luc's, but there are two neatly made beds. Exhaustion, both physical and emotional, creeps over me. All I want to do is crawl in one and sleep away this entire humiliating evening.

After a quick detour to the bathroom, I return to find one of the beds turned down. Sitting on the other, Rafe rests his elbows on his knees, his forehead on his hands. He looks contemplative, as if he's either been praying or thinking, and a strange light surrounds him. I rub my eyes, and the mirage disappears. Man, I need some sleep.

My phone rings in my purse. I fish it out and see it's a call from Luc.

"I, uh, probably should answer. I didn't even leave a note."

"Do you want to go back?" Rafe asks, softly.

I shake my head. The phone stops ringing.

"He knows where you are and that you're safe. Go to sleep; everything will be better in the morning."

I shrug out of my robe and climb in bed. Rafe turns off the light.

"Thank you," I whisper.

He brushes a kiss on my forehead. Like I'm a child, he tucks me in, making me feel safe, secure. He did the same thing when I was a distraught six-year-old. "You're going to be fine," he says.

After he disappears into the bathroom, I stare at the dark ceiling, wondering about my future. I check my phone and find three missed calls from Luc and two texts.

I needed time to cool off. Come back.

I hit delete and read the next one.

Be wary of Riff-Raff's good-guy image.
Things that are too good to be true usually are.

I turn the phone off and pray he doesn't come to the room to cause a ruckus. Did Rafe tell him I was here? Or did he just assume? I can't seem to shut my mind off. How will I ever face Mr. DeVille again? I'm no better than Tweedle Ditz and Tweedle Dumb. What almost occurred is almost as embarrassing as when he saw my battery-operated boyfriend beside my bed. He's my boss; will he think about me half-naked every time I bring him a dadgum cup of coffee?

I have to resign. And without a job, I'll have to quit school and move back home. I can totally see myself ending up as the crazy cat lady in that godforsaken town. It's disheartening to realize I've just blown my chance to escape my roots and get an education. Swallowing this bitter pill unleashes more tears.

Rafe emerges from the bathroom wearing a pair of plaid pajama pants that fit perfectly, revealing the defined V of his pelvis. The city lights filtering through the sheer curtain highlight every dip and plane of his abs. He pauses by my bed and sighs. To my surprise, he pulls the covers back and taps me on the arm to move over.

"W-What are you doing?" I whisper hoarsely.

"Move over, bed hog."

"There are two beds," I squeak, moving over to give him room. I want to curl into his neck and cry my heart out.

He lies down facing me and wipes my face dry. "Stop. He isn't worth your tears; you know this deep down."

"I don't know if I can. It isn't him. It's *me*." And sure enough, a fresh batch pours down my cheeks.

Rafe shifts in the bed, and I find myself on my back as he leans over me. "Please stop, Jo."

The concern in his voice makes me cry harder.

"Stop or —"

"Or what?" I choke.

"Or I'll kiss you."

I don't know who's more shocked by those words, which seem to echo in the silent room, her or me.

I'll kiss her? Sure, kissing her is all I've thought about since the snowstorm. But I don't need to be thinking about kissing her at all, much less doing it. I'm supposed to protect her, not make love to her.

However, maybe Madge is right; I need to throw caution to the wind and just wing it. Nothing about my relationship with Jo is normal, and maybe seducing her will keep her safe from Luc. I can't imagine that danger has actually passed. If I'd acted in the dressing room, we might have avoided this entire disastrous trip...

What the hell am I thinking? I'm her guardian angel. And even worse, I want more than a seduction. I want to spend forever with her. I need her like I've never needed anyone. The impossible has occurred. I've fallen in love with her. The pain this entails feels like hitting a brick wall and will have the same outcome. It can't be, no matter how much I want it.

Having more acute hearing and vision than humans, I notice Jo's eyes widen and her breath draw in sharply. I can tell her mind is working overtime to process what I've just said. So is mine. I've lost focus.

"Okay."

Maybe my hearing isn't that great after all. "What?"

"Kiss me." She's smiling, but her eyes still glitter with her recent tears. "Triple-dog dare you."

"Why?" I'm stalling, and we both know it.

"I'll use it to gauge my current white-trash level."

I frown and sit up, snapping on the light. "What the heck are you talking about?" She's a wreck with her tangled hair, red nose, and swollen eyes. Strangely, it makes me want to kiss her more than ever.

"Tell me something, and be honest." She fiddles with the sheet.

I'm dreading, yet curious about, what she's going to say.

"I know our kiss was a fluke. But…"

"But?" I croak, sounding like a bullfrog.

"Didn't you feel something?" She lowers her eyes, and pink warms her cheeks. "Or am I just a wanton girl?"

I can't contain my grin. Jo and her Word-A-Day. "I'd say more sizzling rice than wonton," I blurt, making it worse. For she is, indeed, sizzling.

"W-A-N-T-O-N, not the Chinese soup, idiot." A hint of a smile plays on her lips.

I want to taste them…I close my eyes for a second, trying to regain control of these wrong thoughts and feelings. "Why would you ever think you're wanton? I think you're perfect." *Where is my filter?*

"Because I was in lust with my boss, yet when other girls flirt with you, I get mad. And when we kissed…I felt something, didn't you? I don't know." She thumps her pillow and rolls over, her back to me. "Never mind. This is embarrassing. Just chalk all this up to a combination of exhaustion and stupidity, okay?"

Thank goodness one of us has some common sense and restraint.

"Good night, and thank you for being my friend."

And there it is. I wonder if this is how He felt when the stone rolled into place at the sepulcher: alone and maybe a bit lost? I snap off the light and lie on my back, staring at the ceiling. I have a new understanding of what Remiel went through when he fell for Evangeline. Being human is bewildering and painful as hell.

"You know I felt something," I whisper hoarsely. "That kiss was special, Jo."

She turns toward me. "How did everything get so confusing? I wish we could go back to being kids."

I nod but don't reply. Within minutes, her soft, even breathing indicates she's fallen asleep. I slip out of bed, on a mission to destroy my despicable brother. My wings ruffle with anger, and I snap them closed as I step into the hallway. I huff with annoyance when I find Madge playing cards with Gabriel, both dressed casually in jeans. No one passing by would realize they aren't of this world. Though they might think it odd to see a couple in the hall playing cards.

Aggravated, I run a hand through my hair. "What are you two doing here?"

Madge smiles up at me. "I'm beating the wings off Gabe. He's too chicken to go to my room for strip poker. I think he's terrified of losing one of his pretty feathers," she purrs, waggling her brows at him.

Gabe frowns. "I am *not* afraid. We have a job, and we're doing it. Trust me, love, I wouldn't lose one precious feather. You, on the other hand, might view heaven in a whole new way."

"Ha! Promises, promises."

Annoyed, I cross my arms realizing I'm in the hallway of a ritzy hotel wearing nothing but plaid sleep pants and listening to inane sexual banter between two angels. I'm living an episode of *The Twilight Zone*. "Stop it. What job could you possibly be doing in the hallway?"

Gabriel's eyes twinkle. "We're here to keep you from doing something stupid, mate. Although it would have been quite awkward to walk in on you and Jolene."

I sputter, "W-What?"

Madge laughs. "Get your feathers out of a wad. He's teasing. We wouldn't have done *that*. We're here to make sure a certain fallen brother doesn't show up to cause problems."

I pinch the bridge of my nose. "I can't deal with this. I'm going back to bed."

"Enjoy," Madge says with a wide smile. Gabe snorts and raises his beer in toast.

"To sleep," I snap, smacking him on the head.

I'm actually a little relieved to have backup. Luc is a formidable opponent, and I appreciate The Boss sending reinforcements. This will allow me time to plan my next move in protecting Jolene. I sneak back into the room and gaze down at her.

Still asleep, she tosses and turns, her cheeks damp from her tears. To heck with planning—I can't stand seeing her suffering, even with a bad dream. I slip in beside her and wrap my wings around her, holding her close. Whispering a prayer over her, I kiss her forehead, feeling more at home than I ever have in my long life. She settles and a soft sigh escapes the smile on her parted lips.

CHAPTER FOURTEEN

The arm wrapped around my waist feels heavy in a good kind of way. Something tickles my nose. I brush at it and nestle into the warmth, feeling secure and at peace.

"Don't wiggle. Please, for the love of all that's holy, don't move," Rafe rasps in my ear.

My eyes fly open. Rafe groans. He's spooning me, and it's very apparent the effect this has had on him.

"Rafe…"

"Shut up. Don't say a word." His voice sounds strangled, and he promptly rolls out of bed. The bathroom door opens and closes.

Sitting up, I frown. Caught in my hair is a white feather. I pull it out and stare at it. It's far too big to be from a pillow. The shower turns on, and I cross my legs, wishing he'd let me pee first. In a few minutes he returns, still damp, with a towel wrapped around his hips. I have an urge to grab that towel but instead dart past him into the bathroom without so much as a *good morning*.

In the shower, the warm water and my soapy hands don't help my attempt to erase Rafe's sculpted body from my mind's eye. I scrub almost to the point of pain, yet my body tingles with need. When did I become so sex-obsessed? Maybe I'm a sex addict. *Great.* I guess it's true; addiction runs in families. Robert Earl's addicted to alcohol, Crimson to her prescription meds, and me, apparently, to handsome men.

I shut off the water and angry male voices filter through the bathroom door. Wrapping a towel around my body, I quietly crack the door. Luc and Rafe are shouting smack like two wrestlers before a match. Pandemonium reigns as Luc argues with Madge, Rafe, and a muscular blond man with long hair and a neat beard. Honest to God, it looks like a convention of angry beautiful people.

Luc sees me first and smiles. He's unshaven and disheveled, looking much like he did the morning of the snowstorm.

"Friday, do you know how worried I've been? Hells bells, you could've at least answered my text and set my mind at ease," he chides.

Behind him, Rafe's eyes burn with anger. "*I* sent you a text telling you she was fine and would be leaving with me and Mar— er, Madge."

He steps toward Luc with his fist clenched. Is my easygoing friend about to take down my boss?

"Easy, mate. Don't get yourself in trouble." The blond guy steps between Luc and Rafe. Judging by his wide grin, he's amused by the entire situation.

"Jolene works for me, and I have need of her *assistance*," Luc counters. "I will see that she arrives home safe and sound."

I don't understand the deep-rooted animosity between these two men, but regardless, I'm tired of being in the middle.

Rafe struggles to break free of the ironclad grip his friend now has on his biceps.

"What's the matter, Riff-Raff? Don't you trust me?"

"Hell, no, I don't trust you, *Lucy*," Rafe roars.

Luc laughs, taunting him.

"Now's not the time to deal with this." Blond-peacekeeper nods toward me, but keeps his attention on Rafe and Luc.

The thermostat in the room must be stuck. Sweat drips down my back, and I'm pretty sure I need another shower. Everyone else appears unaffected. I glance over at Rafe, and the rims of his irises burn red, flames flaring in his pupils. I blink to clear the disturbing vision.

When I look back at him, his eyes are once again dark. Something isn't right. Maybe I have a fever or food poisoning.

A shiver of fear runs up my spine. My limbs feel weighted, and dread settles on my shoulders like a heavy winter coat. Everyone turns to look at me as I clutch my chest, struggling to breathe in the stifling hot room. The room spins and darkens. I can't quite hear the voices around me, and I feel like I'm freefalling down a tunnel.

Luc and Rafe grab my shoulders, and a shock of what seems like electricity surges through me. My body jolts, and my heart skips and accelerates in an erratic pattern. Pain courses through me. Feeling the stagnant, cold hand of death upon me, I begin to pray like a holy roller. I'm scared, and if I knew how to add the rosary into the mix, I'd do so. As a matter of fact, I'd spin a Buddhist prayer wheel, chant Hebrew, and cast a Wiccan spell if I thought it would get me out of this predicament.

"Please help me, God. I'm sorry for all the bad things I've done and for harboring hate in my heart..."

"Oh, fuck," Luc mutters.

The hair on my arms stands on end, and thunder booms, shaking the room so hard the pictures turn topsy-turvy. I jump when the lights flicker. The eerie sound of an impending tornado surrounds us, and it's so loud I cover my ears. My wet hair whips around my face, and I squint against the blast of cold air. Feathers fill the air like we're in the middle of the world's biggest pillow fight.

Madge elbows her way over to me as she glares at Luc and Rafe. Raising one hand, she points toward the door and shouts, "Out! Get out, right now. You're behaving like two spoiled little boys fighting over a toy. Jolene is no toy. She's a *human being*. Now take your idiotic pissing contest somewhere else and let the poor child get dressed."

The last thing I see before she closes the door is the blond guy standing between Rafe and Luc with a hand on each of their chests, separating them. The shouting between the two men continues.

Madge reopens the door and hisses, "Shh! May I point out that you're in the hallway? Keep it down."

Closing the door once again, she turns to me, but her smile looks forced, and lines of anxiety crease her forehead. Still, dressed in tight jeans and a white blouse, she looks impeccable, and not a strand of hair is out of place, which is odd considering what we just went through. I'm sure I resemble a drowned rat. She pulls white and red feathers from my hair.

"Men." She rolls her eyes. "Can't live with them, and certainly wouldn't want to live without them."

"Th-Thank you." The tension in the room has dissipated somewhat, but my unease hasn't. I return to the bathroom and sink onto the closed seat of the commode. Madge stands at the doorway with my sweater and pants. She places them on the counter and starts packing my cosmetics.

"W-What just happened? Am I losing my mind?" I gasp.

"Nice big breaths, darlin'. There ya go. You're going to be fine. Those overgrown brats should be ashamed of themselves, upsetting you with their biggest-Johnson contest. As if size matters. Well, it does, but you know what I mean. I'd rather have an average guy who knows how to use it—never mind, that's probably TMI. Those idiots. They didn't even give you a chance to get ready and have breakfast. Just ignore my prattle and get dressed, sweetie. I'll start some coffee. Would you like me to order breakfast from room service?"

"Ugh, no, thank you."

She breezes out of the room, and I jump into my clothes and yank my hair into a ponytail. None of this seems real. If I'm lucky I'll wake up with Atticus and realize this was a nightmare due to indigestion.

When I open the door, Madge smiles at me. She's already packed my suitcase. I try to deflect any further questions with a few of my own. "Who was that blond guy?"

"Gabe. He works with me."

"Do you only hire good-looking men?"

She laughs. "Looks that way, doesn't it?" Rubbing my arm, she peers into my eyes. "You okay, darlin'?"

I shake my head. "No. I have a pounding headache, and I want to go home. I wish I could just twitch my nose and make it happen." I swallow, trying to understand the entire crazy situation. "Am I asleep or awake? This feels like the reoccurring dream I have where I arrive late to class. The professor is handing out the final exam, and I realize I haven't been there all semester and have no idea what's going on." I zip my suitcase, still putting off the dreaded call to my brother. "I know that doesn't make any sense."

"Actually, it does. I was afraid something like this would happen, but do men ever listen? Noooo." She drums her long, fake nails on the desk. "Do you trust me?"

I hesitate, not wanting to offend her even though I know the answer is *no*. "I don't really know you," I hedge.

"Fair enough. Have you ever seen *The Wizard of Oz*?"

"Of course."

"Well, think of me as Glinda the Good Witch. Close your eyes…"

"What do you mean she's gone?" Back in the room, I glare at Madge and shove Luc against the wall just for the heck of it. After all, this catastrophe is his fault.

He shrugs out of my grasp, and I find myself flying through the air. Feathers float like snowflakes around us. I catch myself just before crashing through the wall. He's strong and didn't hold back. Flames flick the ends of his red feathers. This is just great. If someone complains about the noise and calls hotel security, all of us will be in deep shit.

"*Stop.*" Gabriel's booming voice resonates through the room. His wings flap twice before folding into hiding. A brown-tipped white feather floats to the floor between Luc and me. When Gabe loses feathers, he's beyond pissed. Luc and I share a look and back off. "Now, Madge, where is the girl?" Gabe asks.

"Her name is *Jolene*." Luc straightens his cuff, but his attempt at looking dignified is marred by the scorched red feather sticking out of his hair.

"Not that you ever bothered to learn her name until you thought you could get her in bed," I snarl.

"And get her in bed, I did—"

Before he finishes the sentence, I send him flying across the room. I'm spoiling for a fight, wanting him to pay for every tear Jo's shed because of his sorry ass. Thanks to Luc's flames, the smell of singed feathers permeates the room. Fire alarms sound, and the overhead sprinklers flip on, drenching us.

Luc glares, pointing at the *one* unmade bed in my room. "Don't be casting stones at me. Seems I'm not the only one to bed the fair Jolene…"

That's it. I'm done. I'm going to kill him, and then I'll be forced to take over his job. Not that I can actually kill him, but I'll take great pleasure in trying. I lunge toward him, but Gabe steps between us.

"Stop it, both of you. All three of you have done it now. The Boss is going to be in a rip-roaring mood over how sloppy you've been," Gabe admonishes. "You know better. We're supposed to work undercover."

"*Undercover* being the word of the day," Luc replies with a haughty sneer. "While the rules might apply to those ignoramuses, I'm not really *His* concern anymore."

Gabe rolls his eyes. "Do you really want to go there? Why do you always have to push the envelope? You've always liked being the troublemaker."

As they quarrel, I concentrate, listening for Jolene. If she reaches out needing help, I'll be able to pinpoint her location. It's like having a built-in GPS. But she has to need me in order for me to know where she is. I get nothing. Nada. *Come on,* I silently urge. Just one little ping, that's all I need. I double my effort to latch on to her energy, drowning out the dispute between Gabe and Luc. Still not getting anything, I sigh. Jolene has more guts than most humans and a heart too big for her own good. Luc continues running his mouth, arguing with Gabe.

Desperate, I glance at Madge. She mouths one word. "*Home.*" I'm gone in an instant, willing to pay the price with The Boss for my disappearing act. I have to get to Jolene before Luc does.

I'll deal with him later. I'm tired of being the good angel.

Atticus takes one look at me and turns away with an angry flick of his tail. I sling my suitcase on my kitchen table but make no move to unpack. I'm not even sure how I got home. Everything is a fog, and I wonder if my food was spiked or poisoned. I push that thought away. As much as Mr. DeVille is a jerk, I don't think he's capable of anything so reprehensible. *Reprehensible* is today's word of the day.

Or would he? In the space of forty-eight hours, my world has turned upside down. It's like I don't know who I am anymore, or what I want. For weeks all I've thought about is dating my boss. I worked hard to be a woman he'd want by his side, and I finally caught his attention.

But now? The thought of being with Mr. DeVille makes me uneasy, sick almost. I hear feathers fluttering behind me and whip around to face Rafe. I know for a fact I locked the door. Backing away, I end up sitting on my futon. This place is so small there's nowhere to escape.

I bolt back to my feet. "How did you get in here?"

"I have a key."

"I'm not stupid. You didn't use the key." I lift my chin and cross my arms. "Tell me."

He puts his hands on his hips. "Tell you what?"

I stomp my foot, and Atticus glares at me for disturbing his butt-licking. "Tell me what's going on. You know Luc more than through just work, don't you?"

"I-I'm not supposed to —" He stops and steps toward me. "Yes."

"How?"

"Maybe you should sit down for this."

"Quit stalling and tell me."

"He's my brother."

"Your brother? You two don't look anything alike." The shocked look on her face would be funny if I wasn't so worried about her.

"Neither do you and Johnny Way."

Jo rubs her eyes. "This is all so confusing. I can't seem to sort it out. I really think something's wrong with me." She surveys the room. "I'm not even sure how I got home. Plus, I know I locked the door, and I didn't hear you unlock it..."

I cup her face in my hands. "It isn't you. You're fine. Please, just trust me."

Confusion clouds her eyes, and my heart breaks just a little. I kiss her forehead and stroke her hair. She has no idea what she means to me. I'll do anything to wipe her fears away, even to my own detriment.

Wrapping my arms around her, I hold her close, needing her much more than she probably needs me. I'm in love with this girl. I think maybe I've always been in love with her. I left when she was fifteen, telling myself it was for her own good. Who have I been kidding? I left because I wasn't prepared to see her fall for another guy. The thought of her with anyone else hurts like hell. Luc has reminded me of that.

"I always feel better when you're with me," she whispers.

This time I lower my mouth to hers. It's wrong, but it's all I want to do. I've been lying to myself and everyone else. I'm no longer concerned with just protecting her. This need for her is beyond my comprehension. I want Jolene in every way possible — including biblically. Especially biblically...

Her lips part, and her fingers curl in the hair at the nape of my neck. She presses her body closer, sending me spiraling into forbidden territory. I deepen the kiss, and my hand creeps under her sweater, wanting, needing to feel her warm skin. I pull her closer, but she breaks the kiss and steps away. Her hand shakes as she shoves her riot of waves out of her face.

"Rafe —"

"No, don't say anything. I'm sorry." I back up a step, feeling like the lowest of the low. I need to put my selfish wants aside. I'm no better than that self-serving bastard Luc. I turn to leave.

"Wait." She plucks at my sleeve. I turn and wince at the uncertainty written across her face.

She looks at the floor. "I, uh...just wanted you to know, I think I'm going to go away. I need time to think. It's time I figure out who I am and what I truly want in life. I can't do it here."

"Where will you go?" My heart hammers. Trepidation makes it difficult to contain my wings. "I'll take you wherever you want."

"No. I'm going home, and I'm going alone." She twists her hands together.

"Home?" It's the last place she wants to be; I know this. The fact she's considering it is devastating. "But you left to escape that life."

Jolene shrugs. "Maybe it's the life I was meant to have. Maybe all of this was a lesson to point out that I should be content with the hand I was dealt. Maybe I was too judgmental of others and thought too much of myself."

"No!" I bark, more harshly than intended. I temper my voice before continuing. "Being content isn't good enough. You deserve so much more—passion, joy, and excitement..." It occurs to me I'm not only talking about Jo. It's a lesson I'm learning for myself as well. I grab her shoulders and look her in the face. "Wanting to get an education and change things about yourself is great. Just make sure you're doing it for you, not some asshole like Loser De*Vile*."

She sighs and turns away, busying herself with pulling clothes from her drawers and adding them to her suitcase.

"Jo, he's been around a long time. This is what he does. He seduces with promises he has no intention of keeping. He's not good for you. Think about it. If he's made you feel this bad, something's not right with the relationship."

She whirls around to face me. "This isn't about him anymore. It's about *me*. But I guess you know more about *him* since he's your *brother*. You've never mentioned having a brother. How come I never knew this?"

"He's the black sheep of the family."

"I'm guessing he's older?"

"Yes."

"He doesn't look that much older than you. How come I never met him, and why don't you have the same last name?" She taps her fingers against her crossed arms.

"Uh, it isn't a blood relation. We were foster brothers." I pray she buys my answer. I'm tired of being shady with her.

"I think it's rude neither of you mentioned the fact that you knew each other. It makes me feel kind of foolish. If you hate him so much, why did you work for him?"

Tenacious. It should be her word of the day. "He made me an offer I couldn't refuse."

"Oh, brother. Your last name isn't *Corleone*. Whatever. I get the feeling you're not going give me any real answers, and quite frankly, I'm done trying to sort this out. Just leave."

"I don't want to leave you alone." It's the first totally honest thing I've said to her today. "I'm worried about you. Besides, you said you feel better when I'm with you."

"I do. But I have to learn to take care of myself." She lifts her chin. "I'll endeavor to move forward; I always do."

Ah, there it is, another one of her calendar words. I smile and tuck a strand of her hair behind her ear. "That's one of the things I love most about you." Her eyes widen at my blurted admission, and I want to kick myself. "I can't leave you like this. I promise not to bother you. Tell me what I can do to make this right."

She stomps her foot like a frustrated little girl, and her lip trembles. "Please…just go. Don't make this any harder on me. Don't you see? I have to do this for *me*. I have to grow up. This is real life. There isn't a fairy tale. There will never be a prince whisking me off to live happily ever after. I'm average. I'm just a plain old peony, not an exotic orchid."

"You are far from average. And orchids are overrated." I stroke her cheek. "You're a beautiful, wild summer rose." I kiss her again, softly. "Someday you'll get your fairy tale."

"Please stop." Her eyes shine with tears.

I drop my hand and sigh, defeated. Causing her further pain is not an option. "Call if you need me?"

"Of course." Turning her back to me, she resumes packing.

"Jo—"

"Just go," she whispers without turning around.

I leave, though it's the last thing I want to do.

The door closes behind me, and I sink onto the chair. If he'd stayed one more minute, I don't think I could have held up against the onslaught of his kisses. Rafe's intensity leaves me breathless and wanting more. But I can't make a mess of anything else. I need to get away, think, and regroup. As much as I hate to admit defeat and ask for more help, I grab my phone and dial the one other person who's always been there for me.

"Sanford here." My brother's brusque voice makes me more homesick than I ever thought possible.

"Hey," I croak, doing my best to contain my emotions, but failing miserably.

"What's wrong?" Johnny Way's voice gentles, going from gruff to concerned in one second flat.

"Can I come home?" I correct myself. "May I come home? Please?"

"What happened? Are you okay?"

"Yeah, uh, this job isn't working out."

"Pack up your shit. I'll be there in three hours." My brother hangs up without saying good-bye, probably already headed out to his truck.

I scrounge around the office and bring every empty box I can find down to my apartment. Two and a half hours later, a sharp rap on my door interrupts my packing.

"Who is it?" I ask, praying it isn't Luc or Rafe.

"Who the hell do you think it is?" a familiar voice bellows.

I open the door, and my brother pulls me into a tight hug for about ten seconds before pushing me back to peer into my face.

"You okay?"

I nod, unable to speak with my emotions lodged in my throat. I'm surprised I didn't hear a police siren announcing his arrival. There's no way he drove the speed limit to get here this fast. My eyes shift to the floor. I've never been able to lie to my brother, but I don't exactly want to tell him what a fool I've been.

"I don't want to talk about it. Can we just go?" I shrug out of his grasp and finish taping up the box of books. It hasn't taken me long to pack. The only furniture I'm taking is my bookcase. The uncomfortable futon and dilapidated tables can stay. I squirm under his scrutiny.

"Did someone hurt you?"

"No." I face him, looking him in the eye. It's the truth. It's my own stupidity that has put me in this situation.

He sighs. "Okay. Let's get my truck and your car packed. We'll talk about it later."

"The car is already packed. Remind me to get the oil changed. I haven't had to drive it much here in the city; I'm going to miss public transportation."

"I can't think of anything worse than living in this concrete hellhole." Johnny Way hoists a box to his shoulder.

"You get used to it. I just need to corral Atticus into the cat carrier. All that's left are these boxes and the bookcase. There's a hand truck in the hall."

He huffs and glares at Atticus. No one but me likes my mean old cat—not that Atticus cares.

Johnny Way carts the stuff to his truck, and Atticus hisses and claws my arms as I drop him into his cat carrier. He probably won't acknowledge me for a week. Right now, my brother is the only male in my life who isn't mad at me. How pathetic is that? As I finish cleaning the apartment, a florist delivers a vase of peonies.

"Somebody thinks you're pretty special," the deliveryman comments.

I don't answer and place them on the table as I finish mopping. Johnny Way comes back and gets the last box by the door. "I'm off. Be careful driving and keep a guide to yourself. I'll see you at home."

"Okay, thanks." I smile at Johnny's standard sign-off line. Before leaving, I have one more task to complete. I place the flowers, my keys, and my resignation letter on Mr. DeVille's desk. With one last sad glance around the office I'll never see again, I close the door on this wretched chapter of my life.

When I arrive Monday morning, I storm past Friday's empty desk. Jolene hasn't answered my phone calls or texts. I wasn't surprised when Mrs. Cabot phoned to inform me that not only am I out the best damn assistant I've ever had, we also don't have anyone to clean the office now. The items I find on my desk only darken my mood. Snatching the card from the flowers, I scan it, pretty much knowing what it's going to say.

Thank you for allowing me the chance to see what a douchebag you are.
~Jo

Somehow I don't think *douchebag* is in her stupid vocabulary-building calendar. I have to applaud her panache even as it pisses me off. I open the letter.

I relinquish this job.
~Jolene Sanford

Ah, *relinquish*, the word for January sixth. I shred the note and card and throw them and the flowers in the garbage. My mind races over numerous ways to make her pay for ditching me. A timid knock on the door interrupts my dark thoughts.

"Enter at your own risk." I narrow my eyes and steeple my fingers, waiting to see who has the guts to interrupt.

Mrs. Cabot's pale face peeks around the door. Impatient, I motion her to come in. She stutters and fidgets, asking me about some nonsense with the business. A business I have even less interest in than before—and who knew that was possible? I'm no longer concerned about my job with Him, either.

If Raphael is stupid enough not to open his eyes and seek the treasure known as Jolene Sanford, I'll claim her. Not that I have feelings for her or anything. No, of course not. That would be ridiculous. It's the thrill of the chase. That's all. It has nothing to do with her compassion, sense of humor, or spirit...

Sonofabitch.

CHAPTER FIFTEEN

I've managed to avoid Johnny Way's questions for a week. We've settled into a comfortable routine of sorts. I fix him breakfast before we both head to work, and he usually has something in the Crock-Pot for when we get home. I'm once again the cashier at the Stop-n-Shop. The owner, Mr. Kelly, offered me back the day shift. I used to ride my bike here every day to sweep his store in exchange for candy or a soft drink when I was a kid. In high school he hired me as a cashier, and I worked here until I decided to move to better my life. Ha! That was a joke. I'm thankful he took me back; otherwise I'd probably be picking up stray cats, watching daytime TV, and eating myself into oblivion.

My overprotective brother has never liked me working here. He's afraid I'll be robbed or something—which is kind of silly. I mean, it's just a little country store, and I know everyone around here. Mr. Kelly says I'm his best worker, and he even pretends not to notice when I give poor One-Eye Dooley a free hot dog and a Coke every day. The old man lost his eye in the Korean War and is a little crazy, but he's harmless. He always says he'll pay tomorrow, but he never does.

I'm at the back of the store, stirring the pot of disgusting boiled peanuts, when the bell on the door rings.

"I'll be right with you," I holler.

"My, my, how the mighty have fallen. Reduced to stirring a pot of goobers. I hear you done quit school and that high-falootin' job in the city. I bet that was hard, wasn't it? Havin' to admit you got a little too big for yer britches. How's life treatin' you since you've come back home? If anyone would've asked me, I'd a told 'em you'd be back. You never could stay on task. Git me a six pack of beer—and none of that cheap shit, either."

I lay the ladle down and count to ten instead of spewing the hatred bubbling from the pit of my stomach like a volcano. "How would you know what I have or haven't been up to?" I ask calmly. "It isn't like you've ever kept up with my comings and goings. You've always been too drunk or stoned to care, or just not around." I turn to face the man who is my father on paper only. "When did you get out?"

"You better watch that smart-ass mouth of yours, little girl. I got out today and came straight home. Why haven't you been to see your mother?"

I snort. "I did. The first day I got back. She was passed out on the couch."

He stumbles toward me, and the stale stench of alcohol oozes from his pores. He's lost weight, and his color reminds me of Dijon mustard. His dark hair, now salted with gray, lies matted and un-combed. However, the look of disgust on his face hasn't changed one dadgum bit. I can't remember a time he ever smiled at me. Grabbing a can of pork and beans off the shelf, I ready myself for the blow sure to come. I refuse to run. Never again will I back down from him, and I won't go down without a fight.

The bell jingles on the door, drawing our attention. I'm both relieved to have someone else in the store and worried about what Robert Earl might do.

One-Eye Dooley rounds the corner, leaning heavily on his cane, and waves, his toothless grin stretching across his lined face. "Hey, Jo. I need me a hot dog and a co-cola. I'll pay ya tomorrow." He nods at my no-count father. "Robert Earl. I heard you got out. You glad to see your girl, here?"

Robert Earl grunts. "She was just gittin' me a six-pack." He shoots a warning glare at me. "Weren't you, *Jolene?*"

His use of my name is a warning. He's a walking caricature of every mean-as-a-snake, no-good redneck ever portrayed in a bad movie. If I don't do as he says, things will get ugly. And One-Eye might step in. Robert Earl won't hesitate to hurt that poor old man. I hand him what he wants and watch him leave without a lick of gratitude.

One-Eye purses his lips. "I never did understand how two good kids came from such sorry parents. I figure it must be like math. Two negatives make a positive."

I laugh and on impulse kiss his grizzled cheek. "Thank you."

He winks with his good eye and leaves, eating his hot dog, his Coke swinging from the bag hooked on his cane. I always wonder if it spews when he finally opens it. The next time Johnny Way and I are both home for Sunday dinner, I should invite One-Eye. He needs a good home-cooked meal, not this junk he eats from a gas station food market.

My day continues without further incident until my relief calls in sick. I have no choice but to stay at work, and I text my brother to let him know I'll be home late. He's not happy but grudgingly admits staying is the right thing to do. He's always instilled a strong work ethic in me. I think we both feel the need to make up for our lazy parents.

The evening shift is boring, so I clean the store from top to bottom, even tackling the nasty pizza warmer. Staying busy keeps my mind off my other job and the mess I made. I miss my big-city life, even if it was stressful. I've wondered at least a million times what Mr. DeVille's doing. But while I miss being his assistant, I no longer miss *him* as the object of my affection. I wonder if he's thought of me at all. I doubt it. Less than two days of me ignoring his angry texts and voice mails and he quit calling.

They say hindsight's better than foresight, and looking back, I can see how callous he was toward me. A part of me still hopes he did like me, just a little. I justify my foolishness by imagining Mr. DeVille had a crummy childhood and is afraid to get close to anyone. After all, he didn't live with Rafe and his dad, whom Rafe claims is the best. Personally, I think Mr. Goodman was kind of an absentee parent, but who am I to judge? My life might have been better if Robert Earl had been around less.

I scrub the counter harder, not wanting to explore my feelings for Rafe. I miss him more than I did when he left for college. I can't even watch re-runs of *Friends* without crying. Him coming back into my life was the best thing that happened while I was in the city. And now I know why. He's more than a friend, and we've been skirting around our attraction since we reconnected.

At ten, I lock the store, more than ready to get home and sink into a hot bath. I wonder if Johnny Way knows Robert Earl's out. I forgot to tell him earlier. I know it's a useless waste of energy, but I'm feeling sorry for myself and wish I had someone to talk to.

No, not just anyone—I wish *Rafe* was here. I hope I haven't lost him along with everything else, although if I have, it's my own dumb fault. It's late, but he's a night owl. Pulling out my phone, I decide to see if we can at least patch our friendship. My heart speeds up at the thought of hearing his warm voice. Not only do I miss him, I need him.

A shadow crosses in front of me, and my heart jumps into my throat. I look up to find Robert Earl looming. I could kick myself; I know better. Johnny Way and Rafe have always told me to be aware of my surroundings. The stench of beer and sweat clings to him, and his wild, unfocused eyes are full of hate. He points a shaky finger at me and staggers forward.

"Whoa, now, Jolene. Why don't you march back in there and get your old man some beer?"

"Don't you think you've had enough? You can barely stand or talk. Surely this breaks some rule about your parole." I shove past him, headed toward my car. Robert Earl can smell fear better than a rabid mongrel. So despite my unease, I don't look back, giving a pretense of bravery. But a nervous scan of my surroundings confirms my apprehension: we're alone. There isn't a house within shouting distance. Should I run or call Johnny Way?

Before I can decide, my head snaps back, and I yelp, unable to get away from the grip on my ponytail. His backhand throws me face down on the parking lot. I'm pretty sure I just lost a fistful of hair. Lifting my scraped, burning cheek from the cold asphalt, I glare at my attacker, the man who calls himself my father. No soul resides behind those cold eyes; he's killed it off with hatred and drugs. My cracked phone lies two feet from me, and I scramble to reach it. A worn boot heel crushes it, barely missing my fingers. He laughs as he grinds it with a twist until it shatters into a pulverized mess.

The bizarre thought flits through my mind that the phone represents my dreams. I just pray it isn't an allegory for my life. Panicked, I attempt to crawl away, but a swift kick in my side has me once again kissing the pavement. I curl into a fetal position, my arms protecting my head.

"Now you know your place. Get up, open that damn store, and get me my beer!"

"Fuck you," I gasp, determined to take the beating rather than give in.

"You little smart-mouthed bitch. You'll damn well do as I say, or else."

I'm panting with terror. I've never seen him this out of control before, and my bravado slips. This could well end up being a battle for my life. An overwhelming desire to live drives me to my feet. If I can get away, Johnny Way will arrest his sorry ass once this is over.

Robert Earl grabs my arm, and I try to knee him in the groin. I miss, but it loosens his grip just enough for me to get away. He's like an enraged bull, bellowing and stampeding behind me. I run for my car and tug the handle to no avail, screaming with frustration and genuine fear. The door is locked, and my purse was lost in our fight.

I face off with Robert Earl over the hood of the car. A fiendish smile spreads across his grizzled face. I have no doubt he plans to either take me out of this world or make me wish I'd never been born. He moves to the right; I move to the left. As long as I keep the vehicle between us, I'm good.

Please, God, don't let me die.

The wind gusts, blowing so hard I'm unable to keep my eyes open. I find the door handle, gripping it tight to brace myself against the buffeting blast of air. Is this some sort of polar vortex? I squint and see a wide expanse of white wings. Robert Earl flies through the air, landing on his back with a thud and grunt of pain. Then the winged apparition turns toward me, but I don't wait to find out what it is. I take off running, making it about ten feet before warm wings surround me, and I'm swept off my feet.

"What the fuck?"

Johnny Way would wash my mouth out with soap if he heard me using the F-word twice in five minutes. *Really? This is where my mind chooses to go right now?*

"Shhh, honey. You're okay; you're okay."

Rafe! I sag with relief, safe in his wings. *Wait, what? Wings?* The smell of clear water on a summer night adds to my comfort but doesn't lessen my confusion. I grip a handful of feathers, but when I blink it's an arm. We're now standing across the parking lot near my purse, which he scoops up. The adrenaline that's been coursing through my veins drains like water from a bathtub, and the world around me blurs into darkness. Rafe bends me over his arm, rubbing my back in reassuring circles.

"Nice deep breaths. I've got you; you're safe."

I suck in air, keeping an eye on Robert Earl, who isn't moving.

Rafe strokes my hair, murmuring over and over, "There you go, my darling, brave girl."

The blood returns to my scrambled brain. "Let me up. And I'm a grown woman, in case you haven't noticed," I gasp.

"I noticed. But you're also my girl," he affirms with a kiss to my forehead. He lifts me into his arms and moves toward the car. Yes, arms—I double-check to be sure.

"Okay." Feeling safe, I snuggle into his neck. His scruff tickles my cheek, and I smile. At the moment, I'm exactly where I want to be. I crane my neck around his broad shoulders and see Robert Earl still sprawled on the ground.

"I-Is he dead?" I whimper.

"Nope, just out cold. You can call your mother to come get his sorry ass—or better yet, call your brother to arrest him for assault and battery."

"Did he see?" I swallow, wondering if I'm losing my mind. Or maybe when I hit my head, it knocked me silly. Nope, in my hand is a beautiful white feather. I clutch it tight, afraid it might disappear like Rafe's wings did. "Who are you?" I whisper, terrified of the answer, yet not afraid of him.

He sits on the hood of the car, holding me in his lap. "I'm your guardian angel."

I laugh, but it sounds tinny and weak. "No, really. Be serious."

"I'm dead serious." His eyes crinkle, and he kisses the top of my head.

"No," I gasp, his answer hitting me in the gut. My salty tears sting as they meet my cold, cement-burned cheeks. He holds me closer, and I hear the steady beat of his heart, which adds to my bewilderment, yet gives me comfort. *If he has a heart, he has to be real, right?*

"No need to cry, you're safe now. He'll never hurt you again."

"Please tell me Johnny Way was wrong…" My shoulders shake from the cold and my crying jag. Rafe's flannel shirt is now damp, and I feel guilty. He isn't even wearing a coat, and it's friggin' freezing out here. My nose would be running even if I weren't a tearful mess. "I'm sorry." I run my hand over his shirt as if I can magically dry it.

"Sorry for what? Shh, don't cry. What don't you want your brother to be right about?" He brushes my hair out of my face and wipes away my tears.

"You need a coat. You'll catch your death from cold."

He laughs, and it rumbles deep in his chest. "Not a problem, I promise. I'm fine."

"When I was little, I'd talk about you all the time," I babble between sniffles, wishing I had a tissue. "Johnny Way told me to grow up and quit talking about my imaginary friend." I stop to think. "But at work, other people saw you. Mr. DeVille saw you… Am I losing my mind?"

Rafe rummages in my purse and pulls out four gum wrappers, a tampon, and an expired cat food coupon before finding a tissue. "No, you're not losing your mind. And I'm very real. I'll explain everything, but first, call your brother. We don't want him worrying about why you're so late. Tell him to come haul Robert Earl to jail." He hands me his phone.

"He's a by-the-book kind of guy. He'll want to know what Robert Earl's done. And then the rumors will fly all over town. I don't want to hear whispered gossip about my dysfunctional family. I want to blend in."

"Just tell him he's passed out cold in front of the Stop-n-Shop. It's not a lie."

I narrow my eyes. "Are angels allowed to tell half-truths?"

"It's too cold to discuss theology. Call."

I dial the phone.

"Sanford."

"Hey, it's me."

"Where the hell are you? I tried calling the house. You're half an hour late and not answering your phone."

I smile. My brother still thinks I'm a teenager with a curfew. "I had a last-minute customer; it couldn't be helped. Then as I was leaving, I dropped my phone, and it broke."

"Oh, for heaven's sake, Jo. How many does this make?"

"I'll pay for it. Listen, there's something I need you to do."

"What would that be? You know I'm stuck at the station until morning."

"Robert Earl's passed out in front of the store, and in this weather, I'm afraid he'll die of hypothermia."

"And that would be bad?"

I grin, picturing him rubbing a hand over his tired face. "Come on, I don't want this on my conscience, and neither do you. You brought me up better than that. Just get someone to collect his sorry butt."

I hear him chuckle on the other end of the line and noise like he's getting up from his desk. I knew he'd handle this himself.

"Listen, my friend's waiting on me. I'm tired and ready to go home. You got this?"

"I'm on it."

"Okay, thanks. I'll see you tomorrow. Love you. Oh, and do a drug test on him. I'm pretty sure he's high on something."

"Hey, Jo?"

"Yeah?"

"Be safe and keep a guide to yourself."

"Will do."

Rafe takes the phone from me and turns it off. "Let's go before your brother gets here." He puts me on the ground and opens the passenger door for me.

I frown. "Wait, the doors were locked. Are you magic?"

He jangles my car keys. "Finding them in the bottom of that pit you call a purse could qualify as magic, but no. And I think you have coupons in there that expired seven years ago. Now hurry and get in. Do you really think Johnny Way will miss this opportunity? You know he's on his way."

"True." I slide in and buckle up.

Rafe starts the car and peels out of the parking lot. From a distance, I can hear the wail of a police siren.

My nerves kick in, and I glance over at him. I'm in the car with an angel, going only God knows where. "Should I be afraid?"

Rafe shoots a look at me, rubbing his designer beard stubble. A memory of it grazing my neck makes my toes curl, and I clench my thighs together.

"A rational person would say yes," he admits.

"Are you saying I'm not rational?" We're driving down a long, dark stretch of road. My heart pounds in my chest, and fear whooshes in my ears as realization settles over me like a shroud. "Oh my God," I whisper, too late.

The car swerves as Rafe glances over at me. "What's wrong?"

The finality of my situation takes root. I turn and stare out the window, not ready to face my fate, but not wanting to show my trepidation, either.

"Jo, honey, talk to me." Rafe pulls up in front of my brother's house. The light from the porch is like a lighthouse beacon in the cold, dark night. Those who have died and come back always say there's a light at the end of a tunnel. Is this the light leading to my ultimate destiny?

He throws open his door and hurries around to mine, pulling me from the car. "Jo?"

"I-I'm sorry." His face swims before me, and I fall to my already bruised knees in front of him. My jeans are like a wick on the freezing, damp ground, and I shiver as the cold seeps into my trembling body. I'd better enjoy cold while it lasts; I'm more than terrified of what awaits me beyond that door. Rafe kneels with me, cupping my cheeks.

I grip his warm hands and stare into his eyes. "I know I haven't always done right, and I've been ungrateful at times—"

"Stop," he croons, kissing my forehead and cheek. "What are you talking about? You're the sweetest girl I've ever known."

Known. Past tense. The finality of the word hammers my tortured soul like a nail in my coffin.

"Will anyone miss me?" I sniffle, checking my tears, trying to be brave.

"Miss you?"

"M-My brother. He tried to do right by me. Please make sure he doesn't feel guilty." I cling to his hands to keep from collapsing. "And Atticus—he won't understand…"

"Did you hit your noggin when you fell? Get up and come in the house where it's warm. I'll check out your hard head. Do you think you need to go to the hospital?" His voice resonates with humor and concern.

"At least I'll get to see Lynn again." *Hopefully.* "Want to know my biggest regret?" I breathe, hanging my head, not rising.

"Okay, I'll play. What?"

"I know it should be something noble, like not giving more to charity, or feeling bad for not curbing my tongue. I was terribly snarky at times and cussed a little. I know I'm selfish and vain. I've been accused of thinking I'm better than others, and in truth, I did. I should have been nicer to my mean old cat and given him tuna more often. And I abso-freakin-lutely know I shouldn't have lusted after my boss or hated my parents…" The words pour from my mouth like a creek that's breached its banks. I'm spilling my guts as if it will do any good now. I know it's too late, but maybe I can convert and go to that purgatory place rather than hell.

Rafe stands and pulls me to my feet, chuckling. He holds my face in his hands. He's staring at me with an intensity that gives me naughty thoughts, even though I'll never have the opportunity to act on them. I truly am depraved, feeling lust as I'm about to be sentenced to hell. *Go big or go home.*

"Go on," he encourages with a grin.

"Don't laugh at me. Is it proper etiquette for an angel to laugh at someone in a state of Penzance?"

"Penzance? Are you a pirate?" He cracks up outright this time.

I turn away, not wanting him to see my angry, hurt tears, and swipe them away with the back of my hand. Some angel. *I'm dead, and he finds it funny.* And I can't even stay mad at him, or I'll run the risk of ending up in hell for all eternity. I'm doomed. I didn't realize how good I really had it. Coming home to this backwoods town wasn't so bad.

Turning me around, Rafe gives me a quick hug. "I'm sorry. No, you're right. *Penance* is no laughing matter." He's smiling, but not laughing now. "I'm listening. Tell me your biggest regret, my darling Jo." He tucks a strand of my hair behind my ear.

It takes me three tries to get the words out of my dry mouth. "Not valuing the precious gift I could have had."

He cocks his head to the side. "And what would that have been?"

"You," I whisper.

Jo's eyes shimmer like exotic gems in the dim light. Even with her red nose, scraped cheeks, and tangled hair, she's never looked more beautiful—like a wild pagan goddess. I love this girl, and her whispered confession unlocks the self-imposed shackles on my heart. You can't see the things I've seen—the evils of a world that turns its back on love—without guarding your heart. And in this moment I realize mine's been enclosed in barbed wire, barely beating, to keep from bleeding out over the ugly hatred I've witnessed all these many years. I came here tonight as her guardian. I'm not leaving until she understands the depth of my feelings for her. The cage around my heart is gone, and love courses through me, nourishing my soul.

I'm no stranger to love. Look at Who I work for, He's the Author of it. But this is new. A different kind of love than His *agape* or my *storge*, the love I feel for my brothers and sisters. When I was given Jo as my charge, I loved her. I mean, how can you not love Jolene? She's funny, sweet, and beautiful. But it was a *phileo* love, a commitment to care for her.

Truthfully, I can't imagine my life without Jo. My happiest times have been with her, whether it was sharing a carton of ice cream or fishing at the pond. I still laugh thinking about how her nose would wrinkle when I made her bait her own hook. She's shown me how to see beauty and find peace in the world, despite all its flaws. My favorite thing to do is watch her sleep, when she's at total ease, not stressing about her imperfections—imperfections I find perfect.

Now that I've quit lying to myself about my feelings, I feel free for the first time, ever. It's like running as fast as you can and knowing you might fall, but not caring because you have to do it. Or soaring over the world with the sun on your face. It is joy, pain, and release all at the same time. *I'm living.*

Reckless abandonment is so far out my normal, controlled mentality I almost can't grasp the depth of it. This is *eros*, and I feel drugged—high on the intoxicating allure. Hearing her whispered declaration has unleashed a side of me I've never known. A powerful, all-encompassing hunger to both devour and connect with this woman overtakes any rational thought.

I love her.

I need her.

And I want her.

Now.

I kiss her, my hands snaring in her tangled hair. She scrunches my shirt, and I halfway expect my little tigress to rip it off. Her sweet lips part, and I deepen the kiss, tasting a remnant of breath mint and her cherry-flavored lip gloss. I want to nibble and enjoy every last delicious inch of this girl. I'm a starving angel, and she is an all-you-can-eat human buffet.

She's still unsteady, so I pick her up, walking toward the house. She's mine. I'm hers. I have one sole purpose on my mind. I want to make love to this beautiful woman who holds my heart. Her arms wrap around my neck, and she closes her eyes as tears streak through the dirt on her cheeks.

"Be brave, be brave, be brave," she whispers.

I pause at the doorway and kiss her forehead, realizing I'm not thinking straight. We can't do this, no matter how much I want to. This undisciplined yearning is foreign to me, and I can't seem to get a handle on it. I've got to slow down and start thinking, ignoring my body, which seems to be on the fast track toward desire and irresponsibility. I'm suffering, wanting this woman in every way possible, but my conscience slams on the brakes.

This is against His rules. I'm not of this world. I have to leave when my job is done, and I can't harm her. "I'm sorry. We'll just go inside and talk, okay?" My head tells me this reassurance is the right thing to do. My heart disagrees, and my physical body promises me I'll pay for this later.

"T-Talk? It isn't too late to negotiate?" She opens her eyes and fear lingers in their depths as she struggles to get down. I place her on her feet, keeping a steadying hand on her lower back.

I'm baffled. "What are we negotiating?"

Below my belt, my body stands at attention, cheering at the thought of negotiating some hot, steamy sex with a no-guilt clause. I rub a hand across my face and breathe deeply, trying to regain control.

"I-I'm r-ready. Let's go," she squeaks, squaring her shoulders. Puzzled, I unlock her front door. She flips on a lamp to reveal the cozy room. It isn't fancy by any means, but gives the ambiance of lived-in comfort. There's a faded plaid couch facing the fireplace and a couple of mismatched recliners in front of a bookcase holding a big-screen television.

Jo steps into the room and looks around with wide eyes. Her mouth falls open. "Where am I?"

Concern grips my heart. I grasp her head and examine her pupils. Although dilated, they are equal in size and round. Using my fingertips, I gently check her head for bumps.

"How hard did you hit your head?" I ask. "Do you think you have a concussion? Follow my finger." I mimic what I've seen doctors on TV do to check out people with head injuries.

"What?" She swats at my hand. "Stop it. Let's just get this over with."

"Never mind," I mutter. I don't know what I'm doing, but she's scaring me. What's wrong with her? This is her brother's house; she lives here.

Yawning, Jo rubs her eyes like a sleepy toddler, and I breathe a little easier, feeling stupid. The poor girl's been through a lot and is exhausted. She needs rest.

When Jo turns to hang her coat in the closet, I sneak and start the fire without matches.

Tiptoeing to the fireplace, she holds out her trembling hands, staring into the flames with a pensive look. After a moment, she murmurs, "I'm so confused..." She pales, and her knees buckle.

I'm by her side in an instant, steadying her. I wrap my arms around her waist, snuggling into her neck despite her damp, unruly hair. It might be cold outside, but she smells like roses on a warm summer day. "You always smell so good. You're okay, Jo. You're okay," I rasp, my voice heavy with emotion.

"Oh, no. No, no, no." She shakes her head. Gripping the mantle, she takes in a long shuddering breath. "H-How long?" she stammers.

If she's confused, I'm downright lost. Goose bumps dance across her skin, and she shivers.

"How long what, honey? I think you may be going into shock. Why don't you sit down—"

"I don't want to sit." She shrugs out of my grasp, crossing her arms. I watch as her throat moves up and down, and her bottom lip quivers. "I thought I'd just died—like, you know, within the last hour. I figured Robert Earl killed me over a stupid beer. He's threatened to do it often enough over the years. But now...now I'm wondering...have I been dead longer? Did I die as a kid? Have I been seeing dead people this whole time? Why didn't you tell me I was dead? You figured out that movie long before I did. You could have told me then." Her chest rises and falls as she gasps for breath, and tremors wrack her body. She's babbling nonsense and working herself into hysterics.

I grab her shoulders and stare into her troubled eyes. She's not joking; she's serious. "Why would you think you're dead?"

"Because this can't be real. Am I in heaven or hell? If this is hell, it's warm and cozy and not so bad. Not at all what I thought. Or is this just one level of hell? Do those stairs lead to the fire pit?" She points a shaky finger toward the stairs to her basement. She spins and looks at the stairs leading up to the bedrooms. "But if I'm in heaven, where are the clouds and harp music? And who would've thought heaven would have a fireplace? Crimson was wrong, wasn't she? She always said there was no such thing as purgatory. You're either good or bad. But this must be that purgatory place, the holding room. Who would've thought the afterlife was my brother's home?" She grabs my arms, squeezing tightly. "Please, Rafe. Please let me stay here or go upstairs, not down there."

"*You're not dead.*" To keep from laughing at her, I kiss the tip of her cold little nose. "You're very much alive, and you make me feel more alive than I've ever felt."

"I'm not dead?" she whispers. Her hands wrap around my neck, and we're forehead to forehead.

"Far from dead." I smile and kiss the pounding pulse in her neck, making her gasp.

"I haven't missed my opportunity?" Her warm voice drops to a husky timbre. Her eyes remain dilated, but no longer with fear—with something else...

"What opportunity?" I croak, watching her tongue lick her bottom lip.

"To be with you." She kisses my jaw. "To love you," she whispers in my ear.

They say the road to hell is paved with good intentions.

I have good intentions, but when a match strikes, fire follows.

CHAPTER SIXTEEN

I'm not dead, I'm not dead, I'm not dead! I feel like Ebenezer Scrooge on Christmas morning. And right here in my arms is the best present I've ever had. I want to wrap myself around his solid muscles like wrapping paper on a birthday gift. I want to laugh, I want to cry, and I want to scream with joy.

"No, stop." His hands hold my cheeks, and he closes his eyes, shaking his head.

He might be saying no and telling me to stop, but the hard body pressed against mine says *continue*.

"Jo, wait."

"Do you love me?" I ask, knowing the answer.

"You know I do. More than life itself; that's the problem."

"And I love you, too. And I don't mean as a friend. Although you're that, too. Can't you see? We're perfect for one another. I don't see a problem."

Taking my hand, he leads me to the couch. He collapses beside me as if the weight of the world now rests on his shoulders. Hands clasped between his knees, he hangs his head low. I kick off my shoes and rub his back.

"Rafe, please. I feel like I've been given a second chance. At last everything is crystal clear. I love you, and you feel the same about me. I know I acted silly with that disastrous trip to New York, but don't you see? It made me realize what I truly desire. I want to be loved for *me*. Imperfections included. I want someone I can relax with, who doesn't mind my bad fashion sense, who puts up with my mean old cat, and gets my corny jokes. I want someone who is always there for me, no matter what.

"I'm like friggin' Dorothy, finally realizing there's no place like home. And I don't mean that dysfunctional, crazy, pill-popping family of mine — my brother excluded. Or this house." I motion around us. "I mean *you*. You're my home."

"I want that, too." He sighs and hangs his head. "But I'm not your home. I can't be your home. You're *not* thinking. That's the problem. Do you realize what I am?"

"You said you're an angel. My guardian angel."

"Exactly."

He squirms when I explore the bulge settled below his belt. Grinning, I purr, "Mmm, you feel pretty human to me."

"Painfully so at the moment."

"So doesn't that mean you have, er, all the working parts?"

He chuckles and hardens beneath my hand. "Yes, all parts are in perfect working order."

"Then what's the conundrum?"

"That's December seventeenth's word of the day."

"I guess. You and Mr. DeVille have an uncanny ability to know what each word means and the exact day it falls upon. Is that an angel thing?"

"I guess. Look, Jo, as much as I want this, and need this, we can't. It isn't fair to you. At some point I'll have to leave, and the thought of hurting you…I can't." Elbows on his knees, he rubs his face. He looks like a man facing a death sentence: utterly hopeless.

I rub a hand across his tense back. No feathers. Maybe this is all just some whacked-out dream. "Do you have to leave now?"

"As soon as you're safe."

Squirming in behind him on the couch, I kneel and wrap my arms around his broad shoulders. I kiss the back of his neck, working my way to his ear. "Perfect."

I nibble and flick his earlobe, making him groan. He grabs me, yanking me around to sit on his lap. I'm now staring into his face. Man? Angel? Whatever he is, he's a part of my soul. I am no longer a singular entity. I'm separate yet inseparable from him, from us. He is as much a part of me as the blood coursing through my veins.

"How can that be perfect? I'm pretty miserable at the moment." He traces one finger down my cheek, smiling. Sadness lingers deep in his eyes, and my heart aches. He's going to leave me. This calls for action.

I stroke his rough cheek, rubbing my thumb across his lower lip. "Because I plan to be reckless for the rest of my life, starting now."

"Aghhh! Stop." He pushes me off his lap. "Am I being punked? Did Luc and Remiel plan this all along just to torture me?"

"Who's Remiel? And I'm not speaking to Luc. He's a douchebag. Just call me Grace." Before he can move off the couch, I straddle his lap and kiss him like there is no tomorrow.

"Grace? Why Grace? I'm not Will—*that* isn't the problem," he murmurs, placing soft kisses down my neck.

I giggle. "Not Grace from the sitcom, silly. Grace because you've shown me I'm pretty amazing, and I was once blind, but now I see. You're my soulmate. Don't you get it? Together, we can do anything. With you by my side, I can face my demons and defeat my self-doubts because you believe in me. I can't even imagine not having you in my life. What a fool I've been—"

Rafe starts to protest, but I place my finger over his lips.

"Shh, listen to me. I'm done wasting time. Life is short, and now that I'm not dead, I plan to make the most of it. And that includes seducing my boyfriend." I waggle my brows, trying to coax a smile from him.

Some of the tension drains from his face and one side of his mouth quirks upward.

"Besides, how can love ever be wrong?"

"Love isn't wrong." He points back and forth between us. "You and me together is what's wrong. I can't and shouldn't do this."

"Can't do this as in *physically unable*…" I rock against that tempting bulge between us and whimper. *It feels amazing.* "Or shouldn't do this because of some warped thinking that sex is wrong."

His hands grip my waist, stilling my movement. "Sex isn't wrong when two people love each other and are committed to one another."

"I told you I love you. You said you love me, and you're my guardian angel. How much more committed do you have to be?"

"*People.* I said *people.* I'm good with humans falling in love with each other and having sex. I'm great with it. But the fact remains, I'm not *human.* I can't risk hurting you. I love you too much, Jo. More than you'll ever know or be able to comprehend."

"Hurt me?" I look down at his crotch and smirk. "That big, huh?"

He groans and laughs. "That's not what I meant, and you know it."

"Don't be condescending. Are you saying my love isn't as deep as yours? Or are you against mixed relationships. That's so politically incorrect, I don't even know how to respond." I look away and take a deep breath. "I know my obsession with Luc was irrational, but all that seems so long ago. It's like I was under some weird spell, and it's been broken by my true love's kiss." I look back at him and search his face for the answer I want. "Maybe I should call you Wes."

He smiles and kisses the tip of my nose. "You and your movie references." He pulls me closer, wrapping his arms around me, his face nuzzled into my neck. "I want this; I do. I wish there was a way."

I run my fingers through his hair. "Why can't you just stay here? I'm pretty accident-prone. I'll tell whoever's in charge I need you to protect me on a daily basis."

He chuckles, not lifting his head. His warm breath teases my neck. "I wish it worked that way—"

I silence his words with a kiss and my awareness of him heightens in direct correlation to my desire to take this further, even if he isn't human. This can't be wrong—not when it feels so right. A little breathless, I ask, "Why not? Have you asked?" I whisper. "Please?"

"Jo, when I leave, you won't remember me. Your memory will be wiped clean. It would be morally reprehensible for me to take advantage of you."

"But I want you to take advantage of me. I'm encouraging it," I whisper, nibbling his neck.

"No. It wouldn't be right." He eases me off his lap. I watch as he paces like a caged animal. If he smoked, I'd tell him to do so. He's wound tighter than a two-dollar watch. I'd offer him a drink, but we don't have any liquor. Johnny Way is as against alcohol as I am.

"I don't understand. I've known you since I was six, and even for those years you weren't around, I never forgot you."

"You were young. Kids can see things adults can't. Children are infinitely more in touch with the intangible. Wiping your memory would have been detrimental, leaving you feeling more isolated than you already were. But you're an adult now, and sex changes everything."

"Well, that's just dumb. I've had sex before, and it was no biggie."

"Did you love him?" Rafe's face tightens. Etched there I see pain and sadness.

It feels like my heart is being ripped out of my chest.

He holds up a hand. "Never mind. The past doesn't matter."

"Thank you. I agree. My past isn't any of your business."

He winces slightly but doesn't say anything.

"What about you?"

He looks a little like a buck caught in the crosshairs of Johnny Way's hunting rifle. "A gentleman never discusses things like that."

"Stop stalling. You said you're an angel, not a gentleman. You *have* had sex before, haven't you?"

He crosses his arms in front of his chest. "What about you and Luc?"

My cheeks grow hot. "We've moved on to your sex life, not mine. But no, it didn't get that far."

"Let's just agree to *not* discuss each other's sex lives, okay?"

"Deal. Let's find something else to do." I reach for him.

He looks at the floor. "Did you love Luc?"

"No. That was lust. Pure and unadulterated."

I snicker at his groan of frustration, then stand and begin unbuttoning my blue-plaid flannel shirt.

Rafe remains still, but his eyes drink me in like an angel dying of thirst. "Jolene," he rasps. Wings unfold behind him, stirring and rustling like a peacock's. The white feathers snap like sheets on a clothesline.

"Raphael," I purr, attempting to channel Demi Moore in *Striptease*. In my nervousness, I rip off a button. I leave my shirt wide open and move to my jeans. My hands shake as I fumble with the snap. His throat bobbles and flames flare in his pupils. Slowly, I unzip my jeans and wiggle them down my hips. I look down and realize too late I'm not wearing my new, sexy matching underwear. Nope, they're my oldest, comfiest pair of white cotton panties and a white, unadorned bra. I scrunch my nose with disappointment and glance at Rafe, praying I don't see revulsion in his eyes.

"Sorry, work underwear, made for comfort not seduction," I mumble, stepping out of my jeans and toeing off my socks. In the process, I stumble against him.

"They're fine. More than fine," he croaks, catching me. His wings flutter once and disappear when he closes his eyes.

"I told you my name should've been Grace," I joke in an effort to hide my nerves. His eyes snap open and my skin flushes. He stops me from easing my shirt off one shoulder. His breathing saws harshly as he pulls me closer.

"What about your brother?" he murmurs.

I smile like a cat with cream. "He's pulling the night shift. Now quit stalling."

"Okay." His knuckle brushes the swell of my breast. "Allow me. You still owe me a Christmas present," he whispers.

"I'm afraid it isn't much—"

Stopping me mid-sentence, his mouth ravages mine with skill and finesse. It's a kiss like none we've shared before, one of raw possession. Heat flares from within, scorching my insides and curling my fingers and toes. It's so hot I wonder if I'll combust. Rafe pulls away for a second, breathing heavily. I have no doubt he owns my heart, my soul, and soon my body. Weak with need, I grip his biceps to stay upright.

"Never sell yourself short, Jo. You're the best present ever. But I've never been so unsure and terrified."

"Terrified? You?"

"I'm scared of hurting you. I'd rather die."

I rub his cheek with my thumb. "Go confidentially toward your dream; be not afraid."

He chuckles. "I think you're mixing a Thoreau quote with the Bible."

"Please, Rafe. Give me this one night, even if you think I won't remember it later. *I'll know*. Deep in my soul, I'll *know* you loved me."

"You should consider law as a career. You're quite persuasive and persistent." He trails kisses along my jaw and whispers in my ear,

"I promise you, I will always love you, and you will always know you're loved."

"This isn't some angelic pick up line, is it?" I gasp, throwing my head back.

"Is it working?" He grins, smacks my bottom, and throws me over his shoulder.

I beat his back, pretending to protest this uncharacteristic cave-man-like behavior. Carrying me upstairs, he dumps me on my bed. I watch as he kicks off his shoes and socks, shrugging out of his shirt like a male stripper on fast forward. However, it doesn't surprise me one bit when he takes an extra two seconds to fold it neatly. I giggle as he piles on top of me, obstructing my view of his impeccable pecs. He blows a raspberry on my stomach and tickles my side until I squirm against him.

He stills and his face turns serious. Caging me with his forearms, he pushes my hair off my face with a gentle hand. "One last time, Jo. Are you sure? You understand when I'm gone you'll have no memory of me, or our time together."

"Even if this damns me to hell, I'll risk it."

A horrified look crosses his face. "I don't think that will happen, but it isn't my place to say..."

He moves to roll away, and desperation makes me bold. With determination and surprise on my side, I manage to flip him to his back. Straddling his waist, I hold his hands against the pillow.

"Don't you dare try to stop me; I want my heaven on Earth." I kiss my favorite streak of gray at his temple and spread butterfly kisses down his face until I can nuzzle his neck. I don't care what he says; whenever I smell clean water on a warm summer day, I will remember him.

He grins. "I promise not to move, yet." His thumb rubs a circle on the back of my hand. "I want to see you."

I sit up and shrug my old flannel shirt off my shoulders. My hand shakes as I awkwardly attempt to unhook my bra. I'm pretty sure I look like I'm playing Twister. Seduction always looks easier and sexier in the movies.

Rafe smirks. "Need any help?"

"No, no thanks. I've got it." I gasp, finally getting it unhooked. I twirl my bra in the air around my finger and fling it. "Ta da!" I grab his wrists again and smile, licking my lips.

He laughs, but his scorching gaze locks firmly on my mouth. He wiggles his fingers under my grasp, and I release him. I want him to touch me.

"Perfect," he murmurs, sitting up and wrapping his arms around my back. "You're amazingly perfect."

His lips trace a path down my neck. Tweaking my hard nipple, he rolls and tugs just to the point of a beautiful pain. He stokes my desire into overdrive, and I moan, digging my nails into his arms.

He chuckles and kisses me, his smile wide. "Do you know how long I've dreamed of this?"

"Well, quit dreaming and make it happen." I gasp as he cups my breast in his hand.

He brings it to his hot, greedy mouth and in turn licks, sucks, and nibbles. He labors over each breast, and the throbbing between my legs intensifies to the point I want to scream. I guess he senses my impatience, because I find myself flat on my back. At last, he eases my panties down my legs, following each torturously slow inch with a kiss. In one of those weird random thoughts, I try to remember if I shaved this morning. I wonder if other girls worry about stuff like this.

"More. I want all of you," I demand, ruffling his hair with my fingers.

"Patience is a virtue, Jolene."

I yank his hair, making him yelp and laugh at the same time. "If you don't hurry up and get down to business, I'm gonna pluck you like a Sunday chicken for a Southern Baptist preacher's luncheon."

"You're going to do what?" He's laughing outright now. I smack him hard, which only makes him laugh harder.

"Get busy, mister."

"You're getting awfully bossy. I kind of like it." He winks at me, and I groan, covering my face with a pillow.

His finger strokes my clit in tantalizing circles before dipping inside me. He trails kisses down my thigh, closer and closer to his finger. I'm close to the edge and teetering, so close…I buck, using the pillow to stifle my moans. When his mouth at last follows his finger, I'm done in a matter of minutes, exploding and screaming with my release. My legs quiver in the aftermath, and I keep the pillow over my burning cheeks, trying to regain my equilibrium.

Still he doesn't stop—stroking, licking, and nipping. I feel the crescendo rising once more, and he yanks the pillow from my face, startling me.

"I want to see you this time."

"Please, Rafe," I whimper, gazing at him through lust-clouded eyes.

He kisses my stomach and moves between my legs. "Please, what? Hmm, Jolene? Did that not please you?" He smiles, nibbling on my nipple.

"No. I mean, yes…" I gasp, holding his face in my hands to make him stop. "I want to see you, too. You have on way too many clothes. Let me repay your, er, kindness."

His smile widens. Rolling to his back with his hands behind his head, he waits. I kneel beside him as if he's an altar. It occurs to me that perhaps he's a sacrificial lamb of some sort.

"Rafe?"

"Yes, my love?"

With a tentative finger, I trace the hills and valleys of his carved abs. "Will you get in trouble? If we do this?"

"Honestly, I don't know. No matter what happens, I won't let you get hurt. I promise."

"It isn't me I'm worried about—"

Sitting up, he pulls me into his lap, silencing my protests with a mind-blowing kiss. His fingers twine in my hair, and he whispers, "Hush. I'll be fine. You are my heaven. I just never knew I'd find it here on Earth."

"That's funny," I whisper, using my fingers to memorize his body as if reading Braille. "Because I think I've always known deep in my heart that heaven is where you are." I kiss his jaw. "And here you are." I push him back and attempt to unbutton his jeans, but I can't seem to perform the simple task. I'm as nervous as a cat at a dog show, or a girl that hasn't had sex with a real person in forever. He rolls over and stands beside the bed. As his shirt falls to the floor, huge white wings unfold.

He chuckles. "You okay?"

"They're…" My mouth feels like it's full of sawdust, yet I'm drooling at the same time. "Impressive," I manage to gasp. "Does wingspan among angels compare to human shoe sizes?"

His laughter fills the room. "You know those are myths." He takes mercy on me and shucks off his clothes, leaving nothing to my vivid imagination—which fell woefully short, compared to the real thing.

"Not myths," I breathe. He grins and crawls into bed, kissing my forehead. I stroke up and down his muscles, stopping just short of his waist, feeling strangely shy, which is weird. I've seen Rafe without a shirt countless times. Just never naked, and never with feelings like I have for him now. I don't know if he's right and sex is going to change everything, or if love does. Maybe both.

"May I allow my hand to travail down lower?" I stare at his chest and tracing circles around his nipple.

He chuckles softly and kisses the top of my head. "Travail? When was *travail* the word of the day? I think you mean *travel* because obviously you won't have to work very *hard*...I'm already there."

"It's *upcoming* soon, smartass. I saw it on tomorrow's date." I smooth my hand down the hills and valleys of his taut stomach. Running my thumb across his velvet tip, I watch his abs contract. Air hisses between his teeth. I run my hand down his considerable length before grasping it and stroking.

"Holy hell," he mutters, his eyes drifting closed.

I lick him, tasting the saltiness, and he shifts, gripping the bedspread with one hand, the other stroking my hair. I take the tip in my mouth and ease down slowly, taking in as much I can. His eyes snap open and flames seem to lick his long, dark eyelashes. I continue my slow ministrations, my lips and tongue grazing his shaft. Cupping his balls, I give a slight squeeze as I suck. A low growl at the back of his throat gives me pause, and in an instant I'm on my back with him poised above me. His great white wings expand behind him.

I gasp.

"Don't be scared. Please don't be scared," he whispers harshly, his arms shaking as he holds himself above me. The wings sweep and fold twice before disappearing. He takes several slow, deep breaths.

My heart hammers in my chest, but I'm not afraid. I'm in awe of his beauty. "I'm not scared of you. I could never be scared of you; you're my everything."

His leg nudges mine wider, and he leans in to cover my mouth with his. I taste the lingering essence of myself, and it amps up my desire. I want this, and I want it now. His hand dips lower and lower, caressing my stomach, heightening my anticipation one stroke at a time, until at last, one finger circles my clit. I whimper, rising to meet him, needing more. I'm more than ready when he finally eases in one, then two fingers, crooking them to reach that spot that will send me over the edge.

"Please," I whisper.

"I don't want to hurt you." He nips my neck with his teeth as I tremble beneath him. "But I want you so badly, I'm afraid it might be inevitable."

"Do you have protection?" I gasp.

"Uh, I haven't done this since nineteen fifty-three," he admits sheepishly.

"Whoa. And I thought I'd had a dry spell." I reach in my bedside drawer and pull out a condom.

Once in place, he teases at my entrance, barely penetrating. I wrap my legs around his waist and pull him in deeper.

"Jo…" Sweat beads his forehead.

I wiggle beneath him, encouraging him to continue. "Rafe," I pant. "So help me, if you don't—"

I never finish my sentence because he pulls back and slams farther into me. *Yes, yes, yes,* my heart sings in rhythm with his steady strokes. He kisses my lips, my eyes, my cheeks, murmuring my name like a prayer, over and over. I feel complete and whole for the first time in my entire life. This was meant to be; he is the answer to my prayers. I close my eyes and relax into the free fall over the edge, into the abyss of complete happiness. When his finger flicks over my clit, I'm done. My body shudders, and he soon follows, collapsing on top of me, his damp hair tickling my chin. Something tickles my nose, and I open my eyes and realize it isn't his hair. It's dozens of white feathers floating around us.

I giggle, and he looks up as a feather brushes his cheek before landing on my chest. His eyes crinkle, and he blows a feather off my face. He kisses my shoulder. "Sorry. That was intense. My wings feel like lead." Rolling beside me, he takes a feather and teases my nipple.

I rest my cheek on my hands and face him. We're no longer one, yet no longer separate. I am his. He is mine. We are us. I stare into his eyes and see my love reflected there—but also a breathtaking sadness. My heart lurches and tears gather behind my eyes.

He kisses me tenderly. "No tears, Jo. Please, don't cry."

He hurries to dispose of the condom and pounces back on the bed, kissing me all over. I giggle when he hits a ticklish spot.

"I'm so happy." I attempt a reassuring smile.

It's both truth and a lie. Deep in my heart, I know my happiness is only temporary.

I'm already grieving its loss.

And missing him.

"Jolene…" It's the only thing I can say, as if I've been struck dumb in the presence of such overwhelming joy. If the heavens opened up and an angelic choir sang the "Hallelujah Chorus," I wouldn't be any more surprised.

She presses her fingers to my lips. A tiny smile crosses her kiss-swollen lips, and her eyes close with exhaustion. She's right. There are no words to describe what just happened.

"I love you, Jolene Loretta Sanford." I roll on my back and pull her to me. She snuggles in, kissing my neck.

"I love you, too. I don't care what you say, I'll never forget," she murmurs with a soft sigh as she drifts to sleep.

Guilt washes over me in waves. I hold her tight, kissing the top of her tangled hair, never wanting to let her go. Leaving her will be the death of my soul. For the first time ever, I don't want to go home. Heaven no longer has any appeal, not without her.

After this blatant disregard of the rules, I'm sure I'll be replaced as her guardian angel. It would make sense—and be kindest to her—to leave now, while she sleeps. I can wipe her memory and be gone in an instant. She'd wake never knowing what she's been through. She might seem a bit confused for a while, but her brother will assume it's because she's feeling lost after quitting school, or the fall she took fighting with her father.

But the problem will still be here. *Luc.* She's not safe from him. Or am I justifying my selfishness? I hug her tighter, afraid to let her go. This indecisiveness is a first for me.

I don't want to leave her.

Not yet.

Not until I have to.

Not ever.

Love hurts like hell.

CHAPTER SEVENTEEN

I stir and stretch, not opening my eyes. The warmth and weight of Rafe's arm is uncomfortable, yet comforting—sort of like our newfound relationship. I can sense he's awake. The niggling worry about our future teases the corner of my mind, but I shove it away, determined to live in the moment.

"How long have you been staring at me?" I ask with a sleepy yawn.

"All night."

I glance at my bedside clock. It's five in the morning. My brother will be home soon. It might be best all around if Rafe leaves before confronting my self-appointed keeper. Fatigue circles his eyes. It's as if the fire from earlier has been stamped out, replaced by hard, cold acceptance.

I prop up on one elbow and kiss his chest, over his heart. "Don't."

"Don't?" He smooths my hair and kisses my cheek. His scruff tickles.

"Don't borrow trouble. We have right now."

He smiles, but sadness lingers as his finger traces my cheek and across my lips, as if he's blind and attempting to read my face. My heart breaks seeing his pain, but I put on a brave face, wanting to protect him. I'll think about a future without him later. Or will I? He says I won't remember him. My heart stutters at the thought, but I find it hard to believe. After a lifetime of longing to be loved, I can't believe it's wrong or that it will be taken away from me.

"I'm going to get cleaned up. I have the morning free since my shift doesn't start until one, but it might be best if you leave before my brother gets home."

"I'll join you for a quick shower and then go."

"I'm counting on it. Are your feathers waterproof?"

He looks down to where the sheet tents below his waist and gives me a lopsided, semi-leering grin. "I'm feeling quite human at the moment."

"I see that. Who knew there was such a thing as pervy angels?" I laugh and untangle myself from the covers. "Give me a minute or two alone first. Okay?" I dash to the bathroom and brush my teeth before jumping in the warm shower. I hear Rafe knock. He's ever a gentleman. Or would the correct term be *gentleangel?*

"Come in." I start singing an old song about someone knocking. The curtain snaps open and I jump, dropping the soap.

"Why yes, it *is* the Devil, and you probably shouldn't have let him in," Luc answers with a chuckle.

I shriek, attempting to cover myself with my hands, leaving the shampoo to drip into my eyes.

"Now, now, no need to cry, Friday."

"I have shampoo in my eyes, you jerk."

"Tsk, tsk, surely you can come up with a better word than *jerk.*"

"Get out," I screech, rinsing the shampoo out of my eyes and hair. Cutting the water off, I snatch the towel from his hands, wrapping it tight as if it can somehow protect me. I peer around him, looking for Rafe.

"Whatever are you looking for?" Leaning against the counter, Luc examines his cuticles.

"You know who I'm looking for." My heart hammers in triple time. *Why isn't Rafe coming to my rescue?*

"He's a bit tied up at the moment."

A fierce, otherworldly growl from the other room makes my skin crawl. It's followed by a pissed-off meow. I jump and shove Luc aside.

"What's going on? Atticus?" I stop short and gasp as I try to comprehend the nightmare before me. Flames secure Rafe's arms to the bedposts. Sweat pours off his body, and his ribs expand and contract with his labored breathing. Next to him, Atticus stands with his back arched, fur on end, and hissing at the largest black dog I've ever seen. I say dog, but he actually looks more like a wolf. The demon animal bares his teeth and snarls at my poor cat.

"Rafe!" I dart toward him, but Luc captures my wrist.

"Stop, Jolene. Do you want to be burned?" Luc's grip tightens as I struggle to break free. The rims of his eyes burn red, and flames spark and roar in their depths.

"Why? Why are you doing this?" Despite my effort to control it, hysteria tinges my voice. This seems to aggravate the monster intent on eating my cat. The demon dog snaps his vicious teeth and lunges toward Atticus again. I tug but can't escape Luc's ironclad grasp. My terrified cat hisses and jumps to the top of the dresser.

"Black Shuck."

The beast collapses, resting his head on his giant paws, tail thumping like a death knell. Luc didn't even have to raise his voice to control the creature. Atticus gives one last hiss for good measure and sits, flicking his tail and glaring with typical cat disdain. A moan from the bed draws my attention back to Rafe. I struggle again to free myself from Luc, scratching and kicking to get away.

Luc yanks my arm hard, turning me to face him. "Why am I doing this? I've asked myself the same thing. It was never part of the plan. But regrettably, all creatures have free will, Jolene. Me included. Unbelievable as it sounds, this has become more than a job, or a game to win, or a 'life lesson' as He calls it. I want you by my side. As my consort."

"Jo." Rafe opens his pain-glazed eyes. He pants in short, ragged breaths, and sweat trickles down his chest.

"Stop torturing him," I beg.

"I'm okay." Rafe closes his eyes.

"You're anything but okay," I scream, panic bubbling. "Let him go. I'll do whatever you ask. Just let him go, and stop hurting him."

"*No*," Rafe yells, struggling against the fiery bonds. The nauseating smell of singed skin and feathers fills the room.

Luc smiles at me. "Now we're talking."

I want to slap the smug look off his face, but I'm not stupid. I know antagonizing him won't help.

"Bargaining with the Devil. What a brave girl you are, Jolene. *Negotiation* was one of your calendar words, wasn't it? January second, I believe."

"What do you want?"

"I just want to talk." He looks at me the way I used to wish he'd look at me: as if I'm the only girl in the world. The hair on my arms stands on end. From the corner of my eye I check on Rafe.

"No," he snarls through cracked lips. His skin looks sunburned as he wrestles against his fiery bonds.

"Fine. We'll talk, but let Rafe go, and I'm getting dressed first."

Luc grins. "No need to dress on my account."

"Stop being an ass. You're just trying to make him jealous," I snarl, shrugging into my robe.

"That's an added benefit," Luc replies with a wink.

"Jo, don't trust him." Rafe turns his attention to Luc. "You promised not to hurt her. You harm so much as one hair on her head, and I'll send you back to hell myself."

"Why? Why do you care?" Luc taunts.

"You know you're treading in dangerous water."

"I never tread in water. I have an aversion to it; you know that, Raphael."

"You can't interfere with free will. He doesn't like it. Do you really want to incur His wrath?"

Luc swats the air as if pooh-poohing the idea. "You're blowing this way out of proportion. Jolene, have I ever forced you to do anything you haven't wanted to do?"

Numb with fear, my mind refuses to work. Rafe struggles against his bonds, causing the flames to spark.

"I'm waiting for an answer." Luc's menacing tone snaps me out of my stupor.

Desperate, I respond with the only thing that comes to mind. "I didn't like those fish eggs you made me eat."

"I didn't *make* you eat them. I *encouraged* you to expand your culinary palate."

I heave an exasperated sigh. "Fine, you're right. You didn't make me eat them. Still, they were disgusting." It's true; he's never forced me to do anything. My foolishness where he's concerned is all my own doing. "Why are you being so mean?"

"You do know who I am, right? You're a smart girl. Fire, devilishly handsome…"

I frown as the pieces start to fall together. "But, you can't be the Devil, you're too —"

"Too what? Good-natured?"

I snort. "Good-natured? You?" I rub my eyes. "This must be a bad dream."

"Jo, listen to me." Rafe grimaces as fire licks his wrists. "It's anything but a dream. He isn't called the Great Deceiver for no reason. *Trust me. I'll be fine.* You need to get dressed and leave. Take your cat with you. I'll deal with Ludicrous."

The flames around Rafe's wrists flare and pop like wood shifting in a fireplace. He winces and grits his teeth, which appear even whiter against the backdrop of his burnt face. He hangs his head for a moment, sagging against the burning bonds as if trying to contain his pain. When he looks up, the blaze of Luc's shackles is nothing compared to the smoldering anger in his eyes. His mouth settles into a determined grimace, and not a sound escapes his parched lips.

"Mr. DeVille, please stop. I'm begging you." I refuse to leave. This is surreal, but there has to be something I can do. How can I fight Luc? He is, after all, evil incarnate. *Isn't he?* Although a bossy, manipulative jerk, I've seen moments of kindness. A glimmer of hope begins to build.

Luc smiles. "I do love it when a woman begs."

Rafe flails against his roaring restraints, drawing our attention.

"Stop!" I'm not sure if I'm screaming at Rafe, Luc, or both. Rafe stops moving, and Luc turns his attention toward me. The flames recede a bit. "I said I'd talk to you, so let's talk. Let him go. What you're doing is inhumane."

"In case you haven't noticed, I'm neither human nor humane."

"No, he's an underhanded asshole." Rafe winces as the flames flash, licking farther up his shackled arms.

I grab Luc and pull him out of the room. Atticus zips by us and shoots down the stairs with Luc's beast hot on his trail. I smack him. "Make that damn dog sit."

Luc whistles, and the dog bounds back up the stairs. His tongue hangs between his fangs, and his eyes glow like the ovens at a steel plant. He stops in front of Luc, who motions him back into the bedroom. With a menacing growl, he pads past me, his nails clicking ominously on the hardwood floors.

"Will he hurt Rafe?"

"Not if Raphael doesn't provoke him." He chuckles. "Of course, he's easily provoked. Maybe we could just let him have a go at your cat instead."

"You're a despicable, reprehensible, villainous reprobate."

"I aim to please. Naughty girl, you cheated and looked ahead on your calendar, didn't you? Let's see, you used August fifth, December second, May fourteenth, and my personal favorite, October thirtieth. Don't you just love the way *reprobate* rolls off the tongue? Speaking of tongue rolling, I'd love to roll mine on your hot little body."

"Try this one. You're an asswipe."

"Jolene, don't resort to colloquial vulgarisms. You're smarter than that. Now, are you ready to listen to what I came to say?"

I step back and peek in the bedroom. Drenched in sweat, his teeth clenched, Rafe struggles determinedly against his hellish ropes. Huge blisters have bubbled up and popped, now oozing down his arms.

I glare at Luc. "Talk fast."

He pinches my cheek. "Don't be impertinent, Jolene. I'm the one in control here."

The backs of his fingers graze my jaw before cupping my face. I stare into the blue eyes that used to make me weak-kneed with lust. Lust is the farthest thing I feel for him at this moment. A simmering flame burns in his pupils, but the rims remain blue, not red. I hope this is a good sign.

"I've missed you. More than I thought possible," he murmurs.

I close my eyes to keep from rolling them, knowing he hates that. "What's the matter? Doesn't Mrs. Cabot fix your coffee the way you like it?" Too bad my mouth didn't show the same restraint. I hold my breath and open my eyes. My snippy retort may well be the end of Rafe and me. Will I ever learn to think before speaking?

"Well, there's that, too." He smiles. "It's more than that. I find I miss you as a person. Dare I say it? For a human being, you're pretty damn amazing. You asked me once if you were special, and I gave you a flippant answer. The truth is, yes, you *are* special. Very special."

My brother always told me if something sounds too good to be true, it probably is. I'm not buying it. "How did you get in here?"

He wiggles his fingers. "Magic."

I find it difficult to swallow around the lump of fear stuck in my throat. It takes me a couple of seconds before I can speak. He truly is powerful and holds the fate of those I love in his hands. "What do you want?"

"You, Jolene. I want you."

"You're hurting Rafe because of me? He's your brother. How can you do that?" I clench my fists and tense my muscles — not to strike him, but to steady myself. I may not be dead, but this is a living hell.

"I haven't hurt anybody." Glancing toward the bedroom, his eyes narrow and the red rims of his irises glow before fading back to blue. He winks. "Yet. As for hurting my brother, you of all people should understand that sometimes family bonds don't mean a thing."

I flinch at the truth thrown at me, but lift my chin, refusing to cower. "Why me?"

"It's interesting you should ask 'why me' because this has taken me a bit by surprise as well. This was never part of the plan. I find you fascinating, beautiful, and fun. You intrigue me, and this has become more than the job I was tasked to do. I've developed actual feelings for you, Jolene." His voice sounds uncharacteristically soft.

An agonizing howl of rage has me rushing toward the bedroom, even though there are a hundred questions I want to ask. What plan? Luc grabs my arm. I turn and tug against him to no avail.

"Let me go!" I continue to struggle, determined to get to Rafe.

"If you go in there, you'll be sorry," Luc hisses.

I quit hitting him and still. "I'm sorry. I don't want to hurt you, but I don't love *you*. I love *Rafe*." My tears begin to fall.

He grasps my wet cheeks in his hands, his mouth hovering over mine. "Love is way overrated. What does love have to do with it?"

"What? Love is everything." In this moment my heart breaks just a little for him, which is insane. He's the Devil — why should I care? But I've known him as a man, and even though it was misconstrued, I cared about him. "Luc, have you forgotten what it's like to love?" I ask softly.

For a brief second, a stunned, wounded look crosses his face. Despite everything, I feel sorry for him. Shaking his head, he covers his momentary vulnerability with a sneer.

"Don't be naïve, Friday. Did you love me when you fantasized about me nailing you on your desk in every way imaginable?"

Embarrassment floods my cheeks as my guilt surfaces. "You're right. I used you and objectified you. I'm no better than you are." I sigh, defeated.

"There you go. See? That's why we'll be great together."

I blink and step back. He's right. We're more alike than I want to admit. I used him in a desperate attempt to find love. Some shrink will have a field day with this twist to my pathetic life story.

His smile widens. "You'll find I'm not such a bad guy. Well, that's not true; I'm the ultimate bad boy, so to speak. But we'll have fun, I promise. The world will be yours for the taking. You will be my princess."

I shake my head, looking at him through my tears. "I'm sorry, Luc."

"Sorry for what?" He shifts and looks away, frowning. Fiery red wings unfold behind him, fluttering before disappearing.

"I'm sorry I led you on. It was wrong. I…I'm like a cliché country song. I went looking for love in the wrong place with the wrong guy. I don't love you the way you obviously need to be loved." How sad his life must be. "Who cares about you? Is there no one for you?"

His eyes glow like red-hot coals, and his immense flaming wings quiver and flap without receding this time. "Whatever are you talking about?" he asks in his surly-boss voice. I've touched a nerve.

"I'm saying I understand how you feel. Unloved. Unwanted. And I'm sorry for adding to it, for not seeing you as more than a tool to satisfy my own needs."

"Oh, I'm a tool all right," he mutters, glaring at me with his hands on his hips.

"You like people to think so, but I think you're just protecting your heart."

He laughs. "Heart? I don't have a heart." He points toward the bedroom. "Neither does that do-gooder bastard. We're not *human*, Jolene. You can't ascribe human feelings to non-humans."

"Sure you can. Even my mean old cat has feelings. You do, too, or you wouldn't be here."

I frame his face with my hands. "You told me yourself that you've developed feelings for me. I care for you. I do. But I don't love you like *that*. I'm sorry you're alone—"

He shrugs out of my hands, his feathers bristling. The hall feels like a hot wind tunnel.

"I'm not alone. I can have any woman I choose. That includes *you*."

"You aren't the Great Deceiver. You're the one deceived if you think this is about sex. Don't lie to yourself. Those relationships have no meaning. You're lonely. You think you're the one with power. We both know you can take my body and mess with my mind. But you'll never have my heart or my soul. It may not hold much sway, considering my recent actions, but I'll pray for you, Luc."

"Oh shit, don't go there." Luc frowns. "I don't need your prayers." He looks off in the distance and appears to be struggling with his emotions. "No one prays for me," he adds softly as his wings retract.

"I will."

Flames slither around his feet, and my stomach sinks. I'm too late. We're all going to burn to death. I have to get Rafe out of here. I turn and open the bedroom door, only to have it slam in my face. I fumble with the hot handle, pounding on the door. "Rafe, I'm coming."

Luc grabs me and pain sears my shoulders. I cry out as he spins me around, holding me against the door. His red-rimmed eyes smolder, and heat radiates from his body. Sweat drips down my face, and my lips feel parched, my tongue dry. It's like standing too close to a bonfire.

"Is he truly worth dying for? If you go in that bedroom, you will die. Do you understand?"

I shove him out of my way. "Yes. Yes," I sob. "If I don't go in there, Rafe will die. If he dies, my heart will, too. Rafe! I need you! Dear God, please help me..."

"Well, shit. Now you've done it. You *really* didn't need to go there." Luc sighs. His blazing wings unfurl behind him like a raging forest fire. "Stand back; you're about to see one pissed-off angel barge through that door."

The door behind me swings open, and the cool air on my back feels like a day in early spring. Glancing over my shoulder I see Rafe's wings expand and retract, the flaming shackles gone. "You can't win, Luc. Let her go. She's made her decision."

The acrid smell of burned flesh makes my stomach turn. Charred skin hangs from Rafe's wrists like a blackened spider web. I can't begin to imagine the excruciating pain he must be enduring. "You have to go to the hospital," I whisper.

"I'm fine. I don't even feel it."

"What he isn't telling you is that once he returns *home*, he'll be good as new. This human body of his isn't real. But don't worry, sweet Jolene, you won't remember any of this."

"Trust me, Jo, just trust me." Rafe keeps his eyes on Luc.

"Sure, trust him. My *brother's* always told you the truth, hasn't he? Listen to me. I can offer you so much more. I don't mind this miserable chaos known as Earth. I'm the fuckin' Prince of Pandemonium, and the world is my playground. Plus, I'm my own boss; I can do what I like. Stay with me. I'll take you places you've only dreamed of and do things to you you've only fantasized about. I'll give you anything and everything. I'll lavish attention on you like never before."

He waves his hand in front of my face and images of me in exotic places, wearing beautiful clothes and having incredible sex flash through my mind like a movie on fast-forward. This must be how Eve felt in the Garden of Eden. Luc's offer is tempting. It's seduction, pure and remarkably simple — he framed the offer using my weakness and desires. I don't consider myself overly religious, but I know how the story ends.

"No. You're lying. You can't give me everything."

"Oh, but I can — money, cars, beautiful homes, hot sex, power. I can also take care of those you love, like your brother and that damn cat. You name it, and it's yours."

"You can't give me what matters most. I know Rafe can't stay here with me, but my few hours loving him are better than a lifetime of shallow pursuits with you."

"So you would choose death over a life of privilege?"

"Y-Yes." My knees wobble. I'm truly not as brave as I'm pretending to be. The thought of pain and ultimately death terrifies me.

"What part of *trust me* don't you understand?" Rafe barks hoarsely, his arm wrapping around me.

"Interesting." Luc's long finger taps his lips as he thinks. "One last question: what if I kill him instead?" Luc snaps his fingers, and fire explodes, scorching the tips of my hair and searing what's left of the skin on Rafe's arm.

I scream and turn into Rafe's chest. The smell of burned hair, skin, and feathers permeates the air.

"Shh, shh, shh...You're okay, honey. Firefly's just showing off." Rafe yanks me back into the bedroom, and that horrid beast snarls and snaps at us. Rafe grabs him by the scruff of the neck and shoves him out, slamming the door shut.

I'm shaking so hard my teeth chatter. "He's going to kill us, isn't he?"

"I'll make sure you're safe."

"Can't you twitch your nose or blink and make us disappear?"

He chuckles. "My name isn't Samantha or Jeannie."

I wrap my arms around his waist and press my lips to his scorched, bare chest. It's only then do I realize he's still naked.

"How did you get loose?"

"You did it. You asked God for help, and when you truly need me, I'm summoned."

"I'll pray daily and need you every minute if it means I can keep you here with me."

"I don't think it works exactly that way." Sadness looms in his eyes and his wings dip lower. Swaying, he steadies himself by leaning against the wall.

"I've got to get you to the hospital. Can angels even be treated at a hospital?" I pull myself together and step away. "Can't you call for backup or something? Don't they have some sort of twenty-four-hour hotline for emergencies?"

"What, like a bat phone?" He chuckles and whispers with a dead-pan face, "I'm pretty sure it's called prayer. I'll be fine once I get home."

I pull one of his scorched feathers, not finding his attempt at humor funny. I'm worried. Underneath his charred skin, he's gone gray, and his breathing sounds strangled. His wings droop, bare-ly ruffling.

"Can he kill you? Tell me the truth," I demand.

Rafe shrugs and hangs his head. "Truthfully, I don't know. If it comes to that, I suppose so."

"Can you kill him?"

"No. He is, quite literally, a necessary evil."

"God helped me…why won't He help *you?*"

He lets out a despondent sigh and his wings flutter just a bit. "I haven't asked."

"*You haven't asked?*" I screech.

"No, because if I do, my time here will be done. I didn't want to leave you."

Luc pounds on the door. "Your time is almost up!"

Through my tears, I can barely make out his face, and my voice catches. "P-Please, I can't let you die. Ask! I'll be miserable when you leave, but I'll survive. You're more important than my happiness. There has to be something I can do," I whisper.

"You have five seconds to come out or I'm burning this place to the ground." Luc's voice sounds calm and lethal through the door. The room feels like a sauna on overdrive. "One."

"And you are more important than mine. *I love you, Jolene.* Do not fall for his lies, and absolutely do not go off with him. I don't want you touched by that angel."

I give him a weepy smile. "Only you would make a lousy reference to an old TV show at a time like this." I finger-comb the hair off his forehead. "I love you."

"Two," Luc shouts.

Rafe sways and catches himself. "I love you, too. Always and forever." His wings sag as if their weight is too heavy to hold.

"Three."

CHAPTER EIGHTEEN

This whole business with Luc has drained me, and I'm operating on reserve energy. The painful fire restraints and worrying about Jolene has left me almost as weak as a human. I just pray I've convinced her not to go all Wonder Woman on me.

Luc's always gone in his own direction, but this is not his normal MO, and I have to rethink my position. Maybe it's because Jo told him *no*. Not many have refused his seductive offers over the years. He's a pretty persuasive, self-serving bastard. Maybe she's right and it's time I put my angel pride aside and ask for help. Leaving her is better than seeing her suffer or fall into that bastard's hands.

"Four," Luc intones behind the door.

I try to fold my wings, but I'm done, completely devoid of energy. Jo runs her fingers through my feathers in a soothing motion. Now I know why Atticus purrs having his back scratched.

Jo opens the door, and we find Luc standing with his arms crossed. His fiery wings flap hard enough to blow our hair straight back, and his laser red eyes shift between us.

"About damn time," he snarls.

Jo shakes violently, and I fear she's going into shock. Taking her hand in mine, I give it a reassuring squeeze.

"Since when do you get off on tormenting innocent girls, *Lucy?*"

"Never underestimate me. I've never claimed to be nice." He looks at Jo, and for a brief second his face softens. Is this a chink in his armor? *Does he actually care about her?*

"Jo, go outside. I need to talk to Luc."

She shakes her head. "No, we're in this together."

"Run along like a good little girl. Rafe and I need to have a come-to-Number-One-Son meeting."

Jo gasps. "You're going to go to hell…"

"Good. Warm weather, beautiful faces, it's like being in Beverly Hills. You'd be surprised how many people you know there."

A loud yowl draws her attention, and she runs down the stairs, screeching, "Leave my cat alone, you mangy old dog!"

The ruckus is loud with Jo screaming, the dog howling, and Atticus giving a piercing feline invective as they all race outside. With a quick wrist motion, I slam and lock the front door, then turn to confront my brother.

"Thank you for the distraction, and don't let that beast hurt her cat."

"My pleasure. Seriously? Do you know how annoying that cat is? And folks say I'm possessed…" Luc huffs.

I glare at him, and he shrugs.

"*O-kay*, but I'll let you explain to Black Shuck why he can't eat that disgusting animal."

Exhausted, I sink to the side of the bed. "So what's up with you and Jo? She isn't your type."

Luc's wings bristle. "Why is she not my type? Everyone thinks they *know* me. She's different than most humans."

My wings rise behind me and beat once in warning. "Leave her alone. I mean it."

"Damn. You've got it bad for her, don't you? Is she that good in the sack?"

Using everything I have left in me, I spring from the bed and sling the smug idiot across the room. He hits the wall with a thud, the impact causing a small explosion. Flames lick the curtains and zip across the room, encircling me as if a line of gasoline had been poured. Jo's anguished scream from outside twists my gut. The thought of her trying to come back into a burning building terrifies me, but I'm unable to lift a wing. I've never felt so helpless and frustrated.

"Help me—"

Luc shakes his head. "Don't bother. He knows. He always does, doesn't He? Just accept your fate."

"I don't care what happens to *me*. Save *her*. Please," I gasp as the flames inch higher. Joan once told me being burned at the stake was no Sunday BBQ. She was right.

Luc gives me a small smile. "You haven't figured it out yet, have you? She was never my main concern. You were."

"What?" I must have misheard him. I push my pain to the side, attempting to focus. "What are you talking about?"

"You were the one Boss Man targeted. Your complacency worried Him; He decided to use me to get you fired up about something. You love her, right?"

"Yes."

"Enough to die for her?"

I nod, my mind reeling. "Yes. Don't hurt her."

"Then my job here is done, and I will concede defeat." He gives me a sad smile. "She *is* a special girl. Take care of her."

"So now what?"

"Now you face baptism by fire." He disappears into the flames, and I hear him placing a call and reporting a fire.

But he doesn't offer to save me. He's left me in this fiery hell alone. I don't have a clue what my fate is, or if the call he placed was to The Boss or the fire department. I realize it will take a damn miracle either way, and I fall to my knees, praying for Jolene's safety.

Jolene pounds on the front door. "Luc! Let me in!"

I fling it open, and she attempts to dart around me. Grabbing her by the arm, I drag her out of harm's way. She wrestles against me, cursing with the most ridiculous Southern threats I've ever heard.

"Dog gone it, let go of me! You're lower than a snake belly. If you don't move, I'm gonna whoop you like a rented mule and jerk a knot in your tail."

I roll my eyes. I get so tired of the cliché images of me with a pitchfork and tail. Tugging her by the wrist, I keep moving her away from the burning house.

"Stop!" I roar. Her eyes round into dark disks, and she stops fighting me, at least for the moment. "Your insults are creative but classless. Haven't you learned anything from that damn Word-A-Day calendar? I think the first thing *I'll* purchase for you is a thesaurus. Now, try this instead: Remove yourself, you slubberdegullion! You excerebrose, pygalgious buffoon."

The slap she levels across my face stings, but it makes me grin. This is why I adore her. She's feisty and spirited. If I could just eliminate that annoying core of goodness and draw her to the dark side, she'd be magnificent perfection.

Instead, she continues to struggle against me, but of course, it's impossible for her to break free. She doesn't understand that my feelings for her are genuine. I won't let her get hurt. Hauling her into the yard, I find it nothing short of chaos and confusion. Jolene claws and screams with outrage while Black Shuck barks at the treed Atticus, who hisses his displeasure. To be frank, I'm in my element, enjoying the show. Another explosion rocks the house, and it becomes a raging inferno.

Jolene falls to her knees, covering her face with her hands and sobbing. "Please, God, please," she repeats over and over.

I roll my eyes. Every. Damn. Time. Even atheists in an hour of need call upon Him. "Hmm, no answer. I guess He's on the golf course."

She glares, and I feign indifference with a shrug. I know what has to happen, after all. People think He and I are mortal enemies, but that's not exactly the case. As if on cue, a howl pierces the thick smoke. Jerking Jolene back to her feet, I point to the roof. Raphael appears like a phoenix rising from the ashes. His wings stretch to their full expanse, even as they're going up in flames. It's a glorious, mesmerizing sight.

Not to brag—oh hell, *of course* I'm bragging—Hollywood couldn't have staged the pyrotechnics any better. The Boss owes me for this one.

"Jolene!" Rafe's anguished cry seems to echo in the night.

She jumps to her feet, wide-eyed, and I wince. Rafe and I *are* brothers, despite our differences. Unlike me, he isn't immune to fire, and his pain must be excruciating as his wings burn. A nauseating smell mixes with the smoke from the house. I keep my hand on Jo's neck to prevent her from doing anything foolish, but I needn't worry. She doesn't seem to realize I'm here, holding her. Through her tears, she watches and raises her hands toward Raphael as if in supplication, repeating her mantra, "Please, God, please."

The house implodes with a resounding crack, and flames burst toward heaven in a magnificent spray. The sky explodes like fireworks as Raphael swan-dives toward the ground as Jo screams and sobs. Watching his descent is like seeing a shooting star streak through the air. He lands before her, a broken, charred angel. The heavens open, and rain extinguishes his flaming wings until all that remains is sizzling steam. Thunder rolls in the distance, signaling that my time here is almost up.

Jo crawls to Raphael. Cradling his head in her lap, she rocks him, oblivious to anything or anyone else. He remains still, and if he's breathing, it's too shallow to be detected. Sirens sound in the distance as the burning house crackles and snaps behind them.

I kneel beside her. "Step back, Jolene."

"Leave him alone!" With a feral snarl, she shoves me away, a warrior goddess protecting her mate. She pushes his hair from his face, her tears mixing with the rain to wash some of the soot away. Even with her drenched hair and bedraggled state, there's determination in her eyes. Her indomitable spirit makes me want her that much more — forget the job, forget what I promised Raphael about backing off if I lost. I hate losing.

But one look at her face and I know better. She was never mine. I was a temptation, but she resisted. It's time for me to gracefully concede defeat and move on. Some may say I have dominion on this Earth, but I am merely a counterbalance. And in this situation, good will triumph. Much as I hate to do it, I will bow to His wishes, for her sake.

"Jolene, this has to be done. Trust me."

"Trust *you?*" she shrieks, shoving me away with her fist, one arm still cradling Raphael. "You've killed him!" She tucks her face into his neck, sobbing as if her heart is breaking. Tenderly she kisses his lips. "I love you. Please don't leave me," she begs.

I'm no stranger to war and its aftermath. I've experienced battle wounds, exhaustion, and mental anguish many times during my long existence. But nothing has prepared me for this feeling of being lost and without purpose. I don't know what's happening, and not being in control is beyond frightening. Only Jo's muffled sobs and repeated *I love yous* keep me from giving in to the darkness. Unable to open my eyes, I feel as if I'm buried in mud. Jo needs me, but I'm unable to move. Admitting defeat, I cry out for the One who can help me save her. Her safety matters more than my pride or even my love. I put my selfishness aside. Once I ask Him for help, I know I won't see her again, but she's all that matters.

The pain disappears, and I rush to help her. Instead of soaring, I find myself running down a darkened hallway toward a strand of colorful Christmas lights. Even though I'm not flying, I feel ethereal as I knock on the door.

"Come in, Raphael."

I slip inside and shield my eyes against the blinding light. "Where am I?" Divine love fills the room, and hope replaces my fear. But my joy is tinged by grief.

I miss Jo.

"Close your eyes; you'll burn your retinas. You're in My office." Taking my hand, The Boss leads me to a chair.

I'm confused. I've never taken a dark hallway to get to His office before. Has He moved while I've been on assignment? "Why can't I see You?"

"You're in transition."

I shake my head, feeling muddled and off-kilter. "Transition? I don't understand." I crack open my eyes and squint, but the light hurts like hell.

"You will soon. Don't worry. Keep your eyes closed, son. And watch the language."

"Sorry, Sir." I shrug to stretch my wings, and it's a good thing I'm already sitting. They hang limp and useless, stinking of smoke and burned feathers. I reach behind me, and my back feels like that bubble packing stuff Jo likes to pop. Charred feathers come out by the handful. Desperate, I struggle to recall what happened. She was attacked, I decked her old man, and we went back to her house...

Heat floods my face, and I swallow nervously, shifting in my chair.

He chuckles. "Don't worry, you're not in trouble. Here, put these on." He places sunglasses over my eyes.

"I know, but—" I bite my tongue. It isn't my place to point out that other angels haven't lost their wings over human relations—most recently Remiel. "How long before my wings heal, Sir?" It's still painful to look at Him, even with the sunglasses. I blink and keep my eyes squinted, just peeking every now and then to keep my bearings.

He sits with a loud *oomph* on the edge of His desk. "Tell Me something. If you could have one thing in this world, what would it be?"

"Jo's happiness," I answer without hesitation.

"And what would you be willing to give up for it?"

"Anything and everything." *Wait, was that a trick question? Maybe I should have said something about serving Him? Crap. Shoot, I didn't mean to say "crap."*

"No, it isn't a trick question. Come with Me." I follow and find myself hovering in a tree overlooking a burning building. Jo's house is almost unrecognizable, engulfed in flames. Beside me Atticus hisses, and I scratch him behind the ears. Luc's demonic beast barks below us, his fangs snapping as he jumps, trying to reach the cat. It's then I see Luc kneeling beside Jolene, who is shaking her head and rocking, holding something.

"Jo needs me." I move to leap to her, prepared to send Luc back to hell. But The Boss stops me. "Anything?" He asks, softly.

"I have to go to her; she needs me. Please, Sir. I love her. Jolene is the kindest, most giving person I've ever known. She's everything right about Your humans. You know Luc isn't good for her. He's too self-serving. I know I've messed this job up, and I'm sorry. But please, don't let her get caught in Luc's snare.

"She's my best friend, the person who can make me laugh one minute and exasperate me the next. Sometimes I could throttle her, but honestly—and no disrespect meant—when I'm with her, I feel alive. Being with her is heaven on Earth. I know she isn't perfect. She has lousy fashion sense, is clumsy as all get out, and never did learn to throw a ball with any sense of aim. But I love her for all of those reasons. She deserves someone who sees her and appreciates her for who she is."

"Yes, she does." Warmth infuses my body as His hand glides down my back, hovering over my burned wings. "I will see you both soon enough."

"So I'm free to go?"

"For now." I hear the smile in His voice. "See you in a blink of an eye. And raise your children with love."

Children? This means... I don't understand exactly what's going to happen, but I'm not arguing. I grin. "Yes, Sir."

My spirit returns to the battered body in Jo's arms. Fire seems to sizzle and zip painfully through every nerve ending in my body, but a strange peace settles in my heart.

"Jo," I whisper hoarsely. My lips crack with the effort, and my parched throat begs for relief. I've never experienced such thirst or pain. Even blinking hurts.

"Rafe," she cries, peering at my face, her eyes glittering. "Call an ambulance," she screams at Luc.

"I did."

"Hang on. You're going to be fine." She kisses my face over and over.

"Better than fine — I'm here to stay," I murmur as darkness once again envelops my world.

"Do something! He's dying," Jo cries.

I search her soot-stained face for an answer. I find it, but it isn't the one I'd hoped for. Her love for Raphael is true and unshakeable. Once again, to my dissatisfaction, He was right. She will never be mine. I tell myself I'm only doing this for Jolene. But in truth, it's for my brother, too. She'll keep him on his toes. I kind of look forward to seeing what she'll put him through. What can I say? I'm easily amused.

Grabbing her by the arms, I pull her away from Raphael's lifeless form. "There are many kinds of death. This is but one. Now move. I'm running out of time." I whistle, and Black Shuck leaps forward. He holds her at bay with his bared fangs. "Raphael, can you hear me?"

The rain turns to sleet, bathing him with healing moisture, but he isn't responding. I have to wonder if shock and hypothermia are taking a toll on his changing body. I check his wrist and find a weak pulse. His chest barely moves with his shallow breathing. Is he giving up?

"Dammit, Raphael, Jolene needs you," I shout, shaking his shoulder. A soft groan escapes, and his eyelids flicker open, revealing eyes glazed with pain. I'm about to inflict more, and I swallow my hesitation.

"I'm sorry. Your Boss says this has to be done so you can live fully, my friend. You'll thank me someday—and maybe even forgive me." Taking a deep breath, I roll him over. He moans and swats weakly at me. I focus my gaze and concentrate, gritting my teeth. From my fingertips, an arc of laser light neatly and precisely slices off what remains of his charred wings. His tortured scream makes my wings bristle, and his body convulses as if struck by lightning.

Ignoring Black Shuck's snarling, Jo screams and beats my animal with her fists. He blocks her every move, barking and snapping, but he refrains from hurting her.

This entire experience has drained me, and I'm sick of the cold and the rain. I need a damn vacation, some place warm with women and alcohol. I whistle, and Black Shuck backs away. Jolene darts toward Raphael without a backward glance, and I know I've done the right thing. There's just one last task to be completed. I grab her, turn her in my arms, and cup her face, raising it to mine.

"He'll be fine, Jolene."

"Let me go! I hate you!" she sneers, using her nails to pry my hands from her face.

"As you should. You, Jolene, are a smart, compassionate, loving woman. You almost restore my faith in humanity. I'll miss you." I kiss her forehead, and instantly she stills as I wipe her memory of all angelic knowledge. She will only remember me as her asshole boss.

I let go, and she collapses next to the man she loves, stroking his cheek, kissing his sooty, wet face. It's as if she doesn't see me. Maybe she doesn't.

The sirens scream closer. It's time to make my exit. I look at her one last time, with both regret and admiration. She would've made one helluva consort.

"Rafe," I whimper, falling to my knees beside him and carefully stroking his damp hair. I'm afraid to move him, terrified of causing more harm. An ambulance and fire truck scream down the driveway, their lights circling us. I offer silent thanks. "Help is here; you're going to be fine."

His eyes flutter open, looking very white against his soot-covered face. I kiss the top of his head and continue to stroke his singed hair, needing the reassurance of contact.

"C-Cold." His teeth chatter and body convulses.

"I know. I'm sorry. Just a few more minutes. The ambulance is here. Are you in much pain?"

"Crispy c-critter feels no p-pain," he stutters through chattering teeth. He attempts a smile, and my heart lurches in response. I can't imagine my life without him.

"Hang in there; don't you dare leave me," I whisper. "I love you too much, dammit."

He closes his eyes and murmurs, "B-Back at ya." His body shakes uncontrollably. Despite his charred, dangling flesh, he takes my hand and won't let go.

My brother's squad car flies toward us, gravel scattering in its wake.

"Help's here; you're going to be fine. Think about warm places," I urge.

"No f-fires. Water, lots of water. Even snow, good."

"Sounds perfect to me." I hold his hand next to my cheek, my eyes locked on his, willing him to live.

Two firm hands attempt to pull me away. I'm terrified to let go, as if somehow my touch can will him to hang on. I struggle to stay, but Johnny Way intervenes.

"Let them do their job, Jo," he urges in a firm, quiet voice, pulling me to my feet.

I collapse in his arms. My teeth chatter so hard it sounds like marbles clacking together. He pulls off his coat, enveloping me in its warmth. It smells of his aftershave, and I inhale deeply, trying to rid my nose of the smell of burning wood, flesh, and feathers. *Feathers?*

Behind us, the paramedics talk medical gibberish as they work diligently with Rafe. In a few minutes they load him into the ambulance, and an EMT approaches me.

"Okay, ma'am. Time to check you out."

I shake my head and move toward the ambulance. "I'm fine. I was outside when the house caught fire. I need to be with Rafe."

"Jo, let the man do his job. You won't be any good to him if you're hurt and not treated." My brother tugs me to a standstill.

I allow the paramedic to check me, and I'm grateful for the blanket he wraps around me. "Is he going to be okay?" I sniffle, my eyes watering.

"He's awake, and we're going to do everything we can to help him." He looks at my brother. "It wouldn't hurt for her to be checked out at the hospital. Some sparks singed her hair, and she's been in this cold weather."

"I'm fine. He needs me." They start to shut the doors to the ambulance, and I break free from Johnny Way and rush toward it, screaming, "Rafe!"

Johnny Way catches my hand, and the doors slam shut. "Stop. Let them get him to the hospital. I'll take you somewhere to get cleaned up, and we'll go straight there."

"No, take me now," I demand, determined to be with Rafe. I'll drive myself if necessary.

Then it dawns on me that I'm not going anywhere; my purse is in the burning house. I'm dependent on my brother. Atticus snakes around my feet, meowing and looking pissed off. It's somehow comforting — at least one thing remains normal. I pick him up and snuggle him. To my surprise, he doesn't protest and purrs into my neck. It's as if he knows how close we came to dying. There's no doubt the house is a total loss, and the fire department still works to contain the fire.

Johnny Way guides me by the elbow to his car. I hug my cat so tightly he squirms before jumping out of my arms. "Atticus!"

"He's a cat; he'll be fine," my brother grumbles, fastening his seatbelt. "Besides, that damn animal probably still has all nine lives. He's too mean to die. Buckle up." Johnny Way's voice cracks, and his eyes appear suspiciously moist. "Smoke," he mutters.

I nod, but before I can get my seatbelt fastened, he reaches over and hugs me. "Don't you ever do that to me again. My heart damn near stopped when I got the call about the fire…" He kisses the top of head and pulls back, wrinkling his nose. "Shit, you stink like one of Robert Earl's ashtrays."

I smile. This might be the most demonstrative he's been since taking me away from Robert Earl and Crimson. "I love you, too. I'm sorry about the house."

He starts the car and looks at me from the corner of his eye as he makes his way past the fire trucks and nosy neighbors. I continue to shiver, and he cranks up the heat. "It's just a house. You're okay; that's all that matters. What was Rafe Goodman doing there?"

"Uh, well…" I squirm in my seat. "I'm twenty-five. Do we really have to go there? And how do you know his full name?"

He chuckles. "I reckon the interrogation can wait a minute. I'm a cop, you used his phone to call me, remember?"

"How's Robert Earl?" I ask, redirecting the conversation.

"Pretty miserable. I'm happy to report he's puking his guts up in withdrawals. He won't be bothering you again."

"How do you know he bothered me?"

He takes my hand and squeezes it. *Of course he knows.* "I can take you by Pastor Brown's for a shower, and I think his daughter is about your size. Or we can go straight to the hospital."

"Hospital." I swallow the lump of fear lodged in my throat. "And hurry, please."

"So Rafe Goodman, huh? Same guy from years ago?"

I roll my eyes. "Stop."

"Your minute's up; the interrogation can now continue." He raises an eyebrow and chuckles.

I grin. No way I can stay annoyed at the man who's always been there for me. "Okay, okay. Ask away, even though it's the twenty-first century." My heart fills with love for this good man. "And not to sound sappy, but you and Lynn were better parents than Robert Earl or Crimson ever dreamed of being."

"Now you stop. We're sounding like one of those terrible corny sitcoms you love." He gives my hand one last squeeze before flicking on his siren and speeding after the ambulance.

CHAPTER NINETEEN

Michele adjusts Rafe's IV as he sleeps. His snoring makes both of us giggle. She's been his day-shift nurse throughout his month-long hospitalization, and she's my favorite. All of the hospital equipment still makes me nervous.

The doctors say Rafe's recovery has been "miraculous." He will forever have scars on his back and wrists, but the fact that he didn't break anything when he fell or have any third-degree burns is amazing. No one can explain it. He's still on mega amounts of pain medication, which make him act goofy at times.

"His graft looks great—nice and pink," Michele whispers. "Obviously, his therapy this morning really wiped him out, but he's getting stronger every day."

Rafe stirs and mumbles, "Jo?"

Michele motions me to his bedside, and I hop out of the chair. Timidly lifting the corner of the sheet, I stroke his foot—an area that hasn't had to be bandaged.

"Stop," he croaks. "Tickles. Ice, please."

It's so good to hear his voice, even if he does still sound a little like an asthmatic old man. He moves himself up in bed, wincing.

"Don't be stoic. If you're in pain, punch this button. You won't overdose, I promise." The nurse hands him the button to his pain pump.

"I'm a man." He lets out a slow breath and pushes the button.

Michele chuckles and shakes her head. "Yeah, yeah. So you keep telling all of us. Trust me, even real men feel pain." Handing me a cup of ice and spoon she adds, "Here's his ice. Call if you need me." The door closes behind her.

I dig out an ice chip and promptly drop it near his ear. "Sorry," I whisper, wiping it off with an unsteady hand. I try again and drop it on the pillow. "I suck at being a nurse."

"Yes, you do." His eyes appear heavy-lidded from the narcotics. "But I can think of something you could suck, and I wouldn't mind a bit."

This time I drop the entire spoon of ice. "I can't believe you just said that. I think you're permanently warped on pain medication." I clean up the ice, unable to look him in the eye. I pray we aren't on camera or intercom or something. Picking up the spoon, I attempt once again to feed him an ice chip.

"Quit waterboarding me. Use your fingers."

I plop an ice chip into his mouth. He latches onto my fingers for a second before giving me a lopsided grin and a wink.

"Mmmm, good."

On impulse, I kiss his forehead and murmur, "I know you're playing the sick card. You're definitely feeling better, and you're a wicked man. Are you in much pain today?"

"I'm a man," he repeats. His drug-glazed eyes drift closed for a second before opening again. "Have I slept long? What time do you go to work?"

"You slept about an hour. And I'm off today. Rest." I carefully move the chair and sit next to him. He reaches for my hand and gives it a squeeze before he drifts back to sleep. Although my arm is positioned at a weird angle, I refuse to move. I need this contact as surely as I need water to drink and air to breathe. I came much too close to losing him.

He murmurs something, and I lean forward, straining to hear him.

"Together," he says. "Always and forever."

I kiss the exposed fingertips on his bandaged hand and whisper, "Always and forever."

I open my eyes and try to focus. Thanks to the pain medication, it feels like soaring out of control. As I struggle to sit up, all kinds of whistles and alarms sound. Am I ever going to get out of this hospital of torture? Things are better; at least they aren't inflicting the hydrotherapy on me anymore. The physical therapy is bad enough. But I want to go home, with Jo. My IV beeps incessantly.

"Don't move." Jo jumps up with a panicked look and gently eases me back. Purple circles of exhaustion ring her eyes, and her hair looks a little like one of Atticus's hairballs. She's gorgeous.

"Hey, beautiful."

She smiles, and my outlook on life improves. "Hey, handsome."

The door opens, and a different nurse checks my IV for the umpteenth time today. I have no idea what day it is, or what time it is. A hospital is no place to get rest, and time seems to stand still.

"How are we feeling?" she asks.

"Like death warmed over. I want to get up."

"Let's wait a bit; you're still tired from therapy, and your antibiotic will be done infusing shortly. How about we just dangle on the side of the bed?" The nurse looks at the computer, clicking different screens.

I hate when medical staff talks to me like that. What's this *we* stuff? She isn't going to sit on the bed with me. If anyone sits on the bed with me, I want it to be Jo. "How about *I* get up? *I* need to use the bathroom. I'm sick of this bed. Where's Michele?" I sound like a whining two-year-old.

"She's off today. Well, I suppose I can trust you as far as the bathroom, just be careful and don't get tangled in the IV." She smiles that evil nurse smile. "Or I can get you a bedpan."

Jo's eyebrows shoot up as she bites her lip. I'll take Luc's fire shackles any day over *this*.

The nurse smiles at Jo as she leaves. "When they get cranky, it's a good sign."

"I'm not cranky."

The grin on Jo's face spreads, and she giggles. "You're not?"

"Nope. I'm downright *pissed*. Get me the fuck out of here."

"Rafe," she gasps. "You never talk like that. I'll help you."

"I'm not two, and I'm sick of having to ask for permission to go to the bathroom." I scratch my full beard. I'm pretty sure I can smell myself, and it isn't pleasant. "I want a real shower and something to drink."

"Just relax. You're still a little incapacitated."

I raise one eyebrow, and she shrugs.

"It's my word for today."

"I think *incarcerated* works better in this situation."

My legs feel like rubber when I stand, clutching the gown closed. Who invented these things? Taking a deep breath, I eye the door to the bathroom. I hate to admit it, but it looks five miles away. That damn therapy wipes me out. However, being a man—human or angel—I refuse to admit that Jo and the nurse were right.

I make it in there just fine and even manage to sponge off and brush my teeth, but Jo helps me back in bed when I return. I never realized just how frail the human body is.

"There. Feel better?" she asks, tucking me in like a child.

"The least you could do is give me a kiss."

She wrinkles her cute little nose. "I hate the full beard."

"Pretend I'm Santa. I wish you could sit on my lap and tell me what a naughty girl you've been."

She pecks me on the lips. "You're so silly."

I watch her straighten the room, throwing stuff away and generally clucking like a mother hen. I hate feeling useless. I should be taking care of her. This entire transition has been humbling. I don't see much of Jo because of her work schedule and my therapy. To my dismay, I tend to sleep most of the time when she's here. And I haven't asked what she recalls about that fateful night, fearing she only remembers the bad part.

"Hey, Jo, what happened before the fire? And how did I get here?" My wings are gone, and my hearing and vision aren't what they used to be, but my memory is perfect and intact. I just want to know how much Luc let her retain.

She plumps my pillow and pours me a glass of water. I don't stop her because I crave her touch, and the comforting scent of summer roses covers the antiseptic hospital smells.

"What are you saying? Are you okay?" Her brow creases, and she searches my face as she pushes a strand of my hair off my forehead. Nostalgically, I remember how good it felt when she ruffled my feathers.

I kiss her wrist. "Things are just hazy; fill me in."

She twists her hands together. "Let's see, you showed up at work and knocked Robert Earl out when he attacked me. You took me to my house…" She frowns. "I guess we had a pillow fight or something; there were feathers in my hair." She rocks back and forth on her feet. "I, uh, well, we, er—Johnny Way's gonna want to have a talk with you. He's so overprotective." She blushes and looks away.

"What? We went down that road?"

She looks stricken, and her lower lip pushes into a pout. "You don't remember?"

"Gotcha. Of course I remember. That was the best night of my life." I pull her close. "Come here and kiss me, woman. I'm your man."

"Look, Tarzan, I'm not Jane." She gives me a quick peck on the lips. "The best night? Even though you ended up hurt?"

I gaze at the girl who means more to me than life itself. "The best. But I am sorry about your house."

"It's okay. I've gone back to my roots."

"What do you mean?"

"We're living in a single-wide trailer. Don't worry, Johnny Way's going to rebuild. He's kind of excited; he wants a bigger den for an even bigger TV. Thankfully, his insurance covered the lightning strike."

"Still, it was your home." Guilt eats at me. I'm going to make it up to her and her brother somehow.

"My home is with you. You've always been my home and my sanctuary. That horrible night taught me to appreciate what matters. I came much too close to losing you. I keep having these weird dreams about heaven and hell. The doctor says it isn't uncommon and that both of us might have a little PTSD."

"I know what heaven is."

"You sound awfully sure of yourself—wait, did you have one of those out-of-body experiences? Did you see the white light?" She leans forward, her eyes lit with excitement.

I brush her soft cheek with the back of my fingers. "Heaven is sharing mint chocolate chip ice cream right out of the carton and not caring you only have one clean spoon. It's eating popcorn and watching cheesy sitcoms with your best friend. It's staring at the stars and sharing your secret dreams and fears. It's the ability to say or do terribly inappropriate things because you won't be judged for them. It's burying yourself deep in the woman you love and gazing into her eyes, knowing she's your soulmate always and forever."

Her mouth drops open. It's one of the few times I've seen her speechless.

"You see, Jo, this thing between us? It's greater than the human mind can comprehend, and yet only as humans can we experience it in its fullest." Framing her beautiful face in my bandaged hands, I kiss her. "You are my world, my heaven, my stars, and my sun. You're mine. Always and forever."

"Oh my," she whispers. "You sure you're talking about me?"

"Positive. I will thank God every day for you."

She giggles. "Those drugs must be some good stuff."

"It's not the drugs," I insist. "I love you. You're a woman, and I'm a man. I still can't believe it."

Cocking her head to the side, she grins. "Okay, Tarzan. I love you, too."

I pray I haven't revealed too much, and I'm thankful she remembers me at all. Luc has the ability to wipe her memory completely clean. "The night of the fire, was it my imagination, or was Lunatic DeVillain there?"

"He was there, although I'm not really sure why. The fire happened before I could find out. I guess he came to talk me into going back to work, which I'm not doing. With all the commotion, my memory is kind of vague."

At least she remembers the important stuff. "Let's quit talking and do something more pleasant." I nibble her neck, and her head falls back as she moans, digging her nails into my biceps.

The door to the room opens and her brother strides in, eyes narrowed as if he's just interrupted an armed robbery.

Jo peers at him from almost upside down. Flustered, she snaps up, smacking the heck out of both our heads. "Sorry." She rubs hers and kisses my forehead. "Don't mind my brother. He thinks he's my father."

"It's okay. I plan to make an honest woman out of you."

She sniffs her annoyance. "For heaven's sake, you're as bad as he is. This is the twenty-first century. I'm not a little girl; I'm a grown woman capable of making up my own mind."

"I'm an old-fashioned kind of guy."

"Goodman." Johnny Way holds out his hand. He's visited a few times with Jo.

I do my best not to wince at the tight grip. Once again, he's making his point, and I'm too weak to do much about it. Never in all my eons of existence has anyone thought I was a pussy, but damn if I'm not trembling now. Out of necessity, I ease back on my side. I have no choice. It's either succumbing to the frailty of my human body or passing out cold. This is one aspect of being human I don't like.

"Rafe, have you updated your father on your progress?" Jo asks.

I gaze with adoration and love at this incredibly compassionate woman. How lucky am I to have her in my life? "Yes, I've been in touch."

She sniffs her disapproval. "You'd think he could've put his business aside to visit his sick son. You could have died."

"He, uh, wanted to come. I told him not to. I'm fine. Besides, you're my family now, and you're here. How's Atticus?"

"Annoying as hell," Johnny Way answers for her. He crosses his arms. "Not that Jo would know. She's rarely home, either working or staying here since you've been in the hospital."

Her love and concern moves me. "Thank you." I kiss her hand. "Now that I'm human…"

A shared look between Jo and her brother gives me pause. I've got to quit saying stuff like that.

"How many times has he hit that happy button?" Deputy Watchdog asks. I force myself to maintain eye contact with him and not cave under his scrutiny.

Jo jumps up and pulls him toward the door. "Would you stop? He hasn't done anything wrong. Quit acting like you're going to throw him in jail."

He backs out, doing the I-have-my-eyes-on-you motion. I respond with a one-fingered salute, and Jo's mouth pops open. I kind of like throwing her off balance.

She follows him out the door, but after a few minutes she scurries back to my side. Her brows pull together as she tucks the cover around me. "Look, I know my brother's being a jerk, but for Pete's sake, don't aggravate him. You've never flipped anyone off in your life. Are you in pain? Do you need something?" She reaches to punch the pain button, but I catch her hand.

"No. I'm okay, I just need…" I let my voice trail off and close my eyes. She leans in closer, and her hair tickles my cheek as she strokes my hair. This is just as nice as getting one's feathers ruffled.

"What?" she whispers. "Tell me what you need."

Opening my eyes, I catch her by her neck and pull her face to mine. I kiss her sweet lips and smile at her surprise. "You. I need you. You're all I want." I deepen the kiss until she purrs a soft, satisfied sigh and her lips smile against mine.

"You better stop," she murmurs huskily.

"Why?"

Her eyes crinkle and her smile makes me want to kiss her again. "Because you never know when someone will walk in."

She has a point. "Will you always take care of me?"

"Of course. You've always been here when I needed you." Color rises from her neck to her soft cheeks. "I promise to always look out for you. I'll share my ice cream and not make fun of you for liking *Frasier* reruns, even though *Friends* is way better. I'll pop your popcorn so some of it burns, just the way you like it."

"I don't think I want anything burned for a while."

She leans in close and whispers in my ear, "And I hope you bury yourself inside of me often, making me scream. Just the way I like it."

I harden, and sure enough, the annoying nurse pops back in the room. Jo smirks and sits in the chair, looking a lot like her smug cat.

CHAPTER TWENTY

The car door slams, and I hop off the couch, tripping over Atticus in the process. Darting around the room like a pyromaniac, I light the candles. It sure was easier when I could do this with a snap of my fingers. The wick on one candle flares, and I jump back, a tad unnerved. After being Hansel in Luc's oven, I'm never going to be a fan of fire. But I want to set the mood. It's rare Jo and I get time alone.

For the past nine months, I've lived with Johnny Way and Jolene. Johnny Way's been nice enough to let me bunk up, first on the couch in the trailer and then in the spare bedroom when, two months ago, we all moved into his new house. He's civil, but he has to be more than ready to be rid of me as a houseguest. I've paid a little rent and explained my joblessness by referring to the generous severance package Madge gave me when she sold her company. But now that my therapy is winding down, I seriously have to find real employment.

Anyway, tonight is special in more ways than one. It's the first night I don't have to wear the compression vest since I left the hospital. That contraption has helped my healing process and minimized my scarring, but I'm glad to be rid of it.

Atticus weaves in and out of my feet, hindering my progress, and the front door swings open before I get the last candle lit.

"I picked up a pizza—" Jo stops and takes in the romantic setting. "What's all this?"

The leering grin on my face says it all. "I bribed a guy to call in sick. Johnny Way's having to pull a double." I waggle my eyebrows at her.

Her eyes roam down my body in a leisurely, seductive scan, and her smile widens. "Sneaky. I like it." She hands me the pizza and shrugs out of her jacket.

I toss the fragrant box on the coffee table and grab some bottled water from the fridge. Too late, I realize I should've cooked something special, or better yet, taken her out. She's worked all damn day while I sat around doing nothing, waiting for her to come home. I am officially the world's suckiest boyfriend—human or angel—and I vow to try harder. She deserves the best.

I give her cheek a quick peck and hand her the water, guiding her to sit. She pulls off her shoes and socks and collapses on the couch. I watch her full lips wrap around the bottle as she takes a big swig, and my jeans tighten.

"I needed this. It feels so good to get off my feet." She wiggles her toes, which need their chipped red polish re-done.

I sit beside her and hang my head with guilt. Maybe I should offer to paint her toes, despite her stinky feet. That's what a real boyfriend would do.

She ruffles my hair. "Hey, what's wrong?"

"You shouldn't be working so hard while I lie around doing nothing." I rub my face and jump to my feet, pacing off my agitation.

Jo props her cheek on her hand and gives me her patented indulgent look. "You only have one more week of rehab. That's enough on your plate."

"I hate it. I'm sitting here like a ninety-year-old invalid while you work yourself to death. I feel emasculated," I admit, sinking down beside her and pulling her feet onto my lap. I take them and rub hard, the way I know she likes it. One good thing about being human is a decreased sense of smell.

Her head falls back, and she closes her eyes. "This."

My eyes roam from her mouth to her breasts rising and falling in her red T-shirt. She's always griped about her breasts being too small. She's nuts; they're perfect. "This?"

"*This* is your job." She wiggles her toes.

I'd kiss them, but…even I have my limits. I rub harder, and her moan makes *me* harder.

"I know my feet stink, but please don't stop."

"Are you a mind reader now? Rubbing your feet is not a job. It isn't like I'm going to be doing pedicures for a living. I want to be the man of the house."

"Hush. Don't be silly. You are a man. You're my man," she purrs, pulling at her ponytail holder. The movement stretches her T-shirt tighter as her hair tumbles to the top of her shoulders. I'm not the only one who had to have a haircut to take off some singed ends. She's kept it shorter since then, and I like it. It's all I can do not to pounce and devour her, stinky feet and all. I can tell by her knowing smile she knows exactly what she's doing to me. I once again shift to ease the strain in my jeans.

She moves her feet from my lap and opens the pizza box. "Yum. Thin crust mushroom and black olive. I'm so glad we agree on pizza. Not liking the same pizza could be a relationship breaker."

"That's ridiculous. You can always order half and half."

"No, then the guy knows how much the girl eats. That's not allowed until after you're married." Folding the slice, she takes a big bite, leaving a cheese string between the pizza and her mouth. I nip the string in two and suck on it until our lips meet.

"Are we Lady and the Tramp now?" she asks with a smile against my lips.

"Mm-hmm. And I already know exactly how much you eat." I lick the sauce off her bottom lip. "And I want to eat you…"

"Rafe," she says with a soft gasp. Her smile widens.

Using the distraction to my advantage, I manage to snag a bite from her pizza, and she smacks my arm in protest. "Stop, pizza pig. Get your own slice."

"Hurry and eat. I'm ready for dessert." I nibble on her neck, making her giggle.

"May I shower first?"

"Please do."

She wrinkles her nose. "Are you saying I'm not sexy with my stinky feet, smelly clothes, and unshaved legs?"

"That's a trick question, isn't it?" I nuzzle her neck and nip her jaw.

"No. *Who's on first?* That's a trick question."

I slide my hand under her shirt and snap open the front closure of her bra. Her breathing catches as I fondle her breast. "Not me. I'm sliding into second, praying for third."

"You don't even like baseball."

I look up to see her licking her fingers, her slice of pizza gone. I raise my eyebrows. "Are you kidding me? You're eating through my seduction?"

"Don't judge me. I'm hungry."

I grin. "Are you done?"

She rolls her eyes. "Okay, okay. Continue your seduction."

"I'm hungry, too. Only for you."

"Well, if you put it like that, Shakespeare, let me go shower, and we'll skip right to dessert." She presses a searing kiss to that sensitive spot behind my ear. I swear it just singed more of my hair.

I scramble off of her. She grabs a slice of pizza, and I smack her bottom, urging her to hurry. With a giggle, she races up the stairs, still eating. My stomach rumbles. The shower comes on, so I take a moment to wolf down a slice. I'll need the fuel for my plans tonight, which will start with making her scream for mercy and finish with her screaming in ecstasy. I grab the pizza and saunter to her bedroom.

And I wait.

And wait.

And wait.

I eat two more slices of pizza before the shower stops. I give her all of ten seconds before throwing open the door. A cloud of steam envelops me like we're in an ancient Roman sauna. Reaching blindly, I grab her, laughing when she squeals and tumbles into my arms.

Her lips find mine, and I feel her smile. "I know what you've done, cheater," she whispers.

"I couldn't wait any longer." My hands give her bare butt a squeeze.

"I was talking about eating the pizza." Her hard nipples press into my chest, and my clothes become a towel for her wet, smooth body. "I'm at a disadvantage here. I'm naked." She bites my earlobe and what little blood remained circulating in my lust-filled brain drains below my belt.

"Gah," I mumble, licking the water off her shoulder.

Her hands tangle in my hair, and she tugs my face to hers, kissing along my jaw.

"Gar." I nibble her ear. Her kisses have made it impossible for me to speak in anything but monosyllabic caveman-like grunts.

I plop her on the counter and accidentally hit the faucet. "Ack, I'm getting soaked!" she squeals, her laughter ringing out in the small bathroom.

"Sorry, I'll lick you dry. Mmmm. I like you naked. It's to my advantage."

"Take your clothes off, Rafe. I want the playing field even."

"Sure, coach." I release the nipple locked in my mouth and step back to admire the view now that the steam is dissipating.

Peeling my T-shirt over my head, I toss it with careless abandon.

She claps, and I grin.

"No compression vest! Look at you. No wonder you're in the mood to celebrate."

She unbuckles my belt, but I stop her. I want this to be about her. I drop to my knees to savor that first taste. Pulling her legs over my shoulders, I kiss my way from one knee up her thigh as my fingers find her wet and ready. When I tease her clit with my tongue, her hands tangle in my hair. Her satisfied sighs fill the bathroom as I lap, suck, and blow until she's gasping and squirming. I crook my finger and hit the spot that makes her release my hair and moan.

Over and over I taste, tease, and push her toward her limit. I revel in her frustrated joy, loving the way her body reacts to me.

"Please," she begs. Her eyes close, and she grips the edge of the countertop. "Please, Rafe...I can't..." Once again I bring her to the brink of ecstasy, only to back off.

"Dadgummit, quit stopping or I'm gonna smother you with my wet pussy until you're deader than an armadillo on the side of the road."

I chuckle. "I can think of worse ways to die."

She smacks me so hard with the tissue box I swear I see stars. When she finds the nail file, I redouble my efforts, not wanting to end up on that show about sex and the emergency room. She tumbles into her release with a shout loud enough to raise the dead.

As I rise from my knees, the door to the bathroom slams open, and I throw myself on top of Jo. I'm fairly certain Jo's screams have shattered my eardrum.

"Freeze, motherfucker," a deep voice growls behind me.

I don't move, as a combination of righteous indignation and embarrassment heats the back of my neck. What the hell is he doing here? What happened to his double shift?

Deputy Do-Right starts laughing. "I wish you could've seen how you two jumped."

"Get out, Johnny Way!" Jolene screeches in my ringing ear.

"What the hell was I supposed to do, Jo? I heard you scream—"

Still chuckling, he slams the bathroom door, and I tuck my face into her neck. "That's it. We're getting our own place. I don't care if it's a cardboard box under the bridge."

"Oh my God, these things only happen to me," Jo gasps between fits of laughter.

I growl and nip her neck. The absurdity of the situation is such that I either have to laugh, or climb out the window and run. "How the heck am I going to face your brother after this?"

"Why are you upset? You weren't naked. It wasn't your brother who caught us. And you weren't the one screaming with an orgasm," she chokes out. The horrified look on her face makes me chuckle.

"True," I reply with a smirk, buckling my belt. "You know what this means, right?"

She frowns as she wraps a towel around her. "What?"

"You have to marry me."

"This isn't the eighteen hundreds, and you're not being forced into a shotgun wedding."

I drop to my knee and grab her hand, looking up at her.

"Marry me. Please?" I'd planned to ask her later. But now seems like a pretty good time to jump ahead since her brother's unexpected arrival has ruined my original plan for the evening. I'm getting my money back from the guy who said he'd call in sick…

"What?"

"Marry me."

"You're asking me now?"

"Seems like as good a time as any—"

She storms out of the bathroom without speaking. After a moment Atticus comes to the door, staring at me with a smug look on his face. I sneer back and whisper, "Black Shuck." He turns and leaves, swishing his tail.

I hear Jo stomping around in her bedroom, plainly upset. *What the hell?* I'm certain I've just made the biggest mistake of my short human life. If only I knew what it was.

I slam the dresser drawer so hard stuff falls over. Angrily, I right the perfume bottle, lotion, and cat figurine. *That jerk.* I shrug into my robe and fall to my knees, searching for my slippers. Behind me the door opens.

"Jo, honey. I'm sorry. Whatever I did, I'm sorry—"

"Don't talk to me."

"Why not? Wait…what are you doing, are you praying?"

"No. I'm looking for my slippers. Now get out."

"I love you." He hangs his head.

My anger subsides, but not enough to forgive him entirely. Not yet. He proposed in the *bathroom*, for heaven's sake. And I was butt-ass nekkid. What girl wants to recount her proposal this way?

"Get out. I'm not talking to you!" I find my slippers and fling them at him. One misses, and the other hits his arm.

"That's not true. You just told me to get out. How many times have I told you to focus when you throw? You always veer left of your target."

"Get out of my room, you moron."

Rafe glances at the door and puts a finger to his lips. "Shhh…" He winces as my brother bounds up the stairs. It's our first argument with Johnny Way within earshot.

"What the hell is going on?" Johnny Way's gaze shifts from me to Rafe.

"Rafe asked me to marry him."

Rafe backs up a step, and I don't blame him. My brother packs a mean wallop, and Rafe might not be a match for him yet. But Johnny Way breaks out in a wide grin and punches him on the arm.

"About damn time. So when's the big day?"

"Hold on just a New York minute. What do you mean? You *want* me to marry him?" How can my own brother betray me like this? Atticus jumps on the bed and curls up to sleep.

"You've already gone and put the cart in front of the horse. Time to make things legit."

I look at Rafe, stunned. "Do you hear him?"

"Uh…yeah?" He approaches me like I'm some sort of wild animal with his hands held out. "I love you. You've said you love me. I thought you'd be on board with this natural progression in our relationship. I know it's kind of sudden—"

"*Kind* of sudden? You proposed to me in the bathroom, you inconsiderate, insensitive troglodyte."

"What the hell is a troglodyte? And I should've shot your ass, by the way, taking advantage of my sister like that," Johnny Way adds.

"He didn't take advantage of me. Both of you are asses. Get *out*." I shove them through the door and slam it. Atticus hisses at me for disrupting his sleep, and it's the final straw. Grabbing my cat, I yank the door back open and shove him into Rafe's arms. Before I can close it again, his foot blocks me.

Rafe advances, and I take a nervous step backward. Atticus looks quite smug in his arms, the little traitor.

"Never do that again."

I swallow and lift my chin in an attempt to look braver than I feel. "Or?"

Atticus jumps back on the bed as Rafe closes and locks the door. I back up another step, and the backs of my thighs hit the bed. Rafe now stands toe-to-toe with me, and I watch the pulse at the base of his throat pounding in synchronicity with mine.

"Or I'm liable to turn you over my knee and spank you."

"You wouldn't dare."

I blush at the hopeful note in my voice, and pray Rafe didn't notice. His grin broadens. *He noticed.* He's still shirtless, and my bedside light flatters every beautiful muscle. One tug on the belt of my robe, and it falls open. I never did learn how to tie a decent knot. Now I'm glad. I find myself lying on the bed with my feet still on the floor. Rafe leans over and kisses my throat.

I can't contain my low, guttural moan. "Stop it. I'm mad."

"Quite," he whispers, tugging on my earlobe with his teeth. "Addlepated, even."

"What's that mean?" I push his chest so I can look him in the eye.

He smirks. "An archaic adjective for confused or mixed up."

"Very funny," I mutter and moan as he captures my nipple between his fingers and gives it a tug. "W-What about my brother?"

"He's a crooked cop."

"Why is that?"

"I bought him off. I think he wants us to make up and get married so he can finally have his house to himself." His tongue teases the shell of my ear, and his hand works its way inside my open robe. It's hard staying mad when I really want nothing more than to have him deep inside me.

"That makes for the second-suckiest proposal in the history of proposals — the first being ten minutes ago," I murmur against his lips.

His mouth quits teasing, and he shoves up on his arms to gaze down at me, his brow furrowed. "What do you mean?"

"I mean I want flowers, candles, dinner that I didn't pick up in a cardboard box, and a ring."

"Wait, I had candles."

"One out of four is not a good average."

He blows a raspberry on my stomach. "I'll make it up to you, I promise."

"I know you will." And in my heart, I believe it. I sit up, struggling to find the words. "I love you. I do. It's just that I don't know who I am or what I want anymore. I mean, I know I want us to be together — that's not the issue. But I need to decide about school, and you need to find another job...I just need a little time to sort things out."

He pulls away, tucking a strand of my hair behind my ear. The simple gesture makes me love him that much more. I have nothing to fear. If I say stop or slow down, he will. Looking in his eyes, I see passion and love in their depths. It's as if he can see my soul. *Why am I stalling the inevitable?* I love him. I'm about to take it back, but he speaks first.

"You're right." Rafe carefully reties my robe before crawling on the bed to sit behind me, his back against the headboard. I'm between his legs, my back to his chest. His arms wrap around me, and he leans in and kisses my temple.

"Take all the time you need, Jolene. I've waited a lifetime plus to find my soulmate. A few more days, weeks, months, or even years won't matter. I'll still be here for you."

I rub the arm wrapped around my chest, reveling in the security and strength of the man behind me. He's like none other. He's steadfast and true, the best friend I've ever had. My defender. My lover. I realize in this moment, my dreams *have* come true. I am loved for just being me. Sure, I want to finish school and get a decent job. But right now, in Rafe's arms, I have everything.

I scoot lower in the bed and Rafe follows, spooning, still with a protective arm around me. After a few minutes his snores mingle with Atticus's. I drift to sleep with a smile, knowing I'm where I'm supposed to be.

Twenty-One

The next morning I swat at the annoying sandpaper rubbing my earlobe, and something tickles my back. Then sharp teeth nip my ear. I howl and open one eye to glare at Atticus and his owner, who sits twirling a white feather in her fingers. Atticus stomps around, demanding to be petted, which we both do. That cat owns us.

"How long have you been up?" I stare with horror at the feather in Jo's hand. *What the heck?* "Where did you get that?" It suddenly dawns on me that I'm in Jo's bed, in her brother's house. I bolt up and check to see if there's a gun trained on me. Thankfully, we're alone, except for her annoying cat, which is now kneading the crap out of my arm with his claws.

"Johnny Way's hanging with some of his buddies, and I'm off today," Jo replies in singsong fashion. She runs the feather down my arm. "Did you know the scarring on your back looks like wings?"

I watch the feather twisting in her fingers as if hypnotized and grunt, having no clue how to respond.

"Now get up."

I grin and wink at her. "Already there."

"I mean get your lazy butt out of this bed. *Now.*"

"Why? If your brother's not home, I can think of plenty of good reasons to stay in bed."

"Fine, lazybones. I'm going to the pond." She flounces out of the room. I look at Atticus, who ignores me as he settles on Jo's pillow. Sleep with this feline or spend time with Jo? No brainer. I jump up to get ready.

Fifteen minutes later, I find her at our favorite fishing spot. Seated on a blanket by the bank, she's wearing jeans, a flannel shirt, and a coat. Her hair is tucked under a ball cap, and as I approach, she turns and smiles. Suddenly the day seems a little warmer, a little brighter.

Feeling carefree, I start singing, "You are my sunshine…"

"You're so corny," she says with a giggle, patting the ground.

I sit next to her, and together we stare at the water lapping the bank. Two squirrels jump above us, chattering. It's warm for this time of year; a hint of spring teases the air.

"Why did I ever want to leave?" she asks softly.

"Sometimes we don't realize what we want is right in front of us." I pick up a rock and skip it four times across the water.

"I have a couple of questions for you." She pulls a white feather from her shirt pocket. "Why did you always leave a pink rose and white feather on my desk?"

Crap. "I can explain." I grab her hands and look into her beautiful, trusting eyes. I'm terrified I'm either going to sound crazy, or she'll believe what I have to say and never forgive me for lying to her.

She gives me a smug, Atticus-like look. "Explain away."

"My job is to protect you. It's always been to protect you. I did an okay job when you were a little girl, but then you didn't seem to need me. You grew up, and Luc stepped in to tempt you with a life that would have left you ultimately unfulfilled. I was supposed to keep an eye on you, but I fell in love, and that's not allowed. Pink roses always remind me of you. You know, the ones that grow over there." I point at the dormant bushes.

"And the feather?"

"Uh, well…I, um, felt like your, er, guardian angel. And they say feathers appear when angels are near. I know, I know. Pretty lame."

The words tumble out in a rush. I can't seem to stop. "I'm so sorry, Jo. I screwed up big time, but we've been given a second chance, and

I want to love you forever—just like I always have—but as a man."
I pull her so we're both on our knees, facing each other. I'm pretty
positive nothing I've said makes a damn bit of sense. She doesn't know
the full story. Or does she? *Please help me*, I pray silently.

She laughs so hard she has to wipe the tears from her eyes. "What
are you talking about? I thought you quit the painkillers weeks ago."

"Huh? I did. Never mind." I rub my eyes with the heels of my
hands, frustrated. "I've made such a mess of everything."

"Hey, you're my hero and always have been." She wraps her arms
around my neck and kisses me. "Rafe?"

"Yes?"

"Marry me?"

Stunned, I pull back. "What?"

"I sorted things out last night and realized that with you, I'm the
best me possible. I don't need a fancy proposal. We've got clothes on
now—that's good enough for me. I want to fall asleep in your arms
and wake up there. I want to share my life with you and have your
children. I don't care if we stay in this one-horse town, move to a city,
or live in a cardboard box. I want to be with you forever. It's where
I'm supposed to be. It's as if we were predestined to be together."

I grin. "We were. I have no doubt about it." I hug her tight,
burying my face in her neck.

"For better or worse, which includes baiting my hook when we
go fishing," she says seriously.

"For better or worse, and I'll always bait your hook," I promise,
enjoying the feel of her breasts pressed against my very human heart.
"Want to see my pole?"

She giggles. "Mm-hmm…"

Despite the slight chill in the air, we shed our clothes. She pushes
me back on the bank, and I watch as she tentatively licks up my shaft
before taking the head of my cock in her mouth. Her eyes twinkle.
Closing my eyes, I succumb to the feelings. Up and down, round
and round, she taunts and teases until I'm ready to explode.

Just when I think life can't get any better, she kisses her way up
my body and slowly lowers herself on me. She's more than ready, and
I grab her hips to meet her thrust for thrust. Her eyes close and her
head falls back, extending that gorgeous neck. I rise to capture one

bouncing breast, sucking until she whimpers with need. She pushes me back, gripping my shoulders as she rubs her clit against me. It doesn't take long before we're both spiraling into supreme bliss. I shout some incoherent mumbo jumbo as she collapses against me. We're drenched in sweat and struggle to catch our breath and equilibrium.

"So I take it you'll marry me?" Jo asks. Her satisfied grin mirrors mine.

"Hell yeah!" I give her a resounding kiss.

Jo kisses my chest but makes no motion to move, which is fine with me. We're connected so much more than physically. I stroke her hair, and she purrs like a satisfied cat. After a few minutes, she rolls off, shivering. We shimmy back into our clothes, stomping to get warm.

Jo wraps her arms around my neck. "Thank you."

"For?"

She reaches for the feather in her shirt pocket and traces a heart on my chest. "Giving me a piece of heaven on Earth." Jo tosses the feather into the water.

"I'll love you always and forever," I murmur against her lips.

EPILOGUE

Crossing my arms, I glare at the stage, wondering how the heck Luc finagled his way into being the keynote speaker. We've made peace with each other, but I still don't entirely trust him. To make matters worse, he seems to be directing his comments to my wife.

Thankfully, Jo doesn't appear the least bit interested. She's checking her phone. Looking up, she gives me a small smile. Her mortarboard sits at a jaunty angle, and her eyes are bright with excitement. She's worked hard to be here, but I wish she'd taken my advice and skipped the pomp and circumstance. I make a funny face at her, and she bites her lip, silently giggling.

"Agh! Mommy won again." John sighs.

He's been playing a game on my phone with his mother. I tap his swinging legs and hold out my hand. On his other side, Johnny Way chuckles. We named our firstborn John Luke. I drew the line on the spelling of his middle name. Grudgingly, John slaps the phone in my hand and crosses his arms. It's amazing how much he looks like his mother when he pouts. I've been married long enough — six years now — to know not to say this to Jo.

"This guy is *so* boring," my son complains in a stage whisper.

I grin, knowing Luc's acute hearing means he heard him.

After a standing ovation, Luc leaves the podium and takes his place next to the university president. The graduating class stands, except Jo, who struggles to get up, arms flailing.

"She looks like a turtle on its back," Johnny Way comments.

I agree, but again, I'd never say this to Jo. The young woman sitting next to her helps her stand. Jo grimaces and rubs her stomach. Her graduation gown covers her pregnant belly, which I think is a shame. She's gorgeous.

John crawls into my lap for a better view and cheers excitedly when Jo finally waddles across the stage. Receiving her diploma, she flashes a brilliant smile and waves it in the air at us. John screams, "Mommy!" and I blow her a kiss. Johnny Way whistles. My heart feels like it's going to burst with pride.

I never realized time passed so quickly on Earth. John will be five in a couple of months, and Magda Lynn is due any day. Jo shakes Luc's hand, and then doubles over. Next thing I know, he's lowering her to the ground. I push my way through the crowd, running toward the stage. Sometimes a human body just doesn't cut it. I wish I could fly. John's crying in my arms as I drop to my knees.

"Jolene?" I stroke her hair off her damp face, and her eyes flutter open. "Are you okay?"

"Hell's bells. Of all the time to have a dadgum baby. Let me up."

I realize her gown is soaked. Her water's broken.

Luc chuckles. "Your timing is impeccable, Friday."

John punches Luc. *That's my boy.* "What did you do to my mommy?"

"What a brave young man. Breathe, Jolene," Luc instructs. "Has anyone called nine-one-one?"

Jo struggles to sit up. "No, I refuse to have this baby now. I want to go to the party. I earned it. Help me up!"

"Honey, you're going to the hospital—"

Jolene grabs my tie and yanks so hard our foreheads smack together. "I'm *not* having this baby today. Owwwwwww!" She pants through the contraction.

"Mommy…" John cries.

Through her pain, Jolene comforts him with a hug. "I'm okay. I think your baby sister is being contrary; she wasn't supposed to be here until next week. You need to take care of Daddy. Johnny

Way, will you stop by the house and get my bag? Mr. DeVille, help me get off this stage. These other people need to graduate. Sorry, everyone…Oh!" Her drill sergeant-style orders are interrupted by another contraction. I worry we're going to have a baby any minute.

"Breathe, my love," I remind her, trying to disentangle my sobbing son's arms from around my neck. The familiar wail of an approaching ambulance sounds.

"John, why don't you stand with me, and we'll finish the ceremony," Luc offers. "Afterward, we'll go for ice cream while your father takes care of your mom."

I glare at Luc, not trusting his motives. "No, I'll take care of him—"

Once again Jo grabs my tie, jerking me toward her. "I need you. I'm not doing this alone. This is your fault," she says through clenched teeth.

"My fault? I advised you not to come—"

"You got me in this condition; now you're going to help me out of it. Do you hear me?"

I'm pretty sure the audience in the back of the auditorium heard her, but I keep my mouth shut.

Luc chuckles. "Do you really think you can win this one? The boy will be fine."

I look for Johnny Way, but he's already gone. I don't know what to do. I need help…

"Step aside, godparents coming through," a familiar voice shrieks. I suppress the urge to roll my eyes. *Just what I need.*

Madge sprints up the steps with Gabe on her heels. How she runs in those stilettos is beyond my comprehension. I snicker when she shoves Luc out of the way and drops beside Jo.

"Hey, darlin', help is here," Madge coos.

"Go away. You always look perfect, and I'm a pregnant cow," Jo grumbles between pants.

"Godparents?" I raise one eyebrow.

"Godparents, guardian angel, same thing," Madge replies with a smile and casual wave.

"Not really—" I protest.

Gabe shakes his head and slaps me on the back. "No use arguing over a technicality, mate."

Madge takes a tissue and dabs Jolene's face. "Congratulations on graduating. Accounting, right? And don't be silly. You're a beautiful little mama, and today is about to get extra special. Now breathe, sweetie."

Jolene smiles weakly and breathes with Madge. "This is really happening, isn't it?" Her eyes glitter.

"'Fraid so. I'm sorry, my love." I kiss her forehead.

"I love you, Rafe."

Luc and Gabe each grab one of John's hands, arguing as the president of the university attempts to restore order. No less than six nursing graduates clamor to take care of Jo. *Great.* Is the apocalypse occurring? I can only hope so. Another contraction hits, and Jo groans. She grips my arm with her nails.

"I hate you," she hisses.

I wince and loosen her fingers, which seems to amuse the three angelic beings. Sometimes I wish The Boss had wiped my memory clean of my previous life. "How long have you been having contractions?" I've timed them, and they're now less than three minutes apart.

"Since last night," she pants.

"What?"

"Don't say one word. I worked hard for this diploma. A lot harder than I did for this baby."

"But, Jo—" I stop when she once again tugs my tie in a choke hold.

"Not. One. Word."

"This is priceless. No one's ever been able to shut him up," Luc replies with a smirk.

The EMTs arrive and take over. "Looks like we're going to have a baby," says the older medic with a wide smile.

"Ya think? Even my four-year-old son could figure that out. I'm not having her here. Take me to the hospital," she snarls.

"Yes, ma'am." The younger man chuckles as they lift her onto the stretcher. "But I don't know that we'll make it—"

It's his turn to receive Jo's wrath. "You better get me to that hospital. I want drugs. Matter of fact, I want them now. This hurts like hell. Give me some damn drugs!"

"Mommy said bad words."

I pick John up and give him a kiss. "I know. She's not herself right now. Madge and Gabe will bring you to the hospital to see your new baby sister. I know they're strangers, but in this case, it's okay. They're friends of mine, and they'll meet Uncle Johnny there. I need to go with Mommy in the ambulance."

"Okay, Daddy. But she's not a stranger. I've played with her before."

I sigh and glare at Madge. "Really?"

She shrugs. "I'm his guardian angel. You know children are more in tune with the other realm. I just check on him occasionally." She sniffs and lifts her chin. Looking at John, she smiles widely. "My goodness, you've grown at least three inches."

My son pulls a feather from his pocket. "Look what I found, Aunt Madge. I remember what you told me: *Feathers appear when angels are near.*"

The EMTs are running with Jolene's stretcher to the waiting ambulance.

"Fine, whatever. I have to go. I'm placing my son's safety in your care."

Madge takes John and grins widely. "He'll be fine. Do you like chocolate ice cream? Mr. Gabe has been dying for some since we got here. We'll even make Mr. Luc pay for it."

"I'm beyond tired but in some sort of euthanized state." I smile at the three loves of my life.

Rafe chuckles as he makes silly faces at our daughter. "I think you mean *euphoric*, Ms. College Grad."

"Whatever. My degree is in accounting, not English. I can't contain my happiness. Life is perfect." I give John Luke a kiss on his cheek. He shrugs away as he concentrates on his game. After five minutes, he was totally unimpressed by Magda Lynn, complaining her crying was "annoying."

His father is a different story. A large vase of pink roses with white feathers sits on my bedside table. I pointed out that Magda Lynn got a full dozen, whereas he used to leave me only one when we worked together. But I don't really mind. The baby already has him wrapped around her tiny finger. No doubt, she's going to be spoiled rotten. And I'm perfectly fine with that. He's an attentive dad and puts his family first.

I notice his hair needs a trim. The gray at his temples is more pronounced, and laugh lines crease his face. I find him sexy as ever. Still wearing his suit, he's the picture of casual elegance despite no tie. He removed it on the ambulance ride. A little while ago he admitted he'd been afraid I was going to choke him to death.

I wipe away happy tears. These post-pregnancy hormones make me a sappy mess. I love Rafe more every day, especially when he's with our children. He glances at me, and his grin widens. He hasn't stopped smiling since Magda's birth. He brings her to me, kissing my forehead as he places her in my arms.

"Do you know how much I love you?" he murmurs.

"Ew, stop," John complains.

Rafe ruffles his hair. "Someday you'll understand. Some girl will come into your life, and you'll fall hopelessly in love. It will be the scariest thing that ever happens to you, but also the best."

"Not me. Girls are batshit crazy," my son announces.

I choke, and Rafe's eyebrows rise.

"Where did you hear that?" I ask.

"Mr. Luc told Mr. Gabe and Uncle Johnny Way."

I keep my face straight. "Oh? That isn't very nice language."

"Daddy agreed with them."

Rafe frowns, and the back of his neck flushes — his tell when guilty. "Thanks a lot, son."

Magda lets out a prima donna squawk, wanting to be fed. John puts down his game and stares at the baby. "Even though she's cute, she's noisy. I like Atticus better."

I laugh. "Atticus *is* a great cat. And apparently the only male in my life that doesn't think I'm nuts." I place the baby at my breast, and she latches on like a champ.

John returns to his game and apparently wins big. Excited, he climbs in Rafe's lap and chatters about the move he made that won the match.

Rafe rubs John's back, and his gaze locks on Magda and me. He smiles and mouths, "*I love you.*"

Happy tears once again roll down my face. Rafe frowns and makes a move to come to me but I shake my head and smile, mouthing, "*I'm okay.*"

I'm more than okay.

I have my heaven on Earth. Always and forever.

The End

ACKNOWLEDGMENTS

Thank you to Jessica Royer Ocken, Editor Extraordinaire. Your patience and humor got me through this and I'm sorry for the umpteen edits. I think you are perfect! (I had to get another one in there and added the exclamation point just for you!) I want to give a special thank you to Coreen Montagna for my beautiful cover and the help with line edits and formatting. I know I asked a million questions and changed my mind hundreds of times. Thank you for putting up with me! And thank you to The Blurb Bitch, who is anything but a bitch. Your way with words is amazing!

My family is my life. They keep me grounded and have cheered for me every step of this crazy journey into publishing. I want to give a special shout out to my sister, Carol. I love you, and I'm sorry/not sorry I ruined the ending of every book for you when we were kids. (The plus of being the older sister) And to my agent Victoria Lea, thank you for always believing in me and going to bat for me. You're the best. Special thanks to Carrie for listening to my highs and lows over lunch four days a week.

To my online friends and chosen family, the Cain Raisers: thank you for all the love, excitement and willingness to pass the word about my books. Your posts and support always brighten my days. You all know my not-so-secret obsessions and still love me.

And to my "O" sisters, I wouldn't be here without you. You are the best cheerleaders on social media!

Debra Anastasia, Helena Hunting, and Smut Book Junkies, your friendship and support mean more to me than words can express.

And last but not least, thank you to the best critique partner in the world. Jill, you keep me real.

About the Author

During the day, Nancee works as a counselor/nurse in the field of addiction to support her coffee and reading habit. Nights are spent writing paranormal and contemporary romances with a serrated edge. Authors are her rock stars, and she's been known to stalk a few for an autograph, but not in a scary, Stephen King way. Her husband swears her To-Be-Read list on her e-reader qualifies her as a certifiable book hoarder. Always looking to try something new, she dreams of being an extra in a Bollywood film, or a tattoo artist. (Her lack of rhythm and artistic ability may put a damper on both of these dreams.)

Website: nanceecain.com
Blog: nanceecain.com/blog
Goodreads: goodreads.com/Nancee_Cain
Facebook: facebook.com/NanceeCainAuthor
Reader's Group (Cain Raisers): facebook.com/groups/Cain.Raisers
Twitter: twitter.com/Nancee_Cain
Pinterest: pinterest.com/nanceecain
Instagram: instagram.com/nanceecain
BookBub: bookbub.com/authors/nancee-cain
Newsletter: eepurl.com/bhFMtX
YouTube Channel: bit.ly/2xsU6Ad
Spotify Playlists: open.spotify.com/user/12184539074

Books by Nancee Cain:

Paranormal Romance (Angels)
Saving Evangeline
Tempting Jo
Loving Lili (novella)

Contemporary Romance (Pine Bluff Novels)
The Resurrection of Dylan McAthie
The Redemption of Emma Devine
The Rehabilitation of Angel Sinclair
The Redirection of Damien Sinclair
The Reinvention of Jinx Howell
The Reintroduction of Sammie Morgan
The Realization of Grayson Deschanelle

If you enjoyed *Tempting Jo*, check out *Saving Evangeline*

Evangeline is the town pariah. Everyone knows she's crazy and was responsible for the death of her last boyfriend. Even her mother left her and moved cross-country. Lonely and desperate, Evie decides to end her life.

Rogue angel Remiel longs to return to earth, but there's just one problem. He tends to invite trouble and hasn't been allowed back since Woodstock. The Boss sends him to save Evangeline, but there's a catch: he can't reveal his angelic nature, and he must complete the task as Father Remiel Blackson.

Forced together on a cross-country trip, a forbidden romance ignites and love unfolds. A host of heavenly messengers tries to intervene, but Remiel and Evangeline are headed on a collision course to disaster. Will his love save her, or will they both be lost forever?

Saving Evangline is available now at:

Amazon
Barnes & Noble
iTunes
Books-a-Million
Kobo
Walmart

Continue reading for a sample chapter!
(with permission from Omnific Publishing)

Saving Evangeline
Chapter One

"This is the third time this century we've had this conversation, Remiel."

I watch as the Boss hits the golf ball with a perfect swing and aces the hole. He grins widely and does a fist pump into the air. The odds of an amateur acing that par three shot is probably twelve thousand, five hundred to one, a pro maybe twenty-five hundred to one. But when you're *Him* it happens every time. And every damn — er — darn time He acts surprised.

That's my problem. *Everything here is so predictably perfect.*

He turns to me and I gulp, knowing He's just read my mind. The frown on His face is like witnessing an eclipse of the sun. "Thank you for correcting your language. Now, where were we?"

I take a minute, trying to decide if He's using the royal We, or if he means Him and me. Opting on *us,* I kick at a pebble and mumble, "This is the third time this century I've met with You in regard to my shenanigans." *Shenanigan* is His word, not mine. I sigh and wait for the inevitable *talk.* I concentrate on the ground, gritting my teeth with frustration and trying my best not to roll my eyes. I don't seek trouble on purpose. It's drawn to me like a magnet.

Okay, so maybe that's a lie. I may *occasionally* try to shake things up around here just to break the monotony. The last time I was in trouble, He asked me if I'd changed my name to Legion. I didn't think it was that funny, but everyone else did, especially that old windbag, Peter. Which is precisely why I played that innocent little prank on the old goat.

The Boss nudges my wing with His golf club. "Ah, yes. You know how Peter cherishes those keys. There's no need to test one's free will in paradise. I don't know why you like to torment him by hiding them. And there's nothing wrong with the word shenanigan. It's a lovely word. I like the way it rolls off the tongue. Nice catch on the eye rolling, by the way. You know I find it disrespectful."

"Yes, Sir." *He always knows.*

"Why, Remiel?" His voice is calm and even, not irritating and whiny like Peter's.

"Why what, Sir?" I wish He'd just get on with the punishment and skip the lecture. Oops, not punishment. They aren't called punishments *here*. They're *learning lessons*.

"Why do you insist on going rook?" He leans on the golf club, waiting for my answer.

"Excuse me?" *What the fuck is going rook?* "I'm not sure I understand what you mean, Sir."

"Watch your language, Remiel."

It sucks when your Boss is an om-omni…Dang, I never can keep those "omni" words straight. *Know-it-all.*

He sighs and the trees rustle with the impact. "The word is omniscient, but know-it-all is fine as long as you say it, or think it with respect." His face lights up and I blink from the brilliance, wishing I'd worn my sunglasses. "I need to brush up on modern slang. I'll add it to My to-do-list." Like a kid with a new toy, He whips out His phone and taps in the reminder. It's not that He needs a phone *or* a reminder. He just loves gadgets. He's often said the twenty-first century would be His favorite of all times if people would just set aside their petty quarrels and actually talk to one another. It's His opinion there's no reason *not* to, it's the age of communication, after all.

Putting the phone away, His gaze sweeps over the golf greens. The sigh this time is deeper, causing a rumble of thunder that lets me know He's tired of my stall tactics. "Now back to the issue at hand. Why do you insist on bucking the system, Remiel?"

Ah! He meant going rogue, not rook. I bite the inside of my lip to keep from laughing. "I'm bored," I blurt out. He stares at me and one bushy eyebrow rises. I tag on a hasty, "Sir."

"You're bored?"

I nod, warming to the subject. "Everything is just too perfect around here. It's monotonous. The humans have it made. They get to experience so much more with their free will. I think we should be allowed more than one weekend off every forty or fifty years—"

He holds up His hand. "Enough. Need I remind you, that you get in trouble every time you're away? Hell-raising is never productive, dear boy. Didn't you learn anything from Lucifer?"

I can't contain my sigh of frustration. *He just doesn't get it.*

The Boss pulls on His lower lip and narrows His eyes. "I suppose you think it would be more fun putting out *fires* down below?"

I swallow and back up a step. "Er, well, not *too* far below, Sir. Just say, on Earth." I press my lips together determined to keep my mouth shut before I get in even more trouble. If I'm not careful, I'm liable to be stuck being Peter's lackey forever. My last *learning lesson* occurred after my weekend of excess at Woodstock during the "Summer of Love." I've been manning the registration desk at the Pearly Gates ever since. Talk about a mind-numbing, lobotomizing job. Giving the same old mundane welcome speech to the newcomers is like being a stewardess reviewing airline safety. No one listens or cares.

He clears His throat pulling my attention back to Him. "Using the terms mind-numbing and lobotomizing together is redundant." The twinkle in His eyes make my feathers stand on edge. "I think I have the perfect job for you. Maybe you won't find it too *boring...*"

Oh shi—shoot. This isn't going to be good.

I land on my ass with a thud. I'm in Hell. No, it's too humid to be Hell. Standing, I dust off my pants, careful not to rustle my feathers, which must be concealed when on Earth.

My eyes damn near pop out of my head when I realize what I'm wearing. Dark pants, a clerical shirt, stiff uncomfortable white collar, a rosary in my pocket and a shiny cross on my chest. Aghast, I look toward heaven and glare. "Not funny, Sir."

A gentle breeze rustles the trees in answer. Other than the moon and a dim light from a bridge to my left, it's eerily dark out here. A glance at my watch reveals it's ten o'clock and I'm in the middle of nowhere dressed like a priest. He really should get over my weekend at Woodstock. "Ever hear of forgiveness, Sir?" I mutter under my breath.

Again, a gust whips the trees, reminding me He's aware of everything that's going on and is not amused. My attitude is what always gets me in trouble. Confused, I try to figure out why I'm here in the guise of a priest. I'm sure He and Peter are enjoying a good laugh over this.

Running a finger under the tight collar, I stomp toward the vehicle parked ten feet from me. Muttering one of Luc's favorite words, I open the car door and find keys with a St. Christopher key chain dangling in the ignition. I kind of wish he'd given me back the VW camper I had at Woodstock — the one with peace signs on it. That van saw some good times. Rummaging through the glove box, I find the Florida registration for the car and insurance papers listing Remiel Blackson as the owner. Blackson? Really? I couldn't be Remiel Goodson? A cell phone on the seat rings with the theme from *Charlie's Angels*. It's the Boss's favorite television show from the seventies.

It's passcode protected and takes me three tries to figure out He'd programmed it with *6666*. I get the not-so-subliminal message. I guess even He couldn't get past the four-digit requirement. My tech-savvy Boss has texted my assignment which I read as I exit the car.

You are Father Remiel Blackson,
a Roman Catholic priest on sabbatical.
Save Evangeline Lourdes Salvatore.
PS: Smoking is bad for you,
and don't drink and drive.

Roman Catholic? That means celibate, the spoilsport. I look around in disbelief. I'm on a deserted road in south Florida. How the heck am I supposed to find this Evangeline Salvatore? He hasn't given me any info and I'm not omni — whatever. I'm not a know-it-all. "All due respect, Sir," I add quickly.

Google, of course, it's the twenty-first century answer for everything. I'm excited to get to use the new technology I've been following from Boringville. Thunder rumbles in the distance. *Heaven*, I meant heaven. I type her name into the search engine on the phone and find a few sensationalist articles about her involvement in a tragic wreck that killed a man. It even has her address for home and work. She's a hair stylist, and the name of her salon is The Curl Up 'n Dye. The Boss is right; modern technology is amazing.

I'm about to leave when I notice a lone figure on the bridge. Dark, tangled hair spirals down her back, and her clothes hang loosely on her frame. As I watch, she marches back and forth talking to herself, looking like a wild, sleek panther ready to attack at any moment. Occasionally, she wipes her cheeks and then clenches her fists, but she continues pacing like a caged animal.

The girl stops and peers over the side of the bridge. Swinging one leg over the railing, she freezes. A feeling of dread overcomes me. *Holy shit!* I race toward her in a full-blown panic. I know in my gut it's her and it is my job to stop her.

"Don't do it," a deep male voice commands.

A whisper of a breeze caresses my cheek. With a frustrated sigh, I lower my foot and drag my gaze from the murky, dark water that beckons me with its siren's song. Glaring at the unwelcome intruder, I dash the tears from my cheeks. He stands in the shadow, and all I can make out is that he's tall with broad shoulders. Striding toward me, hands in his pockets, he starts whistling. The thought occurs to me I should be scared and run, but it's as if I'm glued to the spot. As he comes into the light, I see he's a priest. But he doesn't look like any priest I've ever known. This guy is Hollywood gorgeous. Under the dim light, he appears almost incandescent and his emerald eyes seem lit from within. Their intensity burns a hole into my paper-thin bravado, which slips away and disappears like ashes in the wind.

Dammit, I'd just worked up the courage to follow through with my plan to leave this nightmare behind, and this stranger has interrupted, dragging me back to my personal hell on earth.

Feeling naked and vulnerable under his steadfast scrutiny, I cross my arms in front of my chest, desperately trying to contain the welling anxiety building within me. A black mass flutters behind him, and I blink to clear my eyes. *Please, not again, not now.* My mother and the doctor's dire warnings about not taking my medication taunt my tortured mind.

Clutching my head with my hands, I scream to scare my demons away. Sometimes this technique worked when I was in the hospital. More times, than not, it just got me a nice mind-numbing cocktail of drugs, that would leave me nauseated and dizzy for days.

"No, no, no." I march away from the stranger, pacing back and forth, feeling trapped. These hallucinations are part of the reason why I'm here. Now my resolve to end them, once and for all, is shaken. With a trembling hand, I rake my fingers through my snarled hair. Yuck. *When did I last bathe?* My greasy hair feels like tangled string. I must look like a crazy woman.

Laughter layered with a tinge of overwrought hysteria bubbles from deep within me at this last thought. Surely an out-of-control, wild woman will scare this guy away. It usually does. Most folks never look me in the eye. It's like they're afraid my insanity is either contagious or a superpower I can use to slay them.

"Feel better?" His voice isn't patronizing. I'm used to Father Asswipe handing out condescension like communion wafers. This priest asked a simple question, and strangely, I find I *do* feel a little better. He approaches me like I'm a rabid animal, his movements slow and deliberate.

There was a time—not so long ago—when the white collar under his chin would have soothed me. I was raised a good Catholic girl, but we all know the road to hell is paved with good intentions. My descent to non-repentant sinner isn't my mother's fault. I accept full responsibility for fucking up my own life.

Tonight, the sight of the starched white collar does the opposite. It pisses me off as lingering guilt from my upbringing hangs suspended between us like a bridge between saint and sinner. I pull my clenched hands to my waist, preparing for the lecture and platitudes on the sanctity of life. I've heard it over and over throughout the years from my mother, Father Ashton, Sunday school teachers, social workers, psychiatrists, and even the damn cop who arrested me the last time I tried to kill myself.

I'd swallowed the entire damn medicine cabinet and somehow, thanks to my "hearty constitution," made it to the street in front of our house where I was found staggering, oblivious to my surroundings and out of touch with reality. The shrink told me I'd been in the process of being arrested for disorderly conduct when my mom dashed out of the house screaming and crying about what I'd done.

Instead, they rushed me to the hospital to have my stomach pumped. Lesson learned? Plan your suicide. Don't do it on an impulse when your mom is home.

He sighs. "I'm going to say it one more time. Don't do it."

"Don't do what?" I sneer. The nerve of this priest presuming—however correct his supposition is—to know my motives.

"Don't jump." His warm baritone voice fills the air with something akin to the energy felt before a lightning storm. The hairs on my arms stand up.

"What makes you think I'm going to jump, *Father?*" I make no attempt to hide my derision, hoping my rudeness will make him turn around and leave. It worked like a charm with my mother. I've managed to push her clear across the country.

"Let me rephrase. *Please* don't jump. I can't swim," he confesses with a small smile. "Do you want to have to explain my death as well as your own?" His eyes crinkle and seem to dance with amusement, which serves to light the match to my short fuse. The wind picks up and ruffles his hair, causing the natural highlights to dance against his dark brown hair. The ends curl appealingly on the back of his neck and one lock falls on his forehead. It's a bit long for a priest, but the beautician and woman in me wouldn't change a thing. He's beautiful.

"Since I don't believe in God, or the hereafter, no explanations would be necessary. You're boring me, so just leave me the hell alone, and go do your good deeds elsewhere."

His answering bark of laughter triggers my anxiety, and a wall of paranoia flies up around me. *Is he laughing at me?* I square my shoulders and utilize my menacing crazy stare. "What's so funny?"

"I haven't been accused of doing *good deeds* in a long damn time." A rumble of thunder rolls in the distance, and a strong blast of air shakes the trees, signaling a storm is brewing.

"I would think that's your business." I raise one eyebrow, looking pointedly at his collar and the silver cross glinting on his chest. The cross and priest garb are incongruent with his drop-dead gorgeous looks and mild profanity. Of course, the only priest I know personally is old Father Ashton. The ancient priest has to be at least seventy-five and has disgusting nose hairs and bad breath.

He runs a finger along the inside of the collar as if it's too tight. My mind wonders what it would be like to have his fingers run along my body. I shake my head to rid it of the ridiculous image. Maybe I'm sicker than they say I am.

He frowns. "Ah, yes…*this*. It is a bit ironic." He cut his eyes toward the sky with what could only be described as a look of annoyance before settling his curious gaze back on me. His wide, easy smile adds to his attractiveness. "Come on, let's go. You can buy me a drink."

"Excuse me?" My mouth falls open. *Buy him a drink?*

"Vow of poverty, Crazy Girl." His arms sweep out in a self-deprecating manner. "So to thank me, you can buy me a drink."

"I'm not crazy, and what do I have to thank you for?"

He raises one eyebrow and smirks. I huff with annoyance.

"Okay so I'm crazy, whatever. What do I have to thank you for?"

"Why, for saving your miserable, worthless life, of course." He throws an arm around my shoulders as if he's my damn *BFF* and guides me toward the end of the bridge. Strangely, my anxiety—my constant companion for two years—begins to crumble under his casual embrace. This in itself is terrifying. I don't know how to function anymore except in full-blown panic mode.

"What makes you think my life is miserable and worthless?" I shrug away from him, annoyed he's verbalized the obvious. My life *is* miserable and worthless. To be precise, it's downright pathetic.

"Why were you about to jump?" He pats his pockets and frowns. "Hey, you got a cigarette?"

"Ew." I wrinkle my nose with disgust. "No, I don't smoke. It's a nasty habit."

A grin spreads across his face. He's much too handsome to be a cleric with those angular cheekbones and strong, clean-shaven jaw. I bet he has a huge cult following of unsatisfied, female parishioners who love to go into great detail about their non-existent, fantasy-filled sex lives in the confessional. Hell, I'd like to do him in the confessional…

"Not nearly as nasty as Sister Winifred's habit, but that's another story. We all have our vices, don't we? Tell me, Evangeline Lourdes Salvatore, what's yours?"

"I go by Evie—" I stop short and cross my arms in front of my chest, narrowing my eyes. "Wait—how do you know my name?"

"It's my business to know. So what are your vices? Tell me all about them, and if they're really good and juicy, in minute detail, please." Chuckling, he grabs my hand and leads me toward the end of the bridge. I sputter with indignation, sounding like the dying desk fan that sits on my station at the salon. *Former station,* I quit yesterday.

"Your business? I'm none of your business! What kind of sick bastard are you?" I pull away from him again, and my pulse pounds in my ears as the bitter taste of fear floods my mouth. A shiver of apprehension creeps over my body. Trying to be discreet, I take a step back.

It's late and I'm alone on a deserted road in rural Florida with a handsome stranger who knows my name. This is the stuff of low-budget horror movies. *They're out to get me again.* I squelch the thought as my survival instinct kicks into super-drive. Which is kind of bizarre, since just moments ago I wanted to die.

"Leave me alone." I'm not sure if I'm speaking to him or the voices in my head. *Don't panic, this isn't a movie. Don't turn your back to him.* Trying to act nonchalant, I scan the ground searching for anything to use as a weapon. Dammit, I left my purse with pepper spray in it at the edge of the bridge.

"Take the frightened gazelle look down a notch. I'm not going to hurt you." He shoves his hands in his pockets and continues down the bridge — humming of all things — Led Zeppelin's "Stairway to Heaven."

"So says every sociopath in every slasher movie ever made," I grumble. But, for some strange reason, I believe him. Maybe it's the collar. I'm following him like he's the damn Pied Piper of Hamlin.

"Evangeline, if I'd wanted to *hurt* you, I would have done so already. I'm here to *save* you."

My unladylike snort would make my mother twinge. "Seriously. Tell me how you know my name, Father…?" *Please don't say you've heard the gossip.*

"Blackson. Remiel Blackson. But, you can call me Remi. Like I said, it's my business to know. Aren't you a parishioner of Our Lady of Perpetual Chaos?"

This time I laugh at his corruption of our parish church name and the absurdity of his statement. A parishioner? *As if.* "I haven't been to church in a long time, Father. I attend St. Mattress on the Springs. Everyone knows I'm a sinner of the worst kind." I'm not bragging. It's a well-known fact. Ask anyone in the godforsaken town where I've lived my entire twenty-one years. If you can call it living; maybe existed would be a better word.

"Oh, good!" He yanks his hands from his pockets and rubs them together in the worst over-acted imitation of a stage villain I've ever seen. I bite my lip to keep from smiling. "The *worst* kind of sinner is my favorite. You might even say it's my specialty. So, come on, evil Evie, tell me the worst thing you've ever done. Consider the confessional booth open and in business. I promise to go light on penance and heavy on absolution." He nudges my shoulder as we walk toward the end of the bridge.

"I c-can't." For some peculiar reason, even though everyone in the entire damn county knows why I'm a horrible person, I don't want this priest to know—not yet. He'll find out soon enough if he listens to the gossip. I'm notorious, and my reputation is widespread.

"Fine. But if it makes you feel better, I've probably done far worse myself."

I roll my eyes in a childish manner. "Yeah, right. Like what, drink a little too much of the sacramental wine? Trust me, whatever you've done can't compare." Laced with a mixture of shame and anger, my voice sounds bitter even to my own ears. Before I realize it, we're standing next to his car, and I notice he's picked up my purse on the way.

"Evangeline, sins aren't a game of one-upmanship. They're mistakes, and I've made plenty of them. I haven't always been a priest, you know." He opens the car door for me. As I slip past him into the car, the nostalgic scent of fresh cut pine boughs and cinnamon assaults my senses. Damn if he doesn't smell like Christmas in August. He shuts the door, and I reach over and switch the ignition so I can roll down the window and turn on the interior light.

Turning back to face him I ask, "Now what?" My voice trembles a little, which pisses me off. Why is this priest affecting me so?

Remi leans down and peers at me, his clasped hands resting on the open window. A hint of a smile flickers across his face. I like the laugh lines that crinkle by his mesmerizing eyes. He looks to be just a few years older than I am. I realize I haven't been around anyone close to my age since Jack. Lately, it's been my lot in life to attract older men. The worst was old Mr. Locke who couldn't get it up and ended up crying on my chest all night. What's wrong with me? I'm thinking about sex? *This man is a priest.*

"Isn't this where you're supposed to scoot over and drive off in my car, continuously looking behind you while I crash in through the windshield or sunroof?" he teases.

Stunned, I don't know how to react. No one has teased me in a long time. Most people ignore me or walk around me on pins and needles, waiting for either my head to spin around, or for me to vomit pea soup. Or, like old Mr. Locke, men use me for their own pleasure, thinking my reputation gives them license to take advantage of me. *What if he isn't teasing?*

Jesus, what the hell? I bite my lip, realizing my foolishness. I'm sitting in a complete stranger's car. Even if he does wear a priest's collar, it's no reason to blindly trust him. And yet, I don't feel compelled to get out of the car and run. He just isn't scary. *Most sociopath murderers probably aren't, you idiot. Ever hear of Ted Bundy?* I look out the windshield into the dark nothingness of my surroundings. We're miles from civilization.

Who is this priest? I don't remember hearing any town gossip about old Father Asswipe retiring. Where the hell is he from, and how did he get here? It took me hours to walk here. I chose this place because of its remoteness, and I never heard his car drive up. *Maybe he flew here.* I squeeze my eyes shut, shoving the ridiculous thought aside. *Dumb ass, you were busy concentrating on ending it.* He had to have driven up. My breathing saws erratically and blood pounds in my ears as my thoughts scatter like confetti in the wind.

He reaches a hand in the window and strokes my hair, the way I used to pet our cat, Duchess. It's soothing and comforting. "It's okay. I know you're scared," he murmurs. My breathing eases, and my heart quits hammering. A sense of warmth and peace surrounds me. I give in to this strange new feeling, tired of my lifelong struggle to keep my thoughts coherent.

Sucking in a shallow breath, I draw my gaze to his. Flames seem to spark and flare in the depths of his pupils. When I was a little girl I would lie in the backyard staring at the clouds in the blue sky and talk to the angels. At the time, my mother complained about my overactive imagination. I've always maintained it was real, despite the professionals labeling it as a symptom of my *disease*. The feeling of comfort from back then is the one that comes over me now. I blink and the flames disappear. I must be more exhausted than I realized. What do I have to lose by trusting him?

As a matter of fact, he might be doing me a favor. I think suicide is a mortal sin, which would embarrass my mom. If I'm murdered, I could have a full Catholic funeral without the guilt, and she can accept any condolences without the humiliation. *And dead is dead, after all.*

I swallow my fear and take a deep breath as I gaze at the cross dangling from his chest. It sways gently back and forth, and I wonder if a religious magician is hypnotizing me. "If you kill me, will you at least promise to make it quick and easy, with minimal pain?" My question is only half-kidding.

He reaches in the car and tips my chin up so he can look into my eyes. "I don't believe I could cause you any more pain than what you're already dealing with, do you?" The scent of Christmas infiltrates the car, and again, I have the peaceful sensation of staring at the sky and talking to the celestial host. I attempt to swallow the lump in the back of my throat, but it won't go away. All I can do is shrug my shoulders in a combination of pretend indifference and defeat. I realize it isn't him I'm scared to trust. It's me. I don't know how to deal with kindness.

"You're overwrought and tired. I'm going to drive you home, okay?"

"Okay," I whisper.

He's right. My nerves are shot, my battery drained, and my limbs feel like lead. All I want to do is curl up and sleep. And yet, I'm afraid of the nightmares that have plagued me for two years. I never sleep until exhaustion sets in, and then only in two-hour stretches, at the most. The last time I slept was two nights ago.

He walks around to the driver's side and eases into the car, snapping off the interior light. With the darkness, a lost, empty feeling engulfs me. He's taking me home. In my mind, I'm already dead. My house is my tomb. As if sensing my reluctance and fear, Remi turns and pulls me into his arms, holding me tight. Beneath the drab clerical shirt he's all hard muscle and his presence is one of quiet strength. I feel safe for the first time in what seems forever — encompassed in his dark wings. I squeeze my eyes tighter and my finger traces the outline of the cross he wears. *Arms, not wings.* I pull away embarrassed by my whimsical musings.

He smiles as he fastens his seatbelt. "Buckle up, Crazy Girl. If we have an accident, you don't want to die because you weren't wearing your seatbelt, do you?"

My heart sinks into my stomach, and I clench my fists in my lap. *He does know.* Father Asswipe must have given him an earful, or it could have been anyone else for that matter. I'm more than famous. I'm *infamous*. I frown and search his face by the dim light on the dashboard, looking for condemnation, horror, or mocking cruelty, but find none. His lips curl in to a sly smirk. I smack his arm as his warm laughter fills the car. "Nobody likes a smart ass, Father."

"Sure they do. Everyone likes me. And please, call me Remi."

He pulls out to the main road and flips on the radio. Thank God, it isn't a country station. Casting me a sideways glance and an easy grin, he opens the sunroof. I find myself smiling in return and feeling strangely carefree being in the company of someone who doesn't seem to give a damn about my past. I can't remember the last time I've felt this way. Feeling impulsive and reckless, I unbuckle my seatbelt and stand in my seat, squeezing through the sunroof to inhale the heavy, humid night air.

Storm clouds are gathering in the distance, but overhead it's clear and millions of stars twinkle like glitter on black velvet. There's no traffic on the deserted back road, and I squeal with delight when Remi kicks the speed up and cuts off the headlights. We're submerged in darkness, the road lit only by the illumination of the moon. For a brief moment I'm frightened. *Is being scared shitless becoming some sort of warped addiction?* On the radio, Pearl Jam wails "Given to Fly," and Remi cranks it up full blast as we fly down the road at a breakneck speed.

"Spread your wings and give in to the moment," he shouts, followed by a loud rebel yell as he pumps the air with his fist, sounding like a teenager on a joyride instead of a priest saving a crazy girl. His laughter is like a bright light in a dark cavern and fills the empty hole where my soul should exist. I look down at him and find myself grinning. His hair is a disheveled mess, and his pure ecstasy at living in the moment is intoxicating. I want to drink in his bliss. My hair blows behind me in chaotic disarray and goose bumps appear on my arms, but whether from the cold air, or fear, I don't know, or care. In this moment, I'm liberated from the nightmare that is now my life. I throw my head back, shut my eyes, and hold out my arms. It's both terrifying and thrilling.

I'm flying.

I'm free.

I'm alive.

Books by Nancee Cain:

Contemporary Romances

Although each of the titles in this series can be read as standalone stories, this is the preferred reading order:

The Resurrection of Dylan McAthie
A Pine Bluff Novel

Maybe You Can Go Home Again

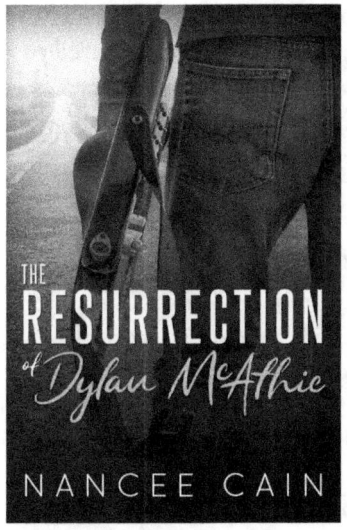

Hounded by paparazzi, Dylan McAthie — the former lead guitarist for Crucified, Dead and Buried — craves quiet anonymity to regroup and sort out his life. An accident leaves him dependent on the family he once ran from, with no choice but to return to the small town of Pine Bluff, Alabama.

Hired by Dylan's estranged brother, private-duty nurse Jennifer Adams remembers the charming boy Dylan was before fame and misfortune. And she notices he's developed a knack for blaming everyone else for his problems, rather than bothering with introspection. She's not having it.

Despite their clashes, as her patient heals, the chemistry between them grows undeniable — until scandal finds Dylan again, threatening to destroy the progress he's made and the couple's growing respect and affection. Can Dylan fix what fame has so easily broken? Or will his public resurrection mean the death of any relationship with Jennifer?

The Redemption of Emma Devine
A Pine Bluff Novel

A Little Shake-Up in Life Can Be Devine

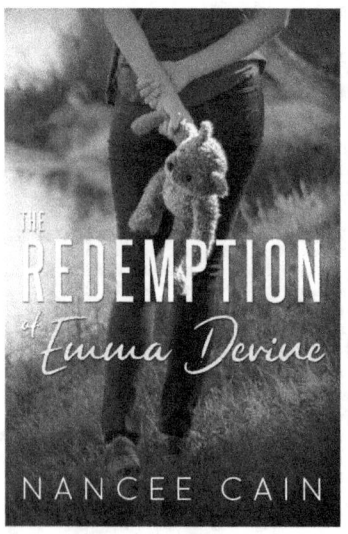

Emma Devine is on the run and fighting to survive. Her tortured past makes trust difficult, especially where men are concerned. But she has no choice other than accepting the help of the man who catches her shoplifting on Christmas Eve.

When not stopping shoplifters, David Patterson leads a quiet life in Pine Bluff, Alabama, working as a high school teacher. His random act of Christmas kindness brings unexpected joy to his life, as he finds himself drawn to the mysterious Emma. When she leaves, his world is turned upside down, and his dreams are changed forever.

Four years later, Emma returns in search of long-overdue redemption. But despite an undeniable attraction between the two, trust is an even greater issue now—for both of them. Can they find their way to a place of understanding? Or have yesterday's mistakes destroyed their chance for a future together?

The Rehabilitation of Angel Sinclair
A Pine Bluff Novel

Love — the Hardest Addiction to Kick

Angel Sinclair arrives in Pine Bluff, Alabama, determined to make amends for his past and move on. But that changes after a chance encounter with a beautiful inn owner, and instead he finds himself pursuing two things that haven't been in his life for years: love and trust.

Still reeling from a bitter divorce, Maggie Robertson wants to focus on making her business a success. Getting involved with anyone in this gossipy little town is the farthest thing from her mind...until she finds herself tempted by a younger man.

Neither Angel nor Maggie can ignore the sizzling heat between them. But Angel's secretive nature soon fills Maggie with doubts about the man she's allowed into her heart.

Was she wrong to believe love could conquer all? Is their age difference an obstacle they can't overcome?

The Redirection of Damien Sinclair
A Pine Bluff Novel

Sometimes You Get What You Need

Acclaimed divorce attorney Damien Sinclair has witnessed more than his share of love's ugly aftermath. He keeps things black and white, preventing anyone from getting too close. But his illusion of control fades when an attempt on his life leaves him struggling with PTSD.

Enter Damien's childhood friend, the free-spirited Harley Taylor. Shrugging off the awkwardness of their teenaged fling and her broken heart, she appoints herself his caregiver. The man needs to learn not to take himself so seriously, and she's hellbent on snapping him out of his brooding funk.

After a decade apart, Harley and Damien find their attraction is stronger than ever. Could Harley's sunny disposition be the bright spot Damien needs in his life? Or will their differences overshadow any hopes of a future together?

The Reinvention of Jinx Howell
A Pine Bluff Novel

Can Love Unmask Their True Selves?

Hiding behind her wigs and heavy makeup, Jinx Howell masks her insecurities — which even she doesn't understand — with bravado, slashing through life with reckless abandon. Lonely, but unwilling to get close to anyone, she finds the ideal solution: a hook-up with the campus's most notorious heartbreaker.

In similar fashion, Mark "Two-Time" MacGregor protects his heart and keeps himself unencumbered through a string of one-night stands. A chance meeting with the edgy Jinx in a dark alley seems like destiny. She claims to want sex with no ties, making her perfect. *Like attracts like.* But this girl with a switchblade has more hang-ups than he does, which is a hell of a lot.

When tragedy strikes, Mark's hit-and-run lifestyle takes a backseat to his need to protect the broken girl whose secrets are unraveling. Along the way, both of them will find their truths unmasked. Can they forge a real relationship, or will they give up on their romance as jinxed?

The Reintroduction of Sammie Morgan
A Pine Bluff Novel

Can Life Get Any Crazier?

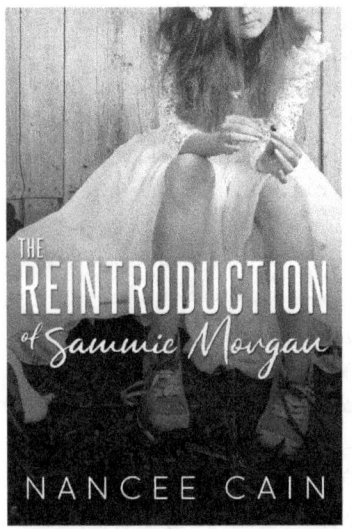

Still reeling from the tragic deaths of his wife and daughter, Matt Tyler trudges through life, caring for his young son, managing his cantankerous father, and working as much as he can. Despite his best efforts, bills are piling up and his vindictive in-laws seem determined to take Luke away from him.

Things change when he stumbles upon Sammie Morgan — with a car that won't run and her mother's ashes in the backseat. Best friends growing up, Matt and Sammie have spent years apart following very different paths. Now they've both run out of options. Without a dime in her pocket, Sammie has nowhere to go. And Matt lacks the stable home life he needs to fight his former in-laws.

Their hasty solution? A marriage of convenience.

But how convenient will this reintroduction be if it means Matt and Sammie have to relive the most painful parts of their past?

The Realization of Grayson Deschanelle
A Pine Bluff Novel

Sex, No Strings Attached

Despite a high-profile clientele, fashion photographer Grayson Deschanelle prefers being behind the lens, away from public scrutiny. After his movie star girlfriend dumps him, he flees to his stepbrother's remote cabin to hide from the paparazzi.

Caught by surprise, Grayson finds Lissy much different than the girl he's known for years. She's no longer a child — though her teenaged crush is still very much intact. Snowed in with her, he tries to fight his growing attraction. But being with Lissy brings what his life is lacking into sharp focus.

The ice melts, and they return home. When their families discover their secret, Grayson must decide what kind of life he truly wants — and whether he'll fight to keep Lissy by his side.

Paranormal Angel Romances

Although each of the titles in this series can be read as standalone stories, this is the preferred reading order:

Saving Evangeline

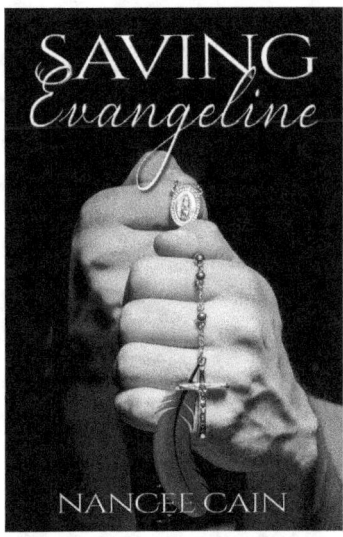

Evangeline is the town pariah. Everyone knows she's crazy and was responsible for the death of her last boyfriend. Even her mother left her and moved cross-country. Lonely and desperate, Evie decides to end her life.

Rogue angel Remiel longs to return to Earth, but there's just one problem. He tends to invite trouble and hasn't been allowed back since Woodstock. The Boss sends him to save Evangeline, but there's a catch: he can't reveal his angelic nature, and he must complete the task as *Father* Remiel Blackson.

Forced together on a cross-country trip, a forbidden romance ignites and love unfolds. A host of heavenly messengers tries to intervene, but Remiel and Evangeline are headed on a collision course to disaster. Will his love save her, or will they both be lost forever?

Tempting Jo

Forbidden love is hell…

Confident and quirky, Jo Sanford thinks her boss is God's gift to women—and she couldn't be further from the truth. Devilishly handsome, Luc DeVille will stop at nothing to lure his administrative assistant right into his arms—and bed.

Over Rafe Goodman's dead body…

Rafe, Jo's best friend, refuses to sit by and watch as Luc tries to win the heart of the woman he's always protected. After all, Rafe is her guardian angel. Suddenly, Jo's caught in the middle of a battle between good and evil. But the closer she gets to the fire, the hotter it burns. Now, Jo's going to learn that when love battles lust, Heaven and Hell collide.

Loving Lili (novella)

Their lovemaking is hot and dirty. Their break ups are nasty and epic.

Tired of taking the blame for every wicked thing that happens on Earth, fallen angel Luc DeVille decides to write a tell-all-book exposing The Boss.

Sharing a long and passionate history, Luc is shocked when Lili Nix arrives to interview for the job as editor. Immediately the verbal sparring begins, but the sexual chemistry remains combustible. Fascinated by this heavenly creature, Luc changes his game plan. After all, she's the only angel who has ever held his attention and understood his intentions.

Being in this world, but not of this world, is a lonely business. Can two lost angels connect and make it last this time?